1/9/92

For Gerald —

With love
from his
eternal pupil

Jon

THE MAN IN THE WINDOW

JON COHEN

WARNER BOOKS

A Time Warner Company

The names, characters, places and incidents either are the product of the author's imagination or are used fictitiously, and any resemblance to actual persons, living or dead, or locales is entirely coincidental.

Warner Books, Inc., 666 Fifth Avenue, New York, NY 10103

W A Time Warner Company

Printed in the United States of America

First printing: February 1992

10 9 8 7 6 5 4 3 2 1

Library of Congress Cataloging-in-Publication Data

Cohen, Jon.
    The man in the window / Jon Cohen.
        p.   cm.
    ISBN 0-446-51534-5
    I. Title.
    PS3553.042433M29   1991
    813' .54--dc20   91-50081
                                                        CIP

Book design: H. Roberts

For Bloop and Hennig

Thank you
Mary Hasbrouck, Kathy Malone, Pete Yee,
Gail Hochman, Jamie Raab, and Liv Blumer.
Thanks, too,
to the National Endowment for the Arts.

The Monster of Waverly

1

ATLAS MALONE SAW THE ANGEL AGAIN, THIS TIME DOWN BY
the horse chestnut tree. Yesterday the angel had stood, in a
floaty sort of way, beside the raspberry patch—Atlas couldn't
tell if its feet touched the ground with any kind of earthly
weight. Indeed, when he inspected the spot later, not a blade
of grass had been disturbed, although an entire cane of
raspberries had been picked. Gracie, his wife, said she had
not gone near his patch.

Today beneath the horse chestnut tree the angel appeared
to have more substance, a physicality it had not possessed
before—gained, perhaps, from stolen raspberries. Atlas turned
to see if Gracie was nearby, but she was still in the front yard
mulching the tulip bed. He opened his mouth to call to her,
but then shut it again. For all he knew, the angel had the
nerves of a cat, and might be scared off by the least little
thing.

The angel, whose face Atlas could not discern, stood
beside the tree. A bright wedge of summer sunlight touched

its wings, and the angel lifted them slightly, flexing, taking in the warmth. Atlas began to walk the length of the backyard toward the horse chestnut tree. He kept his hand extended before him, ready to greet the angel as he might a guest at his weekly Rotary Club luncheon.

The thoughts that came to him were ordinary and peaceful, and for a moment he forgot about the angel waiting for him down at the bottom of his yard. The grass needs cutting, he thought, maybe I'll do it before I take my nap this afternoon. The hedge has filled in well. I should water the zinnias. He paused, then turned and took it all in, his house and yard, the sense of Gracie, busy in the tulip bed, close to him. He brought his hand to his chest and touched it lightly there, mistaking a tingling in his heart for pleasure.

When Atlas turned again, his hand out and ready, he had reached the angel. The angel's head was bent, he was looking down. At his shoes, thought Atlas. I know those shoes, and as Atlas brought his eyes slowly up again, he recognized the pants too, and the shirt. They were his clothes, old and familiar, the most comfortable he owned. Now the angel lifted his face, and revealed himself with a slight smile. Atlas saw that the face also was old and familiar, that it was his own. The angel took Atlas's outstretched hand, and they stood together for a long moment beneath the cool shade of the tree.

Atlas looked into the angel's eyes, eyes he had always known, and said, "This isn't so bad, is it?"

No, said the angel, not moving his lips or making a sound, it's not so bad. Beneath the angel's feet the grass remained undisturbed, as before, but it bent and flattened as Atlas dropped first to his knees, then face forward down into the green.

Coming around the side of the house with a wheelbarrow full of weeds, Gracie watched it happen. She saw Atlas place one hand over his heart and the other straight out in front of him as if he was reaching for something.

"Atlas," she called, and began to hurry, then run to him, her white hair flying. "Atlas."

When he fell to the grass, she knew, even before she reached him, that he was dead.

"Damn you, Atlas," she whispered fiercely, as she drew him to her. She held him, her white hair dropping forward, mingling with his. Somewhere above her came a fluttering of wings, and a rising.

II

The undertaker, Jim Rose, son of Big Bill Rose, founder and owner of Rose's Funeral Home, the only funeral home in Waverly, Pennsylvania, didn't appear to understand what Gracie was saying.

"Mrs. Malone," he said, in a voice modulated by eight hundred and fifty dollars' worth of concern and accommodation—eight hundred and fifty dollars being the price of the cheapest of the cheap coffins, the one Gracie wanted, and a funeral with a minimum of fixings. "Mrs. Malone, if you don't feel you have a suit appropriate for Mr. Malone, Rose's can arrange—"

"My husband, I guarantee you, Mr. Rose, does not wish to travel through eternity in a necktie and a pair of shiny shoes pressing on his bunions."

Louis Malone, Gracie's thirty-one-year-old son, sat at the top of the stairs listening to his mother and Jim Rose.

Gracie held out a flannel work shirt, a pair of corduroys thin at the knees, gray cotton socks, and an old pair of Hush Puppies. Atlas's favorite clothes.

Jim Rose still declined to take them. "Mrs. Malone, really. I just don't feel this is, well . . . I don't feel we'd be doing our job. It's just not professionally acceptable."

Louis coughed. He knew his mother had been given her opening.

"Professionally acceptable," mused Gracie, her hand smoothing back and forth over the flannel shirt. "You have standards, after all."

"Yes ma'am," said Jim Rose. "Of course." He tried a smile.

"Big Bill's standards. Of course."

The smile began to disappear back into Jim Rose's face. "My father's standards, yes."

"Now tell me, Mr. Rose, are those the standards he had prior to the unfortunate incident of the ice, or the new standards that followed the unfortunate incident of the ice?"

Louis shifted on the stair and laughed softly. The unfortunate incident of the ice had been one of Atlas's favorite stories. In fact, everybody in Waverly had enjoyed it for over forty years. Everybody, that is, except the perpetrator and those related to him.

During World War II, Big Bill Rose came up with an idea, or scheme as Atlas would call it whenever he told his version of the story, that was patriotic, enterprising, and good for an easy buck. When he got caught, Big Bill emphasized the patriotic part, and his accusers emphasized the buck part.

Big Bill's was one of the last funeral homes in that part of Pennsylvania that still used ice instead of mechanical refrigeration to maintain the loved one until interment—or, as Atlas put it in his version, to keep the corpses cold and the stink down before planting them, getting his words out quick before Gracie could reach across the dinner table to slap his arm. Wasting so much good, usable ice after each burial had always pained Big Bill. When World War II came along and conservation and thrift became every good citizen's duty, a light bulb clicked on in the dim attic of Big Bill's brain. Without offering too many details as to the origins of the ice, Big Bill approached his sister, Edith, who ran a little catering business out of her own kitchen, with a plan that, as he would later explain to his accusers, "was first and foremost, and originally intended, to ease the burdens of our fighting boys overseas." This was not what he had told Edith. He referred to his "surplus of ice" and a small deal that would be mutually beneficial to them both—whenever Edith was in need of ice for one of her grander events, such as the Waverly Firemen's Ball or the Kiwanis's annual chicken barbecue, Big Bill would supply her at half price. His yearly revenue, for the one year he derived income before his scheme collapsed, came to six dollars and twenty-three cents—an amount, Atlas would say in his version of the story, that even in those days was still a pissy handful of change (Gracie would not even bother to slap at him at this point, he'd used so much dirty talk).

Big Bill's twice-used ice operation might have flourished had Lucy Jameson not ordered a Pepsi-Cola with "lots of ice" at her wedding reception at Waverly Lodge, catered by Edith Rose, in the hot summer of 1943. To his credit, and as he repeatedly explained to his accusers, Big Bill always rinsed his ice, "carefully," he said. Of course "carefully" meant one thing to his accusers, and something else again to Big Bill, who rinsed, carefully, making real sure he didn't melt his profits down the drain—a drain that in this case was located in the center of Big Bill's aging porcelain embalming table. Lucy, impelled by the heat of the day and the anticipated heat of her impending honeymoon encounter, had drained her Pepsi-Cola (chilled with carefully rinsed ice) in one great swallow. When she finished, she continued to hold her tilted glass to her lips. An array of looks flashed across her face, all partially concealed by her upended glass. Surprise. Confusion. And then, slowly, a sort of giddiness. For there, in the bottom of the glass that Lucy still pressed up into her face, came a glint of frozen gold from among the silver chips of ice. A ring, a man's wedding band. Lucy was pleased. She looked shyly at her new husband, Albert Jameson, who stood at her side. She had no idea Al was capable of play, that he was such a trickster, and this odd little game came as something of a relief to her. But when she looked down at Al's left hand and saw his wedding band firmly in place on his finger, her giddy feeling returned to one of confusion.

Al, who was not playful, stared disapprovingly at his new wife as she poured the glass of ice into the palm of her hand, and frowned deeper still when she handed him, embedded in a large chip, the wedding ring. Looking very glum, as if he thought the ring was a mysterious suitor's challenge to his claim on Lucy, Al cracked the ice chip on the end of the refreshment table. The noise captured the attention of all the wedding guests who were not already staring at the strange behavior of the bride and groom.

Al held the ring up and turned it in the sun. "Well, sweet Jesus," he said. The wedding guests pressed closer. Al read out loud the inscription on the inside of the ring. "Norman Keeston. May 10, 1886."

May 10, 1886, was the date of Norman Keeston's wedding day. The date of Norman's demise was just three days ago, and his preservation on ice and subsequent burial yesterday morning was courtesy of Rose's Funeral Home, Bill Rose, director. Lucy fainted right then and there and was immediately attended to by her bridesmaids and all the other women present except for Edith Rose, who remained standing behind the refreshment table beside her ice chest. All the men gathered around Al with one exception, Big Bill Rose, who slipped quietly away to his Studebaker, and sped off for the safety of his funeral home.

It didn't take long for the men to deduce the chain of events that placed Norman Keeston's wedding ring in the bottom of Lucy Jameson's glass of Pepsi-Cola. First, they ruled out that Norman's ring came out of the Pepsi, because it was too large to pass through the opening of the glass bottle.

Then Al remembered that it had been half-frozen in a piece of ice, and all the men turned their eyes toward Edith Rose. Her brother's name emerged unbidden from her lips. "Bill," she said. "I got that ice from my brother Bill."

It took less than five seconds for the wedding guests to understand the implications of ice from brother Bill. A great gasp went up from the crowd, particularly and especially from those whose drinks were cooled with Big Bill ice. At this point in his telling of the story, Atlas would make awful spitting and throat-clearing noises, imitating the guests, then grin at Gracie and Louis.

Weakness of the flesh had been the culprit. Poor Norman Keeston's finger, already contracted with age, contracted further still as he reposed upon a bed of ice on the embalming table. When Big Bill and his assistant had transferred Norman to the dressing table the morning of the funeral, Norman's ring slid off and disappeared among a thousand frosty chips, all bound for the Jameson wedding.

But for a timely catastrophe, that would have ended the career of Big Bill as Waverly's sole funeral director. Sergeant Marple of the Waverly police brought the news, pushing his way through the crowd of men who'd driven to Rose's Funeral Home, until he reached Frank Pearly, his chief. Chief Pearly was trying to keep Al Jameson from strangling Big Bill. Sergeant Marple's news made the men go slack. The Mader twins and Stu Kipner had drowned in Waverly Lake after their boat capsized. No one spoke until Big Bill cleared his throat and uttered the words that saved his career.

"Neighbors. I'm sorry for the unfortunate incident of the ice. Please bring those boys to me and I will attend to their funeral needs at no cost to their families." His voice caught a little on the "no cost" part, but he managed to get the words out. The wedding crowd nodded their silent approval, and then made their way to their cars.

Al Jameson was the last to go. He hesitated in the

doorway, turned, looked Big Bill in the eye, then tossed him Norman's wedding ring. His curse echoed in the funeral parlor as if from the walls of an Egyptian tomb. "May you choke on this ring, you greedy bastard."

For seventy-five cents, his profit from the Keeston/ Jameson ice deal, a profit he didn't even have in his pocket because his sister Edith had yet to pay him, and probably never would, Big Bill got stuck for three free funerals, was shamed before his community, and cursed by an enraged groom. All in all, not a very good day for the funeral industry in Waverly.

Even though he couldn't see them, Louis knew from the silence downstairs that his mother and Jim Rose were reliving the unfortunate incident of the ice. Gracie's eyes had softened, then closed for a long moment as she remembered Atlas telling the story year after year at the dinner table. His details were the details she remembered, even though she had actually been at the Jameson wedding and he had been away at basic training at Fort Jackson. He'd gleaned his story from the stories of others until he formed a version that was his own. "You should have seen Lucy Jameson's face," he'd say, and Gracie would say, "I was there, Atlas, I did see it." "But no," Atlas would say, "you should have *seen* it." And somehow it got to be, from the sheer force of joy he derived from the telling of it, that she saw Lucy or Al or Big Bill or Sergeant Marple the way he saw them, as characters in a wonderful fiction that was true. These people, whom she encountered every day on the streets of Waverly, were elevated by Atlas's recounting of their lives, taking on proportions they did not necessarily possess.

Of course it was unkind of Gracie to use the unfortunate incident of the ice on Jim Rose, Louis knew. Jim Rose probably looked very grim. Perhaps now he would strike back at Gracie through some little unkindness of his own. Do something, say, to Atlas, humiliate the corpse by burying him with no pants on, or with his finger up his nose. But Gracie had not said it, Louis was sure, simply to put Jim Rose in his place. Gracie was a brand-new widow, and the power of her grief, of her missing of Atlas, may have moved her to this exchange with Jim Rose, so that the mentioning of Big Bill and the ice could become inevitable, so that then she could recall a specific moment that was Atlas, could recall him telling his story, and recall further the twenty or thirty times in twenty or thirty ways that Atlas had told the story, and in the specificity of all those moments Gracie would have him again. He would not have left her as he did beneath the horse chestnut tree.

III

Upstairs, watching the flow of bustling women from behind a curtain, Louis thought of trick-or-treaters. Yes, their faces bore that same look of dread and excitement, as on the faces of children in costume, that comes when dead things are in the air.

Gracie let them in, the women who came in twos or threes, never alone, and endured again and again the awful awkward moment as they all stood there in the front hallway. She wished they'd leave their casseroles and cakes on the front doorstep like the UPS man—ring the bell, drop their goods, and disappear. This time it was Kitty Wilson and Bev Howard. Kitty lived next door to Gracie, in the house with the new aqua aluminum siding that Atlas said was capable of causing permanent eye damage in a man of his advancing years. Bev lived four houses down, and had a yard full of topiary hedges, poor abused plants shaped to resemble elephants and bears. Atlas teased Bev and her husband, Bert, no end about those hedges. Atlas never missed an opportunity to be simple and infuriating. He'd stand beside a bear hedge, knowing it was a bear hedge, and say, "My God, Bert. That's more like an elephant than an elephant is like an elephant. Gracie and I were watching the *Nature* show on PBS last night, no, the night before, 'Sunrise on the Serengeti,' and the elephants on that show were nowhere near as majestic or, I'm telling you, Bert, as realistic as this one.'' More than once over the years, Atlas would be walking by and spot Bev on her knees in the ivy, or Bert patching the walk, and he'd stop and stare at them with hard accusing eyes. When he got their attention and then held them with that look until they'd begun to fidget, he'd nod over at one of the bear hedges and say in a low even voice, "One of your bears got into my trash cans last night. See that it doesn't happen again." Then, without a flicker of a smile, he'd say, "Good day," and march off down the block.

Louis loved the elephants and bears, and once he slipped out at night to be with them. While Waverly slept, Louis moved among the animals, then stood very still and watched them move around him. It was in winter after a new snow. He thought it was wonderful to watch the bears and elephants playing in the snow.

Bev scrunched up her face into what was supposed to be, Gracie figured, a mask of neighborly commiseration. But it didn't quite come together somehow, and poor Bev with her drooping mouth looked as if she had suffered a mild stroke. Kitty's face was more composed, held in place by generous layers of makeup. She always coordinated her colors, the lips and eyes matching the stones on a necklace, or picking up a hint of something in a sweater. This time her eyes were rimmed with an intense aqua. Could it be, Gracie wondered, that Kitty is coordinating herself with the new aluminum siding on her house?

Kitty, herself five years a widow, blinked her aqua eyes several times—a display meant to demonstrate the effort it took to contain her tears. Kitty blinked and Bev snuffled, her drooping mouth going up and down. Gracie looked at her two neighbors twitching and grunting before her and thought, Grief is an ungainly dance.

Kitty held her casserole out to Gracie. Unable to say, I am so sorry, Gracie, we'll all miss Atlas, which is what in her own way she felt, Kitty said, "Oh Gracie, here. I whipped this up for you—sweet potatoes with a marshmallow glaze. Put that in the oven at three-fifty for twenty minutes, then take the lid off for ten minutes at the end to let it brown." She placed the dish in Gracie's hands as solemnly as if she were handing over an urn containing Atlas's ashes. Then she stepped back, relieved, and it was Bev's turn.

Bev looked scared, as though she thought widowhood might be catching. Bert, after all, was two years older than Atlas. Maybe there had been some sort of mix-up, maybe it was Bert who was supposed to have collapsed in his backyard. When she heard about Atlas, Bev had whisked Bert out of the yard where he'd been trimming the elephants, and made him lie down on the sofa.

"Gracie," Bev began, then stopped. She gulped.

Gracie said, "It's all right, Bev."

"No, Gracie," she said. "It's just that . . . Here. I made these. The little sugar cookies Atlas liked so much. Remember, at our barbecue two years ago? He ate a full dozen, at least, and Bert, he was so busy at the grill and everything, he didn't even get one, but I guess Atlas didn't notice about Bert, or he just liked them so much he couldn't help himself. Anyway he sure ate them." She thrust the tin of cookies at Gracie.

Gracie remembered things a little differently. The reason Atlas ate the sugar cookies as though they were the main course was because, in the end, that's what they turned out to be. Bert always had a few beers before the annual picnic with Gracie and Atlas, because Atlas made him nervous. He could never quite tell when Atlas was joking and when he wasn't— like with the hedges. Bert must have been extra nervous, because he'd had more than a few beers that day. During two and a half interminable hours, he managed to drop three steaks and most of the chicken breasts on the ground, and the food he was able to keep over the coals he burned beyond recognition. Atlas never looked at a sugar cookie again.

And what do I have, thought Gracie, to comfort me in the hour of my greatest sorrow? Kitty and Bev, a batch of sweet potatoes with a ruinous marshmallow glaze and some sugar cookies. Atlas, save me.

A sudden small sound pattered from above, tiptoes down the hallway, light and quick. Kitty and Bev looked up at the ceiling, then back at Gracie.

Bev said, "Louis is taking it hard, I imagine, Gracie?"

Gracie thought about that. Then she said, "You can't be sure how Louis takes a thing. He carries his sorrow differently than the rest of us."

When she had finally released Atlas's body there beneath the horse chestnut tree, Louis was beside her. He wore, as he always did indoors or out, a purple scarf wrapped high above his nose like a bandit, and a baseball cap, the rim pulled down low. She looked up into his hidden face and saw in his eyes that he understood, but she said it anyway, articulated it for herself. *"Louis, your daddy's dead."* She said it like that, used the word *daddy,* although it was not a word that belonged to Louis, who always called him Atlas. Gracie sat beside her husband, her hand resting on his still figure. Louis knelt down, touched Atlas, then suddenly pulled back and stared down the yard at the lengthening shadows, and pointed there, then there, raising his finger a little each time, until at last he pointed straight up in the air. His head was tilted back, and his scarf fell away. Gracie saw his eyes following a movement, his mouth open, his face bathed in the blue light of the sky.

Kitty pursued what Bev had begun, presuming on the intimacy that seems to form between neighbors after a death.

"Will you, Gracie, do you think you'll be able to care for Louis now that Atlas is gone?" She stood too close and Gracie, as she often did, picked up the fermented scent of wine on Kitty's breath.

Upstairs, a toilet flushed.

Gracie moved past Kitty to the front door and opened it. "You have it quite wrong, quite backward," she said. "Now that Atlas is gone, it will be Louis who takes care of me."

When Gracie closed the door behind the two women, footsteps tiptoed down the hall again.

IV

Gracie remembered what Atlas always told her, what he said right from the beginning. "Gracie, I hope to God I go before you do." He even said it on their wedding night in 1946. She sat at the dressing table in the bedroom of the Tremont Hotel in Atlantic City, and he had come up behind her in his blue silk bathrobe, picked up her brush, and begun to brush her hair. They had kissed before, of course, and more, but nothing approached the intimacy of that moment. She let her head sink back as he stroked. Her hair was brown and long, and it seemed to take the brush forever to move through it. Finally, Atlas put the brush down, and whispered, "Oh, Gracie, I hope I go before you do."

The words did not seem at all inappropriate, or morbid.

Gracie laughed and pulled him to her, and kissed him. They were young, they were just married—he would brush her hair, and they would stay young and married forever.

"Atlas," she said. "Neither of us is going to go. They make special allowances for people like us." She kissed him again.

But Atlas had been to war. "Well, just in case they don't, I hope I go first."

She touched a finger to his lips. "Listen to you," she said. "Listen to you."

He said it many times over the years. But at some point there came a turning for Gracie, and the words took on a measure of menace. The ordinary accumulation of vulnerabilities was the menace, and so were the small shocks that come one after another over the course of a life. The menace was in the slow hollowing of her bones, and in the fragile ticking of the clock. They would not always be young, or forever married, and the hair Atlas still liked to brush for her was going white.

Two years before he died they were at the farm, the hundred acres of overgrown land and small farmhouse Gracie inherited from her mother, when Atlas said those words for the last time. "I hope I go before you do." He floated in the middle of the pond, a seventy-year-old man draped on a black inner tube. She leaned against a piling at the end of the dock, watching a red-winged blackbird on the top branch of a dead willow. It had not moved in five minutes. But when Atlas called across the pond to her, it abruptly took flight. Gracie was sure it was more Atlas's words than the suddenness of his voice that scared the bird. Now she heard the words, too, and they didn't declare love, as they always had, but the loss of love, of Atlas. She felt something rush up out of her chest, felt the frightened beating of wings, and the escape of the blackbird.

Atlas would go before her, he would get his wish. Maybe it would happen now, right now. As he floated in smiling ease, maybe the pond would open up and draw him down. Or his heart would stop, and he would slide through the middle of his inner tube and away. Or something in his brain, something tiny and thin, would engorge and burst, and Atlas would see a brief dim light, one candle lit for one instant, enough to see where he was going, before a slight wind, or the breath from an unseen mouth, cut the flame and left all in darkness.

"Damn you, Atlas," she called fiercely across the water.

Atlas's head was turned, and he didn't seem to hear her. Gracie followed his gaze to the side of the hill which rose beyond the weedy pasture, where a figure moved. Even on this hot day, Louis wore his baseball hat and scarf, though the scarf hung loose and open around his neck—he felt safe at the farm. He sat picking wild strawberries. Gracie saw him find a spot, then his hand going back and forth from the ground to his mouth.

Atlas turned away from Louis and began paddling back to the dock. He pulled himself out of the water, graceful still in his movements. He said, "Well, he sure finds those strawberries, all right. I can hardly see them anymore, but Louis sure finds them, even the ones no bigger than your baby toenail. Boy, I bet—"

Gracie stopped him. "Atlas, don't say that anymore."

He looked at her.

"Don't say you hope you go before I do."

He moved close but didn't touch her. "I'm sorry, Gracie."

"You think you couldn't do it without me. Well, I couldn't do it without you. It works both ways."

Now he touched her lightly on the arm. "You're stronger than me."

She pulled away. "You always say that. How do you know? Everything that's happened we've borne together."

Louis called to them from the hillside. "Atlas. Gracie. I found a big one." Gracie knew from his voice that he was smiling. The line of his mouth would be straight, because his injured lips could no longer define a smile. It was all in his voice now.

Atlas waved to Louis. Then he began to speak, looking at Gracie sometimes, or way off at Louis, or down into the murky water of the pond. Atlas spoke, and Gracie listened, her eyes closing first in the slow heat of the day. She tried to see the world as Atlas described it. She listened, then opened her eyes and watched him intently, as if she hoped to see each word in the tumble of words that rose out of him.

"I got up while you were asleep last night, Gracie," he said. "You're usually the one who gets up, I hear you every time, and I always think, There she goes, she's taking off. Isn't that funny? All you're doing is going to the bathroom, or checking the stove, and I'm as sure as my next breath you're leaving me. Well, I got up, I don't know why. To look out the window, to look at the dark." Atlas stared into the distance. "Up here the dark is different—not just darker, but fuller. I guess all that means is it's fuller of things I'm not used to. At home I know my work shed's out there, and my garden...but up here you don't know. Well, I'm thinking about that when all of a sudden something big pushes around through the tall grass down below the old pear tree, and it's not moving right for a deer, it's too deliberate. I start to get spooked—you know how it is with things in the dark. I move away from the window a little, like it could jump up two stories."

Gracie nodded. She could see it, Atlas peering down at the shadows. "Louis," she said.

"Louis, that's right." Atlas smiled. "There he is, steps out from behind the pear tree, not spooky at all, or playing a joke on me or anything. He didn't even know I was there."

Louis, Gracie thought. Louis in the light of the moon.

"His hat was off. And his scarf, too." Atlas's face went tight, and his voice dropped down. "It hurt me. Even now, even after all these years, it hurts me. With the baseball hat and the scarf, you forget."

The hat and scarf. Was there ever a time, Gracie asked herself, when Louis didn't wear them? Yes—and she saw herself, younger, and Louis a small boy, as she lifted him to kiss the skin on his cheek for the sheer pleasure of it, her lips tasting the coolness of his skin.

Atlas trailed his hand back and forth in the water. "But he never forgets, does he? Wraps himself until he's hidden from us."

"And from Waverly," said Gracie, watching the rippling water behind Atlas's hand. "And from the fair citizens of Waverly."

"Louis, our monster boy." Atlas's eyes cut to Louis crawling on the hillside. "And what was our monster doing last night in the dark below my window? My God—sound the alarm, let the citizens light their torches and brandish their clubs and pitchforks!"

Gracie reached for him, her hand moving out to stop his words from echoing across the water to Louis, to stop them from entering her.

But Atlas caught her hand in his and finished in a whisper. "What was he doing? Catching fireflies."

Gracie's eyes remained on Louis. Not a monster, because what mother could recognize or acknowledge that? What mother could abandon the dream that lived inside her, deny the one thing in this world she knows as certain, which is the absolute and everlasting beauty of her child? Yes, there was a time before he hid himself, a thousand times, and she closed her eyes and immersed herself in them, moments within moments, so that she was able to reconstruct Louis from her memories, at all ages, from all angles, capture simultaneously every mood that had ever shaped his face. For the briefest instant, there on the dock with her eyes closed against the reality of Louis on the hillside, he was hers as he had once been, before he had drawn his purple curtain across his face.

Gracie chose from the memories that swirled before her. "The fireflies," she said.

Atlas turned to her. "Last night, you mean?"

"No," she said. "When he was six or seven." Louis at six or seven. His face, the lashes around his eyes. "Remember?'' she said quickly, speaking before the words caught in her throat. ''How he was about the fireflies, how he wanted to put them in jars and sell them at the hardware store?''

''I remember,'' Atlas said.

''Sell different strengths, he said. Some jars would have five fireflies, some ten. It's funny to think that's how the store seemed to him—a place where his father sold hammers, and paint, and for all he knew, jars with different strengths of fireflies.''

''He loved the store.'' Atlas smiled suddenly. ''That's why he thought of shelves stocked with fireflies, and who knows what all. The store is what he misses most, I think. All these years it's been only four blocks away and he hasn't been able to get to it, could not bring himself to venture out on the streets of Waverly even if he wore a hundred hats and scarves.''

Then Gracie saw Atlas find a memory, saw it take shape behind his eyes, watched him work his mouth in preparation for the telling of it. Here we go, thought Gracie, there's no stopping him now. She was glad though, at least for the moment, to have his recollections quell her own.

''Say,'' he said, ''you know how Louis will ask me about somebody who was in some way connected to the store? How he does because he knows it will make us both remember, and move up and down the aisles again, the way he and I used to when he was little?''

''Yes, I know.'' Gracie leaned against one of the pilings on the dock, braced herself really, because that's what you did when Atlas was about to take off on one of his tales.

''Guess who he asked about last week?''

''Who?'' She knew he didn't want her to slow him down by actually guessing.

''Mrs. Meem.'' And with that, Atlas's flight began. Gracie took a deep breath and climbed on board beside him.

''That's right,'' he said, ''Mrs. Meem and the dog. She

and Louis both felt the same magic in the place, I think, the sheer excitement of being surrounded by so many miraculous things, over your head, in drawers, hanging from the ceiling, spilling out of boxes. Louis was satisfied just to be there amongst it all, but for Mrs. Meem, it was more than she could bear. Brought out her criminal tendencies." Atlas raised an eyebrow.

"Poor Mrs. Meem," said Gracie, smiling.

"Poor Mrs. Meem? Rich Mrs. Meem, you mean, rich with all the stuff she stole from my store! And tricky Mrs. Meem, too, because she tricked me and Louis for the longest time, which was understandable. Who could believe that a fifty-year-old woman with a weakness for flowered dresses and fruited hats would be snatching sixpenny nails and electrical tape? That big pocketbook of hers should have been a clue, but on her frail arm it wasn't, even when it bulged with half the contents of my store.

"But of course, what really confused the picture," said Atlas rubbing his chin, "was the dog."

Gracie laughed. If it was Mrs. Meem who always got Atlas down the runway, then it was the dog who lifted him off the ground.

"Laugh away, but you know that dog was unregenerate. Nothing about it was right. That dog was so wrong you couldn't stop staring at him, he mesmerized you! Which of course, we finally realized, was the plan. To begin with, he swaggered, which is okay for a Newfoundland or a husky, but this dog was terrier-sized, and as a rule you should never trust a little guy who swaggers. His coat was gray, but to say coat suggests it covered him completely, when in fact it only sprouted out of him here and there. That way you got a good look at his skin, which had moist pink areas, partially healed wounds from the battles he waged with his own flesh. And then, of course, there was that smell and those eyes. I believe the two were related in that his god-awful odor, which could not have come from him alone, but was perhaps something dead and rotted he rolled in, something he applied to his pink spots like a salve—I believe this overpowering stink caused his eyes to squint and cross, as if they had done everything they could to get away from it, rolled this way and that with such intensity the damage became permanent. And a dog with crossed eyes is a killer, anybody will tell you that, or at least dangerous, and at a minimum up to no good.''

"Honestly, Atlas," said Gracie, "he was unattractive, I'll admit, but—''

"But nothing," Atlas countered. "He was the absolute worst, and you know it, *we* knew it, me and Louis, and Yank Spiller, and everybody else knew it, were helpless to do anything but eyeball that dog, while unbeknownst to us Mrs. Meem was easing her way to the back of the store. All according to her plan. She'd get herself back there, then to make sure no one looked in her direction, she'd signal the dog with a dainty cough and it would suddenly break away from the crowd that had formed around it, and skitter down whatever aisle Mrs. Meem was not in. Of course we'd chase after it. When a dog runs like that you are compelled to chase after it. But the dog was too fast, and there were too many of us in pursuit, knocking things off shelves and bumping into each other, to gain on it. The dog would suddenly skid to a halt and look over his shoulder and give us a smile. Louis always said he heard it laugh too, but I heard it as a growl, and so did the others. Grin, laugh, or growl, it stopped us in our tracks. At which point, with a steely calm, the dog proceeded to lift its leg and release a mighty stream on my merchandise.''

"Oh, Atlas, please, not this part. How many times . . .''

Atlas grinned at her, pleased to go on. "You would swear, watching him as we all intently did, that he took aim before he fired. I once saw him, Gracie," he said, nudging her with his bare foot when she tried to ignore him, "I once saw him place his flow *between* the claws of a rake, and strike a roll of tar paper. And then there was the episode of the saturation of the cement bags. He soaked five of them, moving back and forth like a fireman working a stubborn blaze.''

Atlas laughed, and so did Gracie. ''Well,'' he went on, ''while this commotion was taking place, Mrs. Meem, alone and undetected in the other aisle, scooped up the contents of my store and stuffed them into her pocketbook. We never would have caught her except for the two cans of yellow high-gloss exterior paint. She was almost out the door, after one of these episodes, when Louis pointed to her pocketbook and said, 'Mrs. Meem, you're leaking.' The paint can lid had opened, drizzling the evidence all over her flowered dress and my wood floor. She broke down, of course, and confessed and generally caused a scene too painful to contemplate. Louis was mortified for her and kept whispering to me to please let her go, which I was certainly going to do.

''A week later she returned to the store, dog and all. It became Louis's job, from that day on, to monitor Mrs. Meem and to account for everything she took. What did she steal? What didn't she steal? Galvanized staples, wood glue, eye hooks, bailing twine, four feet of chain link, pieces of linoleum, a bicycle tire repair kit. Louis and I would go over the list and try to imagine that Mrs. Meem was building something large and complex, requiring odd and unrelated materials. By arrangement with Pastor Meem, I presented him a monthly bill, which he paid in full without comment.''

''You're a good and decent man, Atlas Malone,'' said Gracie.

''Hush, woman, you're trying to distract me from my finale.''

She sighed.

''Well, as you may or may not know . . .''

''Would it matter?'' she said.

"As you may or may not know," Atlas repeated with emphasis, "the business with Mrs. Meem and her dog went on for three years until it came to an abrupt end one cold December morning. It had to do with an electric floor heater and the dog finally picking the wrong target. We chased the dog down the aisle like always, and then when we saw dog, *A,* lift its leg and aim at electric heater, *B,* we all let out a simultaneous gasp. I have to admit, in the interest of scientific curiosity, we did nothing to intervene. The spark that jumped back and forth between the dog and the heater was a sight to behold. The dog died instantly, was thrown five feet into the air, landing in a galvanized bucket which I presented to Mrs. Meem, dog and all, compliments of Malone's Hardware Store."

Atlas stretched out on the dock, grinning up at the sky.

"Every time you tell that story, it gets worse. Galvanized bucket. That's a lovely detail I don't recall."

"Ho-dee-ho," said Atlas.

"A *galvanized* bucket—not just a bucket."

"Truth be told," said Atlas, "it was Louis who provided that little detail. Also the color of the paint. I always thought it was green. Louis was right, though. Yellow."

"You two."

Atlas sat up. "Now if you want to talk details, you should have heard him go on about Harvey Mastuzek last night. There's a story with details." Atlas rubbed his chin and looked away.

Gracie hesitated, but then had to ask. "Harvey Mastuzek in the hardware store?"

Atlas still looked away. "That's right."

"Harvey, who never leaves his house except to buy whiskey?"

"That's right."

"In our store?"

"You want to play Twenty Questions, or you want me to tell you about it?"

Gracie looked at Atlas's back as he sat dangling his legs over the end of the dock. I could just give him a poke and over he'd go. Give him the dousing he deserves. "Tell me," she said.

"Well," said Atlas, suddenly up on his feet and pacing back and forth over the wooden planks, his hands moving, his elbows pumping at his sides, everything charged up and ready to go, "well, Mrs. Meem and her dog, that's a pair we all remember. But Louis, whose intentions are often more complicated than we can know, sometimes he'll reach deep and pull up somebody we would never consider, somebody he'll choose to enliven his recollections of the store. Like Harvey Mastuzek. 'Remember Harvey Mastuzek?' he said. 'Remember the time he came into the store?' No, I said. 'You don't?' his voice incredulous, but kind of sly and amused, too, like he caught you not paying attention to something really important, but on the other hand not important at all, or important in a way you couldn't imagine was important unless you were Louis."

Gracie clutched the edge of the dock.

"He proceeded to tell me the long and complicated story of Harvey Mastuzek, longer and more complicated, if you can believe it, than any of my stories, and filled with nuances inside of nuances, most of which I missed and won't attempt to repeat. Louis went on for an hour, maybe two, about the time, now hold tight, Gracie, about the time Mr. Mastuzek came into the store and bought a black rubber washer. That's right, a thoroughly unremarkable man enters my hardware store for the first and only time in his life, and purchases, in a transaction that could not have taken more than three minutes from start to finish, one thirteen-cent washer for his faucet. Louis's recounting of that transaction was beautiful and frightening. He described Harvey Mastuzek's every feature—

not just how he looked, but right down to speculating on when he last shaved and were those sideburns beside each ear, or simply missed hairs, *missed hairs* for God's sake, Gracie. He went on about his sharp whiskey odor, and the way he spoke and cleared his throat and *breathed*, the way he moved. What he wore, where he might have bought what he wore, whether or not what he wore was appropriate for the season. On and on. Then Louis discussed the journey down the middle aisle with Harvey Mastuzek, and what they saw, what was displayed on the counters, what was on the Peg-Board hooks, the size of the Phillips screwdrivers, how much a ball-peen hammer cost, actually getting the correct cost for that particular year, Gracie. And then the search for the right rubber washer. Louis holding one up, then Harvey Mastuzek taking it and moving under the light to get a better look, then shaking his head no, and Louis holding another one up, until they finally find the right size. That's the transcendent moment for Louis, the look that passes between him and Harvey Mastuzek, the recognition of rightness—the discovery of the rubber washer that will do the job. But there's more, Gracie."

And Gracie thought, Of course there's more. It is the essence of Louis to give more, to reveal, even as he himself remains unrevealed. My shadowed boy, throwing light upon everything, the brilliance of your gaze causing us to look everywhere but at you. "Yes," said Gracie, "more."

"Then he tells me about the return trip up the aisle, past all the same stuff, but the perspective is different now, not just because they are moving up the aisle instead of down it, but because the discovery of the absolutely right washer has colored his view, has put a glow on everything, an aura. At last, they get to the cash register and money changes hands, thirteen cents—that's one buffalo nickel, and one Jefferson nickel, and three pennies. It takes Louis ten more minutes of description to move Harvey Mastuzek away from the cash register and out the door, and when it's all over, Louis lifts his eyes and peers at me from behind his baseball hat and his scarf. He wanted to see if I had gotten it. Of course I hadn't. I was exhausted. I had heard the story, but I hadn't heard the story hidden inside the story.''

Atlas knelt beside Gracie and lightly touched her arm. She looked up at him. "This morning, I got it," he said. "I was brushing my teeth and it came to me, like Louis timed it to go off that way, after a night's rest."

"The story inside the story."

"Yes. The way he saw it, Harvey Mastuzek could walk into the store only one time. It was Mrs. Meem all over again, as Louis perceived it. The magic abundance of the store overwhelmed him, too—the curative potential, the cascade of visual and sensual stimuli—but Harvey responded the opposite of Mrs. Meem. Where she had to immerse herself again and again, to possess because simple contact was not enough, Harvey Mastuzek had to stay away, look once, and then stay away. Like a quick glance at the burning sun. So that's why, in Louis's mind, Harvey Mastuzek's three minutes in the store merited two hours of recollection. And no doubt he gave me the abridged version. A premiere moment in Harvey Mastuzek's life took place before Louis's eyes, so Louis had to give it the meticulous attention it deserved.

"But wait, right? The shelves of Malone's Hardware Store contained no magic, just hammers and saws, and duct tape, and putty knives. Where's the magic that compelled these people? The fireflies, Gracie. Squeezed in between the roofing nails and the wire clippers, or somewhere, who knows where, Louis saw the different strength fireflies. Because Louis saw them, he believed Mrs. Meem and Harvey Mastuzek saw them, too. And the fireflies imbued everything in the store with their luminescent halo. Here's another way of putting it: *To a certain kind of person, a hardware store is a holy place.* There, that's a good moral to the story." Now Atlas was beside Gracie, and together they sat, arms around each other as they watched their distant son moving in the grass of the hillside. When Atlas spoke again, it was in a whisper.

"So last night, Gracie, I got up out of bed and saw Louis out among the fireflies, not wearing his baseball hat or scarf. I tried to see his face in the dim moonlight. I tried to look, as I have never been able to in all these years. But even from a distance, and in the softest light of fireflies and moon, I couldn't. He gave me a chance to see him, because he must have sensed by then that I was there. But I turned away. The slightest turn of my head, away. He knew it. How many times have I done that, and how many times has he known it? When you say, 'Everything that's happened we've borne together,' that's not true, Gracie. You changed the dressings, you applied the ointments, you looked him full in the face and did what had to be done. And I turn my head away."

"Atlas."

"There's too much, and I don't have the strength for it, Gracie. There's too much of everything. I couldn't do it. I couldn't do Louis. And I couldn't live without you. That's why I must go before you. I'm sorry."

Atlas was done. They sat on the end of the dock, and together watched Louis. He knelt in the grass, then a moment later waved and pointed to something he held in his hand. A perfect strawberry.

Atlas reached behind Gracie and found her brush in her canvas bag. He began to brush her white hair. Gracie closed her eyes and mistook the smell of pond water for the sea, and thought she was in Atlantic City.

V

Louis watched the funeral from the car. He had come downstairs an hour before, as Gracie was readying herself. When she turned around he was standing in her doorway dressed in a coat and tie. She expected the hat and scarf—it was the coat and tie that looked odd.

"Look at you," she said.

"Three words guaranteed to make a recluse cringe," said Louis. He made a sound that was his laugh.

Gracie smiled. "I haven't seen that coat in years."

"Since I was sixteen." At sixteen it all stopped for Louis, or was put away, or was in some way changed. "Does the coat smell like mothballs? I mean, I know it does, it's had mothballs in the pockets for sixteen years. But is it overpowering?" He leaned close.

Gracie sniffed. She had been crying off and on since she got up, so she didn't smell a thing. "It's fine, Louis. Really."

"Good," he said.

"You're thirty-one and you still fit in the coat you wore when you were sixteen. That's not bad."

She turned away and began to fix her hair. "Louis," she said at last.

He was at the window peering out at the street. He knew all the windows in all the rooms, and how to look out of them. He knew how not to be seen, of course, knew what the sun revealed as he stood just so behind a curtain or a shade. And the sun was always changing, so on cloudy days he had to adjust himself this way or that, or alter his stance in the afternoon from what it had been in the morning. Bright days, rainy days, light reflected from the white snow or from the green of a summer lawn—all affected the way he stood at his windows. Even at night he was wary, of streetlights, passing cars, and sometimes the moon. Stars, too. For someone who does not wish to be seen, even the light from stars must be considered. Sometimes, though, he did wish to be seen. He liked to play with Kitty Wilson. She couldn't keep her eyes off the windows as she passed by on the street, craning her neck, teeth clamped on a cigarette, squinting through her makeup. He'd flutter curtains and jiggle shades, and her mouth would widen, and if the window was open he could almost hear her panting. When she finally gave up and turned to go, he'd reveal himself completely, there and then gone, and she'd freeze, not knowing if it was a trick of the sun or her imagination, or if he'd really been standing behind the glass.

"Louis," Gracie said again.

He turned and faced her.

"The coat. Were you thinking . . . are you coming to the funeral?"

He moved toward her, then paused and went back to the window. "Jim Rose is here. In a big silver car."

Gracie rose instantly and brushed past Louis. "I told him I didn't want any nonsense. I'm not paying for the privilege of riding in a car owned by Big Bill. I already told Mary Dickson I'd go with her. Those Roses will do anything to squeeze a nickel out of you. Vampires sucking nickels out of the bereaved."

Louis put a hand to her face, and she stopped. He said, "Gracie, I'd like to ride in that car."

"You're coming?" she said, drawing him close. "Louis, there'll be people. All sorts of people."

"I know."

"You're not used to it, honey."

"I know."

"Atlas wouldn't mind. He really wouldn't mind if you didn't come. And neither would I. I'll be fine."

"I'd like to ride in the car. And I'd like to go to Atlas's funeral."

"Louis, why? It's just so much."

He looked out the window at Jim Rose starting up the walk, then he looked beyond him as far as he could see, which was not far enough. "Gracie, I've tried all the windows. Even the tiny dormer in the attic. If there was a way I could see the cemetery from this house, I wouldn't go."

"But Atlas would tell you the cemetery part doesn't matter. It's just a show for his friends, for the people he worked with. He's already gone, Louis, and we're just burying the shell."

The doorbell rang. Then Louis said, "I know he's gone." A movement in the air, a soft beating of wings, and he was gone. "I know. But if I go, I'll believe I've forgiven him. If I can leave this house in daylight, for everyone to see, if I can do that, I'll believe I loved him even when he turned away."

Gracie's voice barely reached him. "He loved you."

"And now he'll know that I loved him."

They held each other, then Louis said, "You sure, now?"

She cocked her head.

"You sure you can't smell mothballs?"

Gracie went downstairs and opened the door for Jim Rose. He was ready for her, getting his words out first. Louis heard him say, "Mrs. Malone, I know that transportation was not part of your original funeral package."

"That's right, Mr. Jim Rose," she said. "And if you think you can bamboozle—"

"Someone has stepped in on your behalf, Mrs. Malone. Someone is satisfying all the financial aspects of this day, so that you may attend to more pressing emotional needs without hinderment." He held out an envelope to her.

"Hindrance," said Louis, stepping into the foyer.

Jim Rose, who had spent years perfecting his professional composure, that look of unflappable blankness, took a large step backwards and widened his eyes.

Louis was pleased, because he was at least as nervous as Jim Rose, but he could see now it would go undetected.

"Hello, Jim. Good to see you." The scarf filtered the shakiness in his voice

Jim Rose took a breath. "Louis. Good to see you." The

words were especially meaningless, since it was impossible to see anything of Louis but his eyes.

The two men faced each other. The last time they had been together was in high school, the day before Louis's accident, showering with the other boys after gym class. The usual chaos prevailed—towel-snapping fights, water skirmishes, tossing soap bars. But one boy didn't join in the fun. Louis spotted Jim Rose scurrying toward his locker, not even bothering to dry off. He was hiding something, something just below his waist. Unfortunately, and of course inevitably, all the other boys spotted him, too. What had happened to Jim Rose was the one thing, that most dreaded of things, all boys pray will never happen while taking a shower with fifty other boys. It could have been any of them, and they were all so grateful it wasn't, they decided to sacrifice Jim Rose to the gods. They immediately attacked, all except Louis and a few other decent souls, taunting him, pelting him with soap bars, snapping at his erection with their rat-tailed towels. Mr. Hollister, the gym teacher, finally broke it up, and then punished the victim, not the victimizers, giving Jim Rose an unprecedented twenty-five detentions. What especially enraged Mr. Hollister was that male sexual anatomy was not going to be taught in health class for another two weeks, and Jim Rose had obviously read ahead in the textbook. The boys added their own little punishment, giving him a nickname, substituting Dick for Jim, so that his name forever identified his sin: Dick Rose.

Louis reached out across sixteen years and offered his hand. Jim Rose didn't take it. Instead he offered the envelope he had held out to Gracie. Louis took it, and handed it to her. She read it aloud.

"My sympathies are with you on this sad occasion. Please accept this small gesture, so that I can be satisfied that my account with Atlas is now closed. Know that God watches over all of his angels. Pastor Meem." She looked at Louis, then said, "Well, well, well."

Gracie called Mary Dickson. Louis and Jim Rose stood silently in the foyer. Jim Rose's professional composure returned. Louis could feel Jim Rose eyeing him. Louis itched beneath his scarf and he reached up to adjust it. Jim Rose sucked in his breath in panic, and Louis realized Jim Rose thought he was about to remove the scarf.

Louis whispered, "No. I'd never . . . ," and then Gracie reappeared.

Jim Rose went out to the car. Louis, with Gracie at his side, stood on the front porch in the sunlight. He trembled. Gracie began to repeat softly, "There, there. Come on now. Come on now," as if calming a bewildered animal.

Which Louis was. From his windows he had seen the front walk, the green grass, the azaleas, the dogwood, every day for sixteen years. And often at night, he had touched the dogwood, moved among the azaleas. But the sun . . . he had lived so long out of the revealing sun. Only at the farm did he dare walk in the light. He looked around, at his street, at the world of Waverly, at everything that was familiar, and knew that he was the object out of place, a shadow on the shadowless land. The sun. The sun in the grass, shining through each blade, and on the leaves of the dogwood, and on the azaleas, impossibly lit, and the incandescent shimmer of the mica in the cement walk. He closed his eyes.

"Flames," he whispered, and hid his face on Gracie's shoulder.

"Come on now, Louis. No flames, no flames," she whispered back. "I'll take you in. Let me take you in."

In. Louis opened his eyes and the flames began to recede. *In*. Where it was cool, and dim, where he could watch the overbright world in safety.

"Take me in," he said. He saw Jim Rose standing beside the open car door, waiting.

In the foyer again, Gracie said, "You'll be all right here, Louis. Wait for me—I'll be back soon. You'll be all right?"

Through the screen door of the house that had been his safety for years and years, Louis saw Jim Rose standing beside the open car door. Without a word, he suddenly brushed past Gracie, pushed on the screen, and broke into a run down the walk toward the car. Jim Rose jumped aside as Louis dove onto the leather upholstery of the backseat. He made it. He made it through the flames.

Gracie hurried up to the car, looked at Louis, then got in beside him. Jim Rose closed the door behind them and walked around to the driver's seat. Gracie adjusted Louis's scarf and brushed at his coat sleeve as the car started up.

"There," he said. "Nothing to it."

He held Gracie's hand as the car moved slowly along. He spared himself, did not look out the window. There was too much to see; he didn't want to use himself up before the funeral. So he watched the back of Jim Rose's neck, or kept his eyes downward and studied the upholstery, the hem on Gracie's dark dress, the tips of his shoes. He imagined leaving a wake of gawking people behind as the car passed along the streets of Waverly to Rose's Funeral Home. Women catching a glimpse of him and dropping their bags of groceries. Children swerving and falling off their bicycles. Old men on their porches slumping in their chairs. Dogs howling, and birds taking flight. Phones ringing all over town: Did you see, did you see? He's out. They've let him out. I'm telling you, I saw him. Louis made himself smaller.

He stayed in the car during the short service at Rose's. The car was parked around back, away from the guest lot. He peeked out the window and saw Jim Rose by a dumpster talking to an immensely fat old man who leaned on a cane. Big Bill. Big for fat, not tall. The cane looked as if it was about to snap. Jim Rose pointed over to the car. Louis pushed back against the seat. Jim Rose had betrayed him. Big Bill would come and press his fat nose against the window. Jim Rose, Jim Rose, I didn't betray you in the locker room. I saw you but did not say a word. Louis closed his eyes and saw himself in the locker room, naked. But it wasn't an erection he tried to hide from the other boys, but his face. He covered his face with his hands as the boys snapped their towels at him, and pelted him with bars of white soap. They pulled his hands away and he was revealed.

Louis opened his eyes and Big Bill was there. Not pressing his nose against the window, but reaching for the door handle. Louis hit the lock before he could open it, then whirled around and hit the other three. The sunlight sparkled on the parking lot and Louis could see tiny flames.

Big Bill backed away, smiling. "No harm, son. Easy now. I just wanted to have a look at you," the words muted by glass.

Louis crouched below the window, and wondered why. Who would want to look? But Big Bill was a looker—at all things dead and terrible. He had seen the worst faces Waverly had to offer. Big Bill was a chronicler of the ugly, a connoisseur of the forbidding. But Louis was not dead yet, so Big Bill would have to wait. Louis saw himself dead, then, and imagined those fat fingers tugging at his scarf, the eager grunts of anticipation.

Big Bill leaned on his cane, still smiling. Louis could feel him, feel the horrible weight of him. The car began to heat up. Louis closed his eyes and saw Big Bill as the devil, his cane a pitchfork, standing in a sea of flames. And then suddenly, through the glass, Gracie's voice. He looked out the window and Big Bill had vanished. Or had never been there at all.

He unlocked the door and Gracie got in. "You didn't miss a thing," she said. "I've been crying all morning, but in there, in that awful place, I was dry as a stone. It's the most neutral place I've ever been—it sucked the emotion right out of me. People were shedding tears, but I was just so furious, Louis. Having left Atlas there for two days—it was worse than leaving him in a McDonald's. And you know how he felt about McDonald's. 'Gracie, don't you ever take me into a restaurant again where they talk into microphones.' He couldn't tolerate that, ordering a hamburger, then having them repeat his words over a microphone. 'Makes you feel like you're wearing your underwear on the outside,' he said.''

She suddenly grabbed Louis's arm. ''Oh Lord. I gave Jim Rose those clothes, remember? Only I didn't give him a pair of Atlas's underwear.'' Now she began to cry. ''Do you think they put a pair on him, Louis?'' Louis put his arm around her.

Up ahead they loaded the casket into a white hearse. The car started up, and Louis leaned back in the seat, away from the window. Everyone knew by now that he was there. The procession to the cemetery snaked down the streets of Waverly, the hearse first, then Gracie and Louis, and a long tail of cars. A lot of people liked Atlas, although very few of them understood his sense of humor. For instance, he probably would have thought it pretty funny, poor Gracie's tears aside, that all these dressed-up people were going to all this trouble to bury a man who wasn't wearing any underwear.

Louis watched the funeral from inside the car. He had whispered something to Gracie, and then she'd told Jim Rose to park in the shade and apart from the others after he let her out. Now Louis sat up, and even rolled the window down. Most of the guests were trying very hard not to look in his direction, some trying harder than others. Kitty Wilson, staring, tripped over a folding chair. Others were more discreet, shooting quick glances at the car. Louis clutched the armrest but didn't hide. The pallbearers eased the coffin out of the hearse, and the eyes left him for a moment. Sixteen years had passed since he had seen the men who now held Atlas's casket. They had become old men, pale as ghosts, six ghosts carrying Atlas to his grave. Fred Nistle, who used to own the bakery next to Malone's Hardware. Jim and Bob Madison, Madison Brothers' Grocery. Ben Hoy, Hoy's Five and Ten. Sam Lester, Sam's Barbershop. And Yank Spiller. Yank was Atlas's assistant at the hardware store, and he was known as "slow." Louis knew that Yank was slow, but that he was wise, too, in things that mattered.

Fred, Jim, Bob, Ben, and Sam were all members of the Rotary Club, as Atlas had been, and they were attempting to honor one of their dead by marching in a kind of dignified military unison. They had either not told Yank Spiller they were going to do this, or, and Louis knew this was more likely, they had told him so many times, and so carefully, the instructions were still whirling around in Yank's brain and not making it down to his feet. The casket moved along like a centipede with a limp. Yank was getting it all wrong, and Louis could see the mourners cringe every time the casket received a particularly strong bounce. At last they got the thing where it was supposed to be and everyone looked relieved, except Yank, who looked a little disappointed because he was just starting to get his steps right.

The men began arranging themselves in the six seats set apart for them, and the rest of the mourners grew quiet. The Reverend Plant opened his Bible and had his mouth around the first word of the eulogy when Yank squinted into the distance and spotted Louis at the car window. He smiled brightly, the smile he always used to greet him with when Louis worked at the store on Saturdays and after school.

"Hey!" he shouted happily, and waved. "Hey, Louis."

Sphincters tightened, lips were bitten, fingers dug into palms, but no one uttered a sound.

"Louis, how you been?" He waved again.

Louis slowly reached his arm out the window and waved back. Yank no longer sat at the graveside—he stood in the middle aisle of the hardware store. Yank waved hello, and nurses worked on his face, they stirred the glowing embers and reignited the flames, and Louis cried out. At the end of the hall his parents wept. To help him fall asleep at night, the nurse with the green voice—he could not see the nurses so he gave color to their voices—turned on the faucet at the bedside sink. Do you feel that? she said. A cool waterfall, the ocean on the shores of Maine, the bluest lake in Colorado. But Louis imagined the Waverly Volunteer Fire Department pumping water out of Waverly Lake, Bernie Stratton manning the hose, dousing his face, for hours, for days. When they pumped the lake dry, Louis would finally fall asleep.

"Atlas," he said, one day. "The store?"

"It's okay, son. You got to it in time. There was only a little damage in the back room."

And Louis squeezed Atlas's hand harder, in relief Atlas believed, but he was wrong. Louis felt regret and sorrow, not for himself, because he did not know yet what lay beneath the dressings, but for the store, that any harm should come to it, even to the back room.

He had returned to the store after dinner, because he needed a jar of rubber cement to finish his senior high school art project. He had his own key, which Atlas had presented to him long ago. He valued it above all his possessions, and he kept it on a chain hooked to the belt loop of whatever pants he wore. The key had barely touched the lock when Louis knew something was wrong. He opened the door and stood by the cash register. The evening glow coming through the front windows turned everything in the store to gold—golden hammers, golden wire, golden pliers. He smelled smoke then, sharp and dangerous, and saw a gray haze seeping from beneath the door to the back room. He ran down the middle aisle, touched the door first to feel for heat, and then opened it. They mixed the paints there, and fixed lawn mowers and storm windows. The old cord to the paint mixer had started the fire, Louis knew—it was spring and they'd been using the machine all day long. A box of oily rags had been jostled too close to the frayed cord, and now the fire spread from there, sending flames curling up the wall in two or three places. Louis opened the door to the alley and yelled, Fire! Fire! Fire! Bob Madison poked his head out from the back of his store and Louis yelled, Fire! again. Then he grabbed a big piece of burlap and brought it down over the box of burning rags. Sparks flew everywhere, and the largest one, the one Louis watched as it moved across the room like a shooting star, landed on the edge of a glass jar half-filled with used paint thinner, teetered there, and then fell in. Louis heard a small explosion, and something bathed his face. That's all he felt, as if he had dipped his hands in the coldest stream in the universe and bathed his face. He opened his eyes once after that, and saw Bernie Stratton in his firemen's hat, holding a fire hose. Louis closed his eyes then, and felt the heat beyond heat, the flames that all the firemen in the world could not begin to extinguish.

Over the weeks of healing, the nurses began to leave areas of Louis's face uncovered. Gracie could stand it, could move beyond it, but not Atlas. Each time a little more of Louis emerged, he'd turn his head, or avert his eyes, some imperceptible distance away. Louis refused to look at himself while he was in the hospital.

On his first day home he went straight up to his room, pulled down the window shade, then slowly turned and faced the mirror above his chest of drawers. He stared straight into his eyes, and only his eyes, because the eyes were a part of himself he recognized. Yes, Louis, it's you. Then he began to move slowly outward, taking in the new terrain of his face. The eyelids, scorched and askew. The eyebrows, the left one burned away completely, the right one half gone and veering crookedly like the broken wing of a bird. The forehead, smeared and waxy, some of it a violent red, some a sickening pale yellow. Down to the nose, what had been the nose. They had tried to fix his left nostril with a strange skin flap that partially covered a moist black hole. When he breathed, the flap jiggled and made a whistling noise. His right nostril was intact. His cheeks seemed to be covered with bunched-up chicken skin, parts of it that terrible red. The fire had burned deep craters into the fat and muscle, the skin grafts had left lumpy scars. His lips had been drawn taut by the flame, pulled into a grimace that revealed several teeth. He could hardly bear the pain of bringing his lips together, to say even the smallest word.

He said a word, finally, after the hour he spent staring at himself in the mirror. "Boo," he whispered.

Louis returned to the hospital one final time. The plastic surgeon spoke proudly to him and Gracie and Atlas about what had been accomplished. "You've been through a lot of operations, Louis, and we have, for the most part, reconstructed your face. Of course, over the years, there will be little things we can do."

Louis stopped him with a question. "You believe you reconstructed my face?"

The surgeon hesitated, then said, "You've come a long way."

"But not all the way?"

"No, not exactly, son."

"Can you return me to what I was?"

The surgeon said quietly, "No. Only God could do that."

Louis stood up and brought a hand to his face. "Well, God did this, don't you think, and maybe we shouldn't tamper any more with his work." And then he left the room, and returned home, where he knew he'd stay forever.

In the beginning, he would stare at himself in the mirror and think, There was the Louis before, and he's gone, the Louis who stopped at sixteen. And now there's me, Louis who is not quite Louis. My name is Louis, he said over and over, relearning himself. My name is Louis and I'm almost human. My name is Louis and I'm not quite human. My name is Louis, he thought one day, and I am a monster, the beast with the soul of a man. Imagine. I lived all these years and never knew a monster lurked beneath my skin, that in a flash of heat and light it would open its eyes, and live. Maybe I should wear a sign around my neck and go out in the world: BEWARE, the sign would read: IF THE MONSTER LIVES IN ME, IT MAY LIVE IN YOU.

These were the thoughts that came to a sixteen-year-old boy staring into his mirror. Not mundane and lovely thoughts of spring, or games of baseball, or high school friends; but visions of dark creatures, and burnt monstrous things.

And so they began their life again. Gracie, Atlas, and their son, Louis, who was Louis, but not Louis. They would talk to him, from time to time, about doctors, and operations, and he would listen quietly until they finished. Each time he gently put them off. No more, he said. If you don't mind me the way I am, then I don't mind either. But, Louis, there's a world out there you're missing. Louis said, That was a world elsewhere. And I don't miss it exactly. It's just available to me in a different way now. In smaller but stronger doses, you might say.

It was available to Louis through the windows of his house. He received bits of the world, its small beauties revealed to him in hidden glances. The unimaginable beauty of the dogwood, the red dogwood Atlas planted on the day he was born, as Louis watched it season after season from his bedroom window. The beauty of the front lawn, as he peered down on it from the attic dormer, not just green, but shades of green, textures of green, even temperatures and moods of green, as the sun arced across the sky, then disappeared at the end of each day. The beauty of the street, the jet-black tar glistening on hot days, the beauty of the garage roof, its peaked angles against a clear blue sky, the beauty, even, of the chain-link fence two backyards away, and of the red doghouse in the Lindstroms' yard, and of the arrangement of the patio stones, and of the rose trellis in any season of the year, whether the roses were in bloom, or it was merely the anticipation of roses to come, or the memories of roses that had been, or no roses at all, simply the trellis itself, or the garage door itself, or the white lawn chair, all of it was lifted into rarity. Because that was his world, everything that he could see from his windows.

Sometimes he entered the world at night, or thought he entered it, because he was never sure whether he dreamed of the hidden backyards and dark driveways on his block, or actually opened his bedroom window and crept out into the night air. He'd do it, or dream it, once or twice a year, be compelled through his window, to move silently to a spot in his yard, or someone else's, that he had watched day after day. Often it was some little thing, or place, he wanted to touch and smell and be near. The bird fountain in Kitty Wilson's yard, a particular root on his own horse chestnut tree, the elephant and bear bushes in front of Bev and Bert Howard's. Once, he watched the elephants and bears play in the new snow, and when they were done he smoothed their tracks with his mittened hands so no one would know.

In time Louis didn't mind that he was a monster. He knew he was a monster without claws, or dangerous teeth, or murder in his heart. I am as harmless as the wind on your cheek, he'd whisper from behind his window shade to the little girl who feared to chase the red ball that had rolled into his yard. I am as harmless as the smell of leaves, he'd say, the words leaving a vapor on the windowpane, when the paperboy on his bicycle gave the house a wide berth. And when Atlas, who could not help himself, looked his imperceptible distance away, Louis would think, Don't be afraid, I am as harmless as the Louis who came before me, and I carry his key. Back in his room, he would lift the key to the hardware store that Atlas had entrusted to him long ago, and touch it softly to what remained of his lips.

Each night before he went to bed, Atlas would knock very lightly on Louis's bedroom door. "Louis," he'd say. "Are you there?"

Louis lay in the dark listening to his father's words. He thought it such a funny thing to say, and very sweet. He was the Waverly recluse—of course he was there. He'd answer back. "Yes, Atlas, I'm here."

Atlas wouldn't open the door, not because he was afraid of Louis, not then at least, but because the words he was about to say made him shy. "I love you, son. Goodnight, and I'll see you in the morning."

The words that came to him in the dark were so sweet Louis almost forgot that Atlas could not look at him.

Once upon a time, Atlas knocked on Louis's door and whispered, "Louis, are you there?"

Louis looked out of the car window at all the mourners seated in the distance. Reverend Plant's words were lost among the sound of birds and the buzzing of insects. Behind the reverend lay Atlas's casket, the brown wood gleaming in the sun. Louis stared at it for a long time and then he said, "Atlas, are you there?"

He heard a soft beating of wings, and felt the car jostle slightly on its springs, then a voice said, "Yes, I'm here." Louis turned toward the other side of the car, the side not facing the funeral ceremony, and saw Atlas, in his corduroy pants and his old Hush Puppies. Out of the back of his flannel shirt a pair of magnificent pearly wings with gold-tipped feathers swayed in a gentle breeze.

Atlas spoke, but his lips did not move. "Come to the window, son."

Louis slid across the car seat. He thought of all the time he'd spent at his windows. This was a different window with a different view.

"You believe what you see?" Atlas said, touching the car door.

"I always believe what I see," said Louis.

"Then remember, Louis, that on this day you saw your loving father." And with those words lingering in the air, Atlas reached slowly into the car with both hands and removed Louis's hat, and unwrapped the purple scarf from his face. Then he leaned forward, just inside the car, and kissed the scorched skin of Louis's cheek. Louis closed his eyes and felt the kiss.

When he opened them again, Atlas had disappeared, and a figure in white, leaving the sidewalk and approaching the parking lot, walked toward his car. Louis looked anxiously around for his scarf and hat, and then realized the hat was on his head, and the scarf still hid his face. Atlas...

The figure in white was a nurse, a short squat nurse, and she walked right up to the car. "Excuse me," she said. "Pardon me. But do you know whose funeral this is?"

Louis looked at her looking at him. She didn't seem to find it the least bit odd talking to a man who was invisible except for his eyes. Clearly, she had seen stranger things. She waited for him to answer.

"Um," said Louis. He was out of practice talking to people. "Atlas Malone's," he said. "This is Atlas Malone's funeral."

The nurse pondered this. Then she said, "Nope. I don't think he was ever a patient of mine. Don't remember seeing him at the hospital."

"No. He was pretty healthy. He just... went."

The nurse said, "He was a relation of yours?"

"My father."

The nurse looked at him some more. "I'm sorry. You knew that it was bound to happen, though?" She spoke the words without sounding unkind.

Louis said, "Yes. Bound to."

"I have to go, my shift's starting soon. I'll be seeing you."

I doubt it, thought the recluse of Waverly, thought the man who was not seen.

The nurse turned away, took some steps with her short legs, then turned back again. "There are worse things than death, you know."

"Yes, I know," said Louis, pulling his hat a little lower, and his scarf a little closer, as the nurse moved across the parking lot, and away.

The
Man
in the
Window

1

WHEN IRIS SHULA, THE NURSE, SAID THERE WERE WORSE things than death, she knew what she was talking about. She looked over her shoulder at the funeral, just ending, and the mourners heading for their cars, and thought, Death—now, that's the good news. The bad news was Mr. Brenner in bed 12 of the Intensive Care Unit of Barnum Memorial Hospital. Mr. Brenner, or the Tube Man, as the nurses called him, had been in a coma for five months, or as the nurses put it, he'd been dead for five months but didn't know it yet. The nurses, Iris included, were not a mean lot—they just called them as they saw them, and over the years they'd seen a lot of them. The Tube Man looked dead, felt dead, and smelled dead, but despite all that accumulated deadness, once a month on the full moon, the night-shift nurses swore the Tube Man spoke. Iris raised a silent eyebrow because everyone knew that the night shift, due to sleep deprivation or boredom, often stretched the facts. A sigh maybe, or a groan, comatose patients did that, but a word, from someone with a tracheotomy who was on a ventilator? The first word, according to the night shift, was *the*. *The* what? said Iris, who didn't believe it was *the*, but maybe *thhh* or *uhhh*, some kind of neutral mouthy sort of sound. The next month the night shift reported another word. *Man*, they said. The following full moon, the Tube Man spoke again. *In*. The nurses put all the words together, made a sentence out of them, or the beginning of a sentence, because they figured the Tube Man was making a sentence, at the rate of one word a month, which was damn good for a comatose patient. Even Iris was hooked. The next month she said, Well? to the night nurses, when she came in for her morning shift, what did he say? *The*, he said *the* again. That made it "The man in the."

Iris watched the mourners start to pull out of the cemetery parking lot. She walked on. Last month the Tube Man completed his sentence. "The man in the window." Whatever that meant. She knew it meant something, though, because every time she said it, she got a nervous, excited feeling, a strange sense of anticipation. Over the years she'd heard many odd words from her patients: delirious cries, jumbled utterances, fragments from drug dreams, mumblings from the dying. Just one week ago she'd taken care of a man with a stroke who, when you asked him if he needed a urinal, or if he was hungry, always replied, "The cat in the hat? The cat in the hat?" He said it so that it came out a question. And the old Italian lady last year, Mrs. Mellace, who did not speak a word of English until the moment of her death, which Iris witnessed. Mrs. Mellace, who hadn't moved in three days, suddenly sat bolt upright, her eyes huge and white-rimmed, and said, "I feel a certain clarity." Then she died, still sitting, her eyes unblinking. Iris had heard plenty over the years, but she'd never carried anything with her, or pondered a set of words as she had the Tube Man's "The man in the window."

The poor Tube Man, Iris thought, he doesn't have much longer. The poor part wasn't that he'd die soon, the poor part was that he'd lived so long, and in such discomfort. Iris believed, even though she knew that it couldn't really be true, that a comatose person still felt things, in a kind of way. Felt the *presence* of the tubes, the humiliation of all the wiping, and the suctioning, and the bed baths, felt the pain of constant exposure and the endless days in bed. The Tube Man had tubes in all his orifices, and in some places two or three. When he ran out of orifices, the surgeons made some more, one in his belly, another in his chest wall. He had IV tubes in three different veins through which he received, according to the time of day or night, three different fluids, clear, yellow, and thick white. Yes, there were worse things than death.

The cars from the funeral drove past and Iris looked up. She recognized the man in the hat and scarf in the window of one of them. Without thinking, she nodded ever so slightly as he went by. And did he nod back, or had the car window reflected the passing road? Why had she done such a thing? The last of the cars in the procession disappeared into the glare of the afternoon sun.

II

Herb, the ancient security guard, held open the door to the employees' entrance for her.

"Iris, my love," he said.

Iris pushed past him to the time clock. "If I'm your love then you're a desperate man, Herb."

They'd had variations on this dialogue for two years. Herb sidled over to her. He always got close enough to touch, but never did. He knew better. "A man my age knows a thing or two about love," he said.

Iris looked him over with a nurse's eye. "A man your

age knows a thing or two about blindness and senility. You got to be afflicted with both to love me.''

"You're a peach.'' Herb tried a smile, and his dentures dropped down about a quarter inch.

"Herb, take a deep breath and get some oxygen to your atrophied brain, then squint your cloudy eyes in my direction. I'm four foot seven, weigh one hundred and fifty-five very poorly distributed pounds, have a nose like a boxer's, and the complexion of a corpse.''

"I'm in the market for a woman like that.'' Herb let out a wheezy laugh.

"You don't sound so good, Herb.''

"If I collapse, you're the one I want doing mouth-to-mouth.''

Iris started off down the hall. "If you collapse, I'll help put you in the body bag.''

"You're a peach!'' he shouted after her. "You're my love!''

Iris stopped at the soda machine to get her two Pepsis, which she always drank regardless of which shift she was working. Then she put forty cents in the candy machine for her candy bar. She was working evening shift so she got a Mars bar. On nights she bought a Goldenberg's Peanut Chew because it didn't matter that her breath smelled of peanuts, since all the patients were asleep. On day shift she bought a Three Musketeers, which she immediately washed down with her first Pepsi for the double sugar kick that would get her through the morning craziness. She caught a glimpse of herself in the vending-machine glass. Like peering in a fun-house mirror—she looked stepped on, like she should pop back to her normal shape, lithe and long. Nope, she thought, that's me. Sometimes her unattractiveness surprised her. The only thing I haven't got is bad breath. Except on nights with my Peanut Chew. She had her body odor under pretty good control, too. So what? Who'd answer a personal ad that read:

"Short, dumpy, thoroughly unappealing woman, who bathes regularly and flosses nightly, seeks mate, preferably not Herb."

Iris walked down the back steps to the Intensive Care Unit, absently devouring the Mars bar she usually managed to save until just before dinner.

"Ooh. Calories, calories," came an all-too-familiar voice.

Iris looked down at Leona Richards, the hospital dietitian, prancing up the stairs. Shit, she thought, here we go. Leona obviously had never partaken of a Mars bar in her life. She packed her petite frame into the tightest white slacks in the hospital, and the only male Iris had never seen react to her was the Tube Man. Even Iris always turned her head to watch Leona's ass move down the hall, with a feeling of one part awe and two parts despair.

Iris bit into her Mars bar defiantly, and said, "How's it going, Leona?"

"You should at least be eating a granola bar," said Leona.

"Not enough sugar." Iris sucked a piece of caramel off her front teeth.

Leona winced at the sight. "I'm giving a talk on alternative carbohydrates tonight at seven in classroom B if you'd like to come."

"Sweet of you to offer . . . get it, sweet? But I'll be too busy."

Leona pressed. "Don't you care about your body? I can get you a free pass to my aerobics club."

"I couldn't even squeeze my left thigh into one of those little leotards."

"Well, wear shorts."

"Leona, this conversation's absurd. I have to get down to the Unit."

"How about walking? You can burn off—"

Iris had reached it. "Hey. What do you think will

happen if I lose some fat? There's just more fat underneath. It's fat all the way. And here's something else. Has it ever occurred to you that I like being fat and ugly? You ever thought about that? Huh?'' Iris's voice boomed in the stairwell.

Leona backed away, then turned and ran up the stairs. Iris couldn't help herself—she watched until Leona's marvelous ass disappeared from view.

Iris put a quarter in the pay phone just outside the Unit, the one anxious family members always used to relay bad news about a relative. There'd be four or five of them, looking shocked and blank, handing the phone back and forth, probably scaring the hell out of whomever they were calling, because each of their stories would be different, even though they had all talked to the same nurse or doctor. Fear caused them not to hear straight, and Iris knew that even when they nodded their heads yes, little of what she said ever got through. They saw her lips move, but what they heard was, It's bad, then it's going to get real bad, then it will get worse.

Iris dialed her father's number. She had moved up from Maryland two years ago to look after him when her mother died. Her father, Arnie, and mother, LuLu, had lived in Waverly only five years—Iris had moved ten times since she was born. Arnie, a retired auto mechanic, would suddenly say at dinner, "I feel itchy, you know?" and Iris and her mother would sigh. They knew that before the month was out, they'd be sitting down to dinner in a different house in a different town. When LuLu died, Arnie went into a deep funk. Iris said, "You going to get itchy again?" Arnie said nope, he didn't think so, looked like Waverly was a keeper. That scared Iris, so she invited him to stay in her little twin in Towson, Maryland, but he said nope again. Which scared her even more, so she moved up to Waverly to keep him from going out to the garage and inhaling carbon monoxide, or taking a big gulp of battery acid—she imagined that if he did himself in, he would honor his profession and somehow involve a car. Not kill himself in a crash, he'd never take a car down with him, but maybe plug himself into the electrical system and hit the ignition, something like that. Arnie never actually brought up the possibility of suicide after LuLu's death, but Iris, ever the nurse, had to consider it. She'd worked a year in Emergency and had seen people who killed themselves for the smallest and unlikeliest of reasons.

The phone rang seven times before Arnie picked it up. Iris held the receiver away from her ear in anticipation of his clearing his throat loudly, which is what he always did before he spoke. "Hello," he finally said.

"That's a disgusting habit," said Iris.

"Hello?" Arnie said again. He used his deaf left ear, the ear he'd pressed against car engines for forty years to listen for the little clicks and gurgles only a mechanic can decipher.

"Don't clear your throat—"

"Wear my coat?" said Arnie. "Who is this?"

"Iris!"

"Iris? What you calling for, girl? You forget your coat?"

"It's summer, Arnie. Why would I be wearing a coat?"

"I don't know. You're the one who called."

"Forget it."

"Okay, then. See you later."

"Arnie!" Too late. He'd hung up. The pay phone swallowed her quarter. She waited for the dial tone to return, then she put in another one. Fifty cents to talk to that old fool, she thought, dialing.

She waited for him to finish with his throat noises. "Hello," he said.

"Arnie, this is Iris. Don't hang up."

"Why would I hang up?"

"Well, you hung up on me last time."

"Girl, don't they give you enough to do at that job of

yours, you got all this time to spend on the telephone? It's no wonder people are always dying in hospitals.''

"Arnie, you're a pain in the ass," Iris said. A visitor frowned as he walked by, and she frowned back at him.

"That's why patients are dying, because nurses are talking dirty and spending all their time on telephones."

"You're in rare form today, Arnie."

"Thank you. That's the nicest thing you've said to me in forty years."

"I'm thirty-seven."

"It seems like forty years," Arnie muttered.

"Listen, will you please. I forgot to feed the dog. Will—"

"Need a dog!" Arnie shouted. "What the hell do we need another dog for, girl?"

Oh Jesus. Iris slumped her head against the pay phone.

Arnie's pump was primed. "Another dog. Ain't we got enough piss on the floor, you want two dogs pissing all over the place? And you know how much a can of dog food costs? Kal-Kan went up to fifty-three cents, and you multiply that by two dogs, and that comes out to something like five million dollars a year for dog food. And they won't eat the dry stuff you see taking up all that room in the stores. Fifty-pound bags. Who buys fifty-pound bags, and what do they use it for? Mulch? 'Cause no dog will eat it. Ours won't, anyway, and if you think I'm going to take that from *two* dogs, you're wrong, girl."

"Arnie. Arnie, I have to go now," Iris said, restraining herself mightily.

"Do you? Too bad. Enjoyed talking to you. Call anytime."

III

Arnie hung up the phone. That's a strange girl, he thought. How old she say she was? Thirty-seven? How'd she get to be thirty-seven? I thought I was thirty-seven.

"Where's the time go, eh, Duke?" Duke was Arnie's dog, a big reddish-brown mutt he'd hit with his car on the way home from the grocery store five or six years ago. Arnie had stopped the car and gone over to the dog, and when the dog licked his hand, that added another layer to Arnie's guilt, so he gathered him up and took him home. The dog's recuperative powers were remarkable—all it took was one big bowl of Kal-Kan, and he turned absolutely frisky. Arnie eyed him, and decided he'd been had. The dog was probably an old pro at throwing himself in front of cars for a free meal. Arnie said to him, "Okay, Duke," (he didn't know why he called him Duke, the name just came out of him) "you're welcome to stay as long as you pull your own weight." Arnie wasn't sure what he meant by that, since he had no sheep to herd, or dogsleds that needed pulling, but he thought he'd better put his foot down, especially with a dog that made its living throwing itself in front of cars. Over the years Duke proved himself better at gaining weight than pulling his weight.

"Where's the time go?" Arnie said again. "Come over here and get your scratching, Mr. Duke."

Duke ambled across the kitchen to Arnie, then turned himself one hundred and eighty degrees and let out a kind of sigh. The scratching would begin at the base of his tail, then move up his spine, and leave him paralyzed with pleasure. Duke sighed again. Only Arnie could deliver this sort of scratching, which had less to do with technique than with equipment. Arnie had a metal hook where his right hand used to be—he'd lost his hand twenty years ago when an engine block from a Chevy Impala snapped a hoist chain and crushed it. The hook, with its opposable device for grasping, while something of an inconvenience on his job as a mechanic, was great for scaring children, and even better for scratching dogs. Arnie gave Duke a long one. When he finished, the dog shuddered, then collapsed in ecstasy on the floor.

Iris kept bugging him to "update your prosthesis. You don't have to look like Captain Hook, you know. They got better things on the market these days. You'd have more freedom, and you wouldn't be scaring the hell out of little kids anymore. You notice how the Girl Scouts avoid our house during cookie season? I haven't had a chocolate mint Girl Scout cookie in ages because of that hook of yours."

But Arnie wasn't having anything to do with any "prosthesis." Prosthesis sounded like *prophylactic* to him, which shifted matters into the realm of the sexual, a place he never liked to be in discussions with Iris.

He rubbed Duke with his toe, thinking about Iris. He wondered, not really wanting to wonder, what she knew about sex. As a nurse, she had to know something, they take all those body courses in school, but what did she, and this made him really uncomfortable, know on her own? He came, as always, to an immediate and inevitable conclusion. Nothing. Not one damn thing.

Iris had been an unappealing baby—and babyhood, as it turned out, was her physical high point. She went from unappealing to unattractive, and by the time she moved into adolescence she'd become undeniably homely. Even her parents, who loved her, who gave her every benefit of the doubt and then some, could not dispute the evidence. LuLu would despair, "She's just so, just so . . ." "Homely," Arnie would finish for her, because he thought it best to face the facts. "But what's it matter?" he'd say. "In the end who gives a good goddamn?" And then he'd think, Just about the entire male population of the world, that's who.

Like the boys in Iris's senior high school class. Iris's looks compelled them, as beauty would have compelled them in the opposite direction, toward unkind acts. During the month before the senior prom, she received a phone call every night from some unknown, and ever-changing, male voice. "Hey, Iris, how about it, you wanna go to the prom? Just get a face transplant and I'll take you." Hysterical laughter from five or six boys. "Hey, Iris. If the prom was a costume party you could go as a bowling ball." Ha ha. Click. Arnie caught the tail end of one or two of these, and when he went downstairs to comfort his ugly duckling of a daughter (who would never become a swan), she shrugged him off. "Fuck 'em, Daddy. I don't care." Quite a word to come out of his teenage daughter's mouth, but he let it pass. Of course he let it pass.

Duke groaned and shifted on the kitchen linoleum. Now that Iris had moved back in after seventeen years out of the house, not this house of course since he and LuLu had moved four times since Iris left, she had become his burden again. When she arrived she said, cheerfully, "Well, Arnie. Looks like you're face-to-face with my face again." He could not pretend, as he and LuLu had tried, that away from home Iris might have some sort of luck. Seeing her every day, his bowling ball daughter, rolling around the house, made him smile at the folly of his hope, as thin as it had been.

"She's my burden, Duke. And I'm her burden. And you're everybody's burden, ain't that right?" Duke got up and went over to his bowl and let out a low whine. Arnie regarded him for a moment, then said, "I forget to feed you? Is that right? Now where'd she get a notion we needed another dog, I can't even feed you." Arnie reached up in the cupboard and snared a can of food with his hook. He opened it, then dumped its contents into Duke's bowl. Duke stared at the bowl, then gave Arnie the dog equivalent of a puzzled look.

"What's the matter with you?" Arnie examined the contents of the bowl, which *did* look kind of peculiar. He picked up the can. Spaghetti-O's. He'd just filled up the dog's bowl with Spaghetti-O's.

He tried to cover for himself. "Hey, look. I thought you might like a change." Duke stared at him, unblinking. Obviously he wasn't buying it.

"So I screwed up, okay?" He tossed out the Spaghetti-O's and filled the bowl with Kal-Kan. "You won't tell Iris? It's between you and me, right?" he said, half-jokingly.

Spending too much time around the house, he thought. That's the problem. You get a little dippy. Last week, instead of his Polident tablets, he'd dropped two Alka-Seltzer tablets into his denture cup. His dentures turned a light green, which Iris had not failed to notice. The week before that, he had poured V-8 juice on his Frosted Flakes, and ate three spoonfuls before he caught himself. Fortunately, Iris had not yet come down to breakfast.

Christ. I'm deaf in one ear, I got no teeth, I'm missing my right hand, and now I'm going senile. Senile's the thing.

"Senile's the thing, right, Duke?"

You go senile and they put you right in the Home. Course now, this ol' hook may present them with a little problem. Yep. I'll be able to fend them off for a while. Unless of course I lose the damn thing, which is likely the way things are going. Hell, Iris's a nurse, she'll take care of me. I don't know, though, being a patient of hers might go pretty rough. No. I'd rather be in the Home. No. They'd take my dentures, take my hook—I'd sit around in one of those rolly chairs and pee-pee on myself all day. Least Iris would keep me tidy.

Duke licked his bowl clean. "Think I'm getting dippy, boy? No, I'm just cooped up here too much."

The thing was, he never thought he'd have to live without LuLu. They just snatched her away from him, like they snatched his hand. He thought the two of them would go together, in bed, like it was their honeymoon—instead of their whole lives stretching before them, the end of life would await them, and when he'd imagined it that way, he wasn't frightened. But with LuLu gone—the entire business scared the bejesus out of him. He'd never, ever discussed it with LuLu, but he'd been counting on her. He should have discussed it—maybe she would have hung on, waited for him. But she couldn't have waited. The stroke would've got her, just like the engine got my hand. Things get you. Iris'll tell you about that, all her hospital stories.

"Come on, Duke, let's go for a walk. Maybe we'll see somebody we know." A joke, of course, since he didn't know anybody in Waverly. He wasn't much for knowing people. He had LuLu and he'd figured that would be enough. And all the moving from town to town. You don't get attached to people that way. Iris helped to fill up the hole a little, the hole that LuLu left. She knew how to get on his nerves, which helped to pass the time.

Arnie started off down the block with Duke up ahead, trotting along dragging his leash. Sometimes he'd be on his walk with Duke and he'd stop suddenly, almost midstep, and look around, and not know where in God's name he was. Which town, of all the towns over all the years, was he in? Not only which town, but what year? It started happening after LuLu died of her stroke—she was his bearing, and she'd left him, stranded on a sidewalk, lost in time and place. Where was home? Home was where LuLu was, and LuLu was nowhere. He'd come in after an hour or two, and Iris would look at him a minute and then say, "Boy, that was a long walk." You don't know the half of it, Arnie would think. He was lucky he made it back to the house at all. He'd go right upstairs and lie on his bed, sweaty and nervous, and try to recall LuLu's face, place her firmly in this room, in this house, so he wouldn't lose himself again.

Arnie tipped his hat as a middle-aged couple walked by. They barely looked at him. See? They know. I'm unconnected and they know it. LuLu, I didn't learn how to do it. Even at work, all the different auto shops and garages, I paid attention to the cars, not the guys I worked with. I should've had beers with them, I should've stayed put in one town. LuLu, we were supposed to go together, that was the plan. Why didn't you know that?

He walked on for a few blocks, following Duke. Finally, Duke stopped and waited for him. They stood together, and Arnie lifted his hat and mopped his brow with his handkerchief. The pincer mechanism on his hook jammed and he had to work the thing loose, then he put the hat back on his head.

"Don't ever get one of these, Duke, they're a pain in the ass." He almost stepped off the curb when he saw a whole parade of cars heading up the street. A funeral. The lead car, a big silver Lincoln, kind of jerked to the left as it drove by, and the engine sputtered and died. The other cars jammed on their brakes as the Lincoln coasted to a stop. Duke wagged his tail, which he always did when a car was near. Arnie figured he was remembering the old days when he used to throw himself in front of them.

Jim Rose got out of the car, looking like he wanted to say a few dirty words. Arnie remembered Jim Rose because he'd used Rose's Funeral Home when LuLu died. He wouldn't ride in the Lincoln, though, as hard as Jim Rose tried to persuade him. First, what was the point in having a fancy car with no parade behind it—it was only him and Iris, and another carload of ladies from LuLu's church. Second, a Lincoln was a piece of shit under the hood, and he wouldn't soil his pants by plunking his ass down in one.

Arnie stepped off the curb and joined Jim Rose and the other men who'd pulled over to have a look at the jumble of wires and metal, which obviously baffled the hell out of them. He enjoyed himself a minute, listening to their expert advice. Then he said, "Mr. Rose, you need some assistance?"

Jim Rose, looking real hot and real close to letting loose with a string of those dirty words, eyed Arnie, then eyed Arnie's hook, and said, "No thanks, old-timer. We got it."

Arnie smiled. So you think. He moved away and idly walked around the car. Two people sat in the Lincoln, a woman about his age, and a . . . he guessed it was a man, wearing a baseball hat pulled low and a purple scarf. How about that? Arnie nodded and the fellow nodded back ever so slightly, then scooted down in his seat. Mighty peculiar business, Arnie thought. He glanced at the woman again; she looked pitiful and wilted from the heat.

Jim Rose tried the engine, but the only thing he got was a clicking sound. Arnie looked again at the woman, then moved to the front of the car. "Here. I'm a mechanic. You stay put, Mr. Rose, and hit the ignition when I say." Arnie fiddled with the distributor cap a minute. "Okay, now hit 'er." The car kicked to life. Arnie went around to the driver's window. "You need a new cable."

"Thank you," said Jim Rose. He turned his head and said, "You all right, Mrs. Malone?"

"I'm fine." She craned herself over the man in the hat and scarf and said through the window to Arnie, "Thank you, sir," and smiled.

The man in the hat and scarf stared at Arnie's hook. Arnie looked at him and then said, "Yeah, son. I guess we all got something."

The man looked like he was about to speak, but Jim Rose touched the accelerator and the Lincoln moved off down the street.

IV

Iris sat in the conference room at the far end of the Intensive Care Unit, waiting to take report from day shift. The Unit looked wild. They had a new one in bed 7, a gastrointestinal bleed. Two docs were in there, and three nurses, trying to hold the guy down. GI bleeds were almost always alcoholics, about as messy and ornery a patient as you could get. Respiratory and a bunch of other people crammed into bed 8, tubing somebody and setting up a vent. So a bleed in 7, thought Iris, someone crashing in 8, the Tube Man in bed 12, and one other ventilator patient in 5. So that'll be three people on vents when they finish tubing 8, and the rest of the beds were stable cardiacs, and stable post-ops. A full house—twelve patients.

"Place looks crazy," said Libby, a permanent evening nurse, walking into the conference room and glumly dropping into a chair.

"Tell me about it," said Iris. "You see what's in 7?"

Libby did a cheerleader chant. "Give me a B, an L, a double E, D. What's that spell?"

"Alcoholic," said Denise, walking in. "Let's hear it for the alkies."

"What's your guess?" said Libby. "A fifth a day, or a case of beer a day?"

"Both," said Iris.

They peered out the door and saw the bleeder pull free from a nurse and take a swing at the doctor who was trying to insert a Blakemore tube down his nose.

"Naaah," said Denise. "Looks like a social drinker to me."

They all laughed. What else could they do, with eight hours of trying to subdue a bloody wild man ahead of them?

Libby said, "It's not just us three, is it?"

"No way," said Denise. "I'll quit. I'll go up to the nursing office and rip up my time card in front of them."

Iris nodded at Denise's threat, then picked up the phone and paged the supervisor. The call-back came immediately. "Mrs. Beeman, Iris here. You sending us anybody else?... No, we don't have two empties, the place is full.... No, the bleeder didn't die in the Emergency Room, he's in bed 7...."

Denise and Libby rolled their eyes. Denise mouthed "Tell her I quit."

"... Yeah, and somebody's crashing in 8. ... I don't know who, I just got here. ... Okay. Okay. Good. Good, we'll take her. Fine. Bye."

"Let me guess," said Libby. "They're sending us a nurse's aide from Rehab."

"Nope, an RN from Orthopedics."

"A real live RN? Honest-to-God competence?"

"It's Dolores Winston."

"Oh shit," said Libby and Denise in unison, "the Terminator."

Dolores had earned her nickname a year ago when she was pulled from the floor to work in the Unit. She had removed the tape from the airway of a patient on a ventilator, then left the airway hanging there to go answer another patient's call light. Then she forgot about the ventilator patient and went into the back room for a cigarette. The patient coughed out the unsecured airway and coded. They managed to resuscitate him, just.

"We'll give her the stable patients," said Denise.

"Give her the dead patients, that'd be safer," said Libby. "Give her the Tube Man, he's a no code."

"I'm taking the Tube Man," said Iris, who was charge nurse for the evening. She felt something strange in her chest when she said his name, and swallowed hard.

"Suit yourself. Then give her a couple of cardiacs and a post-op," said Denise. "I'll take the GI bleed, what the hell."

Libby and Iris clapped. Libby said, "Give me the guy crashing in 8, and split the rest however you want."

"You two are wonderful," said Iris.

"Just keep the Terminator out of my patients' rooms," said Denise. "Here she comes."

Dolores walked in. Cute as a button and dumb as dirt. She had the second nicest body in the hospital, after Leona. What, are they testing me tonight or something? thought Iris.

She had never trusted beauty. She didn't believe it somehow, that it lasted, that the right people had it, that it wasn't in some way corrupting. She frowned at Dolores, cute Dolores with her little nose and her bouncing honey curls.

"Hi guys," said Dolores. "Looks like I'm in the Unit tonight." She turned and surveyed the chaos in 7 and 8, then demonstrated her usual understanding of critical situations. "Doesn't look too bad out there."

Libby and Denise rolled their eyes behind her back. Iris bit her tongue.

Report from day shift was a disaster. Even Dolores seemed to get the message. "I don't think I want to be here," she said when report ended.

An encouraging sign of intelligence, thought Iris. "That's the correct response, Dolores." No nurse from the regular floors liked to be pulled to the Unit. The Unit was the dumping ground for all the patients too sick for anyone else to handle. Very few were "walkie-talkies," patients who could engage in normal human communication and locomotion. Most were bed-bound and had a minimum of two IVs and a drainage tube. Even the so-called stable patients were time bombs, especially the cardiacs who looked good one minute, then you'd glance up at the EKG monitor and their hearts would suddenly start pumping at 180, then go flat line.

Iris said to Dolores, "I'm going to have to give you three patients, Dolores, you see how busy it is."

Dolores swallowed.

"But they'll be pretty stable," said Iris, hearing in her own head the tick tick tick of the time bomb. "Beds 1 and 2 are both cardiacs who are doing pretty well. Keep your eye on 2, he goes into heart failure at the drop of a hat. You heard in report how they had to load him up on digoxin and Lasix, so stay on top of his lungs. I'm also giving you 6, who's a fem-pop bypass second day post-op. They're not sure if his grafts are working, so watch his circulation, especially his right foot—it looked dusky on day shift, and they couldn't get all his pulses. Okay? Shouldn't be too bad, really, Dolores.''

Dolores smiled weakly, and her honey curls seemed to lose the bounce they had before she'd heard day shift's report.

Iris went into 7 to help out with the GI bleed. He'd thrown up a good basin or two of blood, she could tell from looking at his gown and the saturated bed sheets. This guy looked like he belonged in a big city hospital, not in a place like Barnum Memorial. Barnum served Waverly, Upper Providence, Smithfield, and three or four other towns. They all had their alcoholics, and more than a few of them came in just like this guy. Iris read the patient's name posted on the door: Harvey Mastuzek. Denise had hold of Harvey's thrashing legs, and Libby pressed against the upper part of his body. The house doctor still hadn't gotten the Blakemore tube in. Blood dotted the doctor's white coat, as well as the bedside table and commode. Harvey jerked his head violently every time the doc tried to get near his nose with the tube. Nobody in the room looked like they were having much fun.

Iris marched up to the bed. The bed was in its highest position, and she could barely peer over the edge of the mattress. She gave Harvey the long hard nurse's look she'd learned over many years of nursing. Daniel Boone might have used the same look to stare down a grizzly. It caught Harvey's attention.

''Who the fuck are you?'' he snarled. A line of blood bubbled down the corner of his mouth.

Iris smiled sweetly. ''I am an angel of mercy, and I want to help you.''

''Then get these people the fuck off me.''

''Harvey, we have to get this tube in your belly to help stop the bleeding.''

"I'm not bleeding." Harvey was more than a little out of it. He blinked blearily at her.

"Harvey, you are bleeding, and if you don't let this kind and patient doctor put that tube down your nose and into your belly, you will bleed to death."

Harvey stared at her a minute, then he mumbled, "Fuck him, and fuck you. I don't like you. I don't like your face."

Libby and Denise tensed and looked away. The house doctor fiddled with the Blakemore tube. Iris moved to the head of the bed. "Excuse me, Harvey?"

Harvey said, "You heard me."

"I don't think so. I heard something rude, but I really don't think that's what you meant to say." Her face was inches from his.

Harvey pushed against the pillow. "Stay away from me, you little troll."

Iris went up on her toes, her mouth almost touching his ear. "I'm only saying this once," she whispered. "You cut the shit right now and let us put the tube in, or I'll come in here when no one's looking and slice off your balls with a dull scalpel."

Harvey opened his mouth as if to speak, but nothing came out.

Iris looked at the house doctor. "Okay, Doc. Harvey says you can put that Blakemore in now."

Harvey lay perfectly still as the tube went in. He kept his eyes on Iris the entire time, as she stood in the corner of the room smiling at him.

V

Other jobs, thought Iris at about 9 P.M., couldn't be like this. Other jobs, you get to sit down once in a while, you get to eat your supper, you're not running your butt off every second, picking patients up off the floor and putting them back to bed, fighting with docs and X-ray techs and pharmacists and lab, cleaning up blood and packing wounds, suctioning and turning and injecting and irrigating and draining and bandaging, transferring patients out and getting new ones from the ER, hanging IV meds. And all the rest of it. And that was when things were going normally, thought Iris, downing a warm Pepsi, her third of the evening—that was before crunch time.

Crunch time had come at 8 P.M. when Dolores's patient, bed 1, coded. When they saw what bed the code was in, everybody thought: the Terminator strikes again. But it wasn't her fault, except for the kind of evil magic she seemed to work on her patients. Bed 1 had been the most stable heart patient in the Unit, a resolving myocardial infarction. He was an MI who hadn't even suffered that much damage to his heart muscle; he was due to go up to the regular floor the next day. Iris was standing beside Dolores, checking a chart, when Dolores said, "That looks funny."

Dolores had been looking at the central EKG monitor, and since she didn't know how to read heart rhythms, they all looked funny to her. Iris finished reading her chart, then followed Dolores's gaze.

Iris swore. The rhythm that had caught Dolores's eye, that would have caught anyone's eye, was bed 1's. The other patients' rhythms beat with regular electric jiggles. Bed 1's chaotic jags meant only one thing.

"V-fib," shouted Iris, already running for the room. "Call a code, Dolores."

Bed 1, Mr. Beck, sat up in bed, his eyes rolled back in his head. He was making the "gh-ghhh" sound. The gh-ghhh sound was not a good sign, Iris knew. Most of the patients who reached that stage didn't make it. Libby came in with the emergency cart as Iris put the head of the bed down and started CPR. Short Iris always had difficulty getting a good position for CPR; she had to climb in bed and kneel beside the patient so she could do her chest compressions. This always led to a lot of teasing from the docs about how Iris would use any excuse to get in bed with a man.

The code finally came over the hospital address system: "Code ninety-nine, bed 1, ICU." It seemed to take forever for help to come, and as always, the nurses were on the front line holding things together until it did. Iris continued compressions, while Libby bagged Mr. Beck with 100 percent oxygen. Denise arrived and charged up the defibrillator. Dolores stood in the doorway, mouth open, doing nothing.

"Dolores, go out there and keep your eyes on the other patients, will you?" Iris grunted between compressions.

Despite their efforts, Mr. Beck began to turn a mottled blue. His gh-ghhs grew faint. Respiratory arrived and slid a tube down his throat and into his lungs. The IV team stuck some lines in him, and two docs showed up and started ordering meds. They shocked the patient seven times and administered all the emergency drugs at least once, and hung up all the IV meds you could hang. Still, Mr. Beck turned an eggplant blue, and stopped making sounds. His EKG slowly smoothed out from jagged V-fib to flat line. Iris pumped his chest the entire time, pumped even after one of the docs said, "Okay, it's over. Let's call it." She was the last to stop working on the patient.

After the family had come and gone, Iris went in to help Dolores and Libby wrap the body. Iris didn't mind the look of a dead body lying in bed. Wrapping the body in the plastic shroud sheet, however, gave her the creeps.

"When I die," she said, "don't you dare wrap me in plastic."

"How about aluminum foil?" said Libby. "You'll stay fresher longer."

"You guys!" Dolores frowned. Floor nurses rarely appreciated the humor of the Unit nurses, the darkest and dirtiest in the hospital.

"I'm serious," said Iris, holding Mr. Beck's hands together as Libby tied them across his chest. "I'm afraid of suffocating."

"You'd be dead," said Libby. "Here, Dolores—put your finger there so I can tie a knot."

"Even so," said Iris.

"One of his eyes is open," said Dolores.

"He's winking at you," said Libby.

Iris thought, Yeah, Dolores, you're so cute even a dead man winks at you. Out loud, she said, "Why don't you close it if it bothers you?"

"I can't do eyeballs," said Dolores softly.

"You know what I can't do?" said Libby. "Toes. I don't know. For some reason toes really get to me." She handed Iris a card with Mr. Beck's name and related information stamped on it. "Here, Iris. You tie the toe card on for me, pretty please?"

"You guys are such chickens. So I got to do the toe *and* the eyeball?" She reached up and touched her finger to his left eyelid. When she got it down, the right one went up.

Dolores jumped back as Iris and Libby tried not to laugh. "You did that on purpose," she said.

"I didn't do it on purpose, *he* did it on purpose."

"Yeah, Dolores," said Libby. "Sometimes these guys aren't as dead as you think. Remember Mr. Harvard?" she said to Iris.

"The only time I thought I was going to lose it."

"We had him all wrapped up like a mummy—"

"A *plastic*-wrapped mummy," said Iris. "Ugh."

"—and just as we were about to slide him from the bed onto the stretcher, he sits up."

"And I mean up," said Iris. "Right up, like he was getting out of bed in the morning. I'm telling you, I screamed."

"Everybody in the room screamed," said Libby.

"So he wasn't dead?" whispered Dolores, keeping one eye on Mr. Beck.

"Oh, he was dead," said Iris. "He was just squeezing the last bit of goody out."

"Usually they just fart," said Libby.

"Or jerk an arm or a leg."

"Or groan. A lot of them groan."

"Some of them speak outright. How about that guy last year, what was his name?" said Iris.

"Lauber? Stauber? Something like that," said Libby.

"What'd he say?" whispered Dolores.

"He was another one we had all wrapped up," said Iris. "But we heard him clear as day. Really creepy."

"What'd he say?"

" 'Pepsodent.' "

"Pepsodent? That's creepy?" said Dolores. "That doesn't seem creepy to me."

Iris looked at her. "The word itself wasn't creepy, Dolores. The creepy thing was that he spoke at all. Since he was dead and everything."

"Why'd he say Pepsodent?"

"We couldn't figure it out. You see, the whole time he was in the Unit, he brushed his teeth with Crest," said Libby.

"I think it was a regret thing," said Iris. "Like probably all his life he wanted to try Pepsodent, but he never got around to it. He carried the regret to his death. Beyond his death, really. Because he was definitely dead when he spoke."

"Definitely," said Libby.

Iris often wondered what word she'd utter beyond her own death. What regret would rise to her dead lips, what longing? "Beauty," perhaps? Is that what she'd say? It would have been nice to be beautiful for a day, to try it, to see what all the fuss was about. Maybe "Love"? That's another one she'd never get close to. She embarrassed herself. She didn't have time for foolishness. "All right, guys, let's finish this."

They got out the white plastic shroud sheet and slid it under Mr. Beck. They taped it around his feet and legs, his chest.

Iris said, "You guys don't do eyeballs and toes. Well, I don't wrap heads. Dolores, he's your patient."

Dolores made a face. "He's still kind of winking."

Libby took the tape from her. "I'll do it." She pulled the last corner of the plastic shroud over his face and taped it.

Then they all stood there and stared at the mummy that had been Mr. Beck. A minute or so passed. Nope, thought Iris, didn't look like he was going to sit up or speak or even fart. Looked like winking was it. "Okay. Two more hours and this night is over."

Time to do right by the Tube Man. Iris had given him maintenance care all shift, performing the essentials while she kept the chaos in the Unit under control. She'd turned him on his left side at seven P.M., two hours ago, and he hadn't moved a molecule since. The ventilator hissed and puffed in the corner, delivering its twelve automatic breaths per minute. Every other minute it administered a sigh, lifting the Tube Man's chest an inch or so higher than usual. Three IV pumps clicked and bipped on their poles beside the bed, steadily infusing the Tube Man with fluids. Iris hung two new IV bags. She spoke to him as she worked.

"Hello there. This is Iris again. I'm going to get you straightened up for the night, all right?" She always spoke to the comatose patients, told them what she was doing. If they could still hear, it was the polite thing to do, and if they couldn't, well, what the hell.

"It's been really busy tonight, sorry I couldn't get to you sooner. I'm going to suction your breathing tube now, then clean around it a little bit." Suctioning terrified most patients. They coughed and turned maroon, and usually fought it. Because he was so far gone, the Tube Man didn't react at all. He turned quietly dusky as Iris suctioned the mucus out, then quietly pink again when she bagged him with 100 percent oxygen.

"I'm going to wash your back and bottom now, and change your sheet." Iris had no problem turning him, he'd lost so much weight. His skin was pale and papery, and it sometimes tore when the nurses changed his dressing.

"You been here a long time, haven't you?" she said as she powdered his back. "You must be getting pretty tired of all this, of us coming in here and bothering you, and jabbing you with needles and all. We don't mean to hurt you, do you know that?"

The Tube Man gave no sign of knowing, or not knowing. She turned him on his back again and saw that his eyes were open. But that didn't mean anything. Sometimes they did that. If they were open too long, the nurse applied artificial tears. Artificial tears, and artificial breaths, and artificial food—she wondered how much of the Tube Man was real anymore. And what was behind those open eyes? Was he in a long coma dream, or was there nothing going on in his brain? She imagined a kind of wind whistling in there, like the wind that might be whistling across a distant planet. Pluto. When she was little, Arnie had told her about the planets. Mercury, the hot one. Venus, the green one. Mars had Martians. All the way to Pluto, which Arnie didn't describe as cold or dark, but as having an undying wind that blew across its surface. It never changed, never blew harder or softer. "How did it get there?" Iris had asked. Arnie thought a minute, then he said, "Well, God had just about finished creating everything, and He was real tired. And the last thing He created was Pluto, which He let out into the sky with a big sigh. The sigh became the wind that always blows across Pluto." Maybe that's what it was like inside the Tube Man's head. A wind blew there, God's long, tired sigh.

She swabbed out the Tube Man's mouth. There was the usual puddle of thick drool on the pillowcase, so she changed it. She washed his face, which was all hard bone, and then suddenly loose over his caved-in cheeks, because he had no teeth. The Tube Man watched her actions with unmoving eyes. She took his blood pressure and temperature, and wrote them on his bedside chart. Then she opened a can of nutritional supplement and poured its creamy gray contents into a bag that hung on a pole above the Tube Man's head. The bag was connected to a long tube that entered his left nostril and ended in his stomach. The supplement flowed day and night at sixty cc's an hour, an unending blur of breakfast-lunch-dinner.

The ventilator alarm suddenly buzzed, and the high pressure limit light flashed on. The Tube Man turned dusky. Iris popped open a suction kit, went down his airway, and sucked out a big mucus plug. His color slowly returned to normal. She half smiled: she'd just saved his life, for the umpteenth time. He'd been getting a lot of plugs lately. His heart had been slowing over the last few weeks, too, and going into wacky rhythms. He didn't have much longer; something would finally get him. Then the nurses would pull out all his tubes, tie a toe card on him, and wrap him in his shroud sheet—and that would be that.

The last thing Iris did for him was comb his hair. When he came in five months ago, he'd had a fine full head of gray hair. Hardly any remained. She combed the wispy strands anyway, and restrained herself from saying, "There, now you look nice," which is what she usually said after fixing a patient's hair. Nice? You couldn't make a dying skeleton who was full of tubes look nice. No wonder no one came to visit the Tube Man anymore. Who could bear to look at him? Only the nurses, whose job it was to care for all the abandoned bodies, to touch the untouchables.

Iris straightened up the room and checked the supplies, then she emptied his urine bag and totaled his intake and output on the daily chart. His urine output had tapered to practically nothing over the last couple of days. No, it wouldn't be long.

"Okay, sir. I'm going out of the room now." She clicked off the overhead light, and turned to walk out the door.

And then behind her, rising above the sound of blips and beeps and sighs from all the machines crowded into the room, a word, a single word:

"Is."

Iris slowly turned and looked at the Tube Man. He had spoken again. She could see in the dim light that his eyes had closed; otherwise, everything about him was exactly the same. The same, except that he had moved from the depths of his coma and said a word. Was he starting a new sentence? A sentence beginning with "Is"? He'd never get it out—he didn't have five more months to speak another sentence.

She went over to him, went up on tiptoes, and repeated his word in his ear. "Is? Is?" And then she waited a moment, as if there was some kind of real and actual chance he'd speak again. Despite herself she said, "Give me more, can't you?" She felt funny in the chest, nervous, and her mouth was dry. The Tube Man lay motionless. She could almost hear the winds of Pluto whistling through his brain.

"You have to finish it, don't you see?"

She said the word to herself, trying to imagine how he would work it. "*Is* this a hospital?" "*Is* this fair?" "*Is* this it?"

She had a thought then. "Is" wasn't the start of a new sentence, but a continuation, maybe, of his first one? "The man in the window." She'd assumed that was all of it. But no, the Tube Man was still working on it. "The man in the window *is* . . ."

Iris hugged herself as she watched the ventilator puff breaths into the dying figure beneath the white sheet. She knew that someday soon, he would speak the name of the man in the window.

VI

Arnie sat on the front porch steps in the late summer dark. Duke wandered around in the yard, trying to eat fireflies. Arnie couldn't see too well, but even with one deaf ear he could hear Duke snapping at them, and then there'd be a lot of spitting and chewing sounds when he caught one.

"Duke. What the hell you doing out there? What are you eating bugs for?"

Duke snapped and spit again.

"You swallow enough of those fireflies, your balls will light up. What'll Iris say, she comes home and sees your balls blinking on and off?"

A window slammed closed next door. Guess you aren't supposed to shout about dog balls in this neighborhood. Arnie smirked, then took another sip from his beer. His hook crunched into the can, and a few drops foamed out of a hole and dripped on his knee. Iris would be getting home pretty soon. He figured he'd wait up for her. What a shitty job, working evenings and getting home after eleven. How'd she stand shift work? He took another sip of beer and watched all the fireflies that had escaped Duke's jaws of death. LuLu had liked the fireflies. In a summer long ago they had sat together on a front porch holding hands and kissing, and watching fireflies. Holding hands. He lifted his arm and stared at the dull silver hook on the end of it. The hand that had touched LuLu was gone. They take your hand, they take your wife—Jesus, what a world.

The lady today in the backseat of the Lincoln, who'd they take from her? Mrs. Malone, Jim Rose called her. And the strange-looking guy in the hat and scarf beside her, her son probably. He looked young around the eyes. It had to be Mr. Malone who'd died, her husband. Welcome to the club, Mrs. Malone. Arnie raised his beer in a salute, then downed a big gulp. Poor lady. She had quite a smile. Even under those circumstances, she managed to smile and thank him for fixing the car. She was a hell of a lot more gracious than that stiff, Jim Rose.

LuLu had a smile on her, too. She didn't smile so much the last couple of years before she died, though, because of her dentures. She was terrified they'd fall out of her mouth. She must have gone through a tube of Dentu-Grip a week— you couldn't have pulled the damn things loose with a pair of pliers. She never let him see her without them. At night, she'd work on herself in the bathroom, then scurry across the room in the dark to bed.

"You're going to kill yourself, running around in the dark like that," he'd say to her.

"If I do," she whispered, her words mushy and tooth-less, "don't you dare look at me until they get my dentures in."

"Hell, LuLu. What you so sensitive about your teeth for? I got a hook! I'm missing my entire hand! I'm the one who should be sensitive."

"But you're a man, Arnie. It doesn't matter to you in the same way. I was pretty once," she said softly.

Arnie reached out to touch her, with his hook he realized at the last moment, so he shifted around and reached again with his good hand. "Not once. Still. You're pretty, still."

"Sure. In the dark."

"In the dark I got my hand again, you got your teeth. There's nothing wrong with the dark. You're pretty, I'm handsome. We get to do it all over again."

"I'd like to do it all over again, Arnie."

"All of it?"

"Most of it," said LuLu. "The parts with you. The parts with you when my teeth were good."

Arnie sat on the porch steps, Duke at his side, remembering

LuLu as she wanted to be remembered: young, her smile bright, her teeth good.

He jumped when an apparition in white suddenly appeared before him.

"Iris girl, don't be creeping around this late at night. You want your old man to piss himself?"

"You'd just be joining the club," said Iris. "Most all the old men I took care of tonight pissed themselves. And worse, let me tell you."

Arnie raised his hand. "No, don't tell me. You're always wanting to tell me. How come is it you health people got to be so quick with the bad news? I never saw a group of people so eager to give all the nasty details."

Iris stood before Arnie and looked him in the eye, which she could manage only because he was sitting on the porch steps. "All the details? You'd piss yourself for sure if I ever gave you all the details."

"So, good. You keep your details and I'll keep my pants dry."

"Well, you're certainly in a feisty mood. What are you and that ratty dog of yours doing up so late?"

Arnie looked past her to the dark and the fireflies. "Oh, I don't know," he said. "Didn't seem like much of a night for sleeping. Thought I'd wait up for you. You know."

Iris put her pocketbook down and sat on a step below him. A good deal of her round fat bottom hung over the edge. She looked out into the night for a while, then she said, "So, thinking about Mom, are you?"

"Sure. You know it. Thinking about LuLu."

Iris wondered what that would be like, to love someone so much. She knew that somewhere in the dark, amidst the glow of the fireflies, LuLu was there for Arnie. A love that conjured up the dead. In the hospital when someone died, they died, that was it. Nothing you could bring back, nothing in between about it. Well, that wasn't quite true—the Tube

Man was certainly in between. Great. Arnie has LuLu, and I have the Tube Man.

Arnie was thinking along the same lines, missing LuLu and feeling sorry for himself, but feeling sorry for his unnaturally homely daughter, too, because she had no one to miss. He tried sometimes to see in her some extraordinary hidden gift, some thing of great beauty, the pearl that would make her attractive to a man. But if there was a pearl, it lay deeply and irretrievably buried. Where she was not unsightly, she was merely ordinary. Her voice didn't dazzle, she had no great brains, she cooked but with no particular interest or talent for it, she couldn't dance and didn't want to (a wise choice—when Arnie imagined Iris throwing her concentrated weight around a dance floor, his stomach went acidy). Her hair didn't shine, her feet were not small, the clothes she wore didn't enhance her qualities, because she had few qualities to enhance. She could be funny at times, and kind at times, but not overwhelmingly, not to a degree that might cause a guy to give her a second look. The best Arnie could come up with for Iris's main selling point was that she did what she was supposed to do. Which wasn't so bad really, in a world where you couldn't depend on anybody. Iris showed up for work on time, she bathed regularly with sensible soap, and she paid her bills. Arnie doubted there was anyone out there staying up nights fantasizing about a woman like that.

So the two of them sat on the steps looking out into the night, Arnie feeling sorry for Iris, and Iris feeling sorry for Arnie, but neither of them really wanting to talk about it, because what, after all, could you say?

Iris took off her nursing shoes and wiggled her white-stockinged toes. "Any more beers left?"

Arnie stood up, relieved to escape his thoughts. "Sure, sure. Stay there, I'll get you one."

"Great," she said, rubbing her feet. "I wore the treads off these babies tonight."

"Bad night?"

Iris opened her mouth to speak.

Arnie pushed on the screen door and hurried inside. "No details! No details!"

Duke yawned and regarded Iris. A crushed bit of firefly flickered weakly on the corner of his mouth. Iris brushed it off. "Why don't you be useful and eat something like cockroaches or ants?" Arnie came back out with her beer and a fresh one for himself. They drank, and listened to the crickets. Iris felt the alcohol ease through her. She thought about her night—the GI bleeder, wrapping bed 1 in the shroud sheet, the Tube Man, Libby and Dolores and Denise. She let the beer flow around all of it, and through it, until the edges were a little less sharp, the particulars less defined. She let herself drift, all the way back to the encounter she'd had on the way to work. Now she had time to think about it, to wonder about the man in the baseball hat and purple scarf.

She'd wondered about it all night, of course, but didn't have enough time to really get to it. She kept meaning to ask Libby or Denise about him, they'd both grown up in Waverly, but it had been so damn busy. Something was wrong with him, obviously. As a nurse, she'd seen lots of people attempt to conceal or disguise their disfigured parts. The ladies who wore bright scarves around their necks to hide their tracheotomies, or the ones who wore gloves on their arthritic hands, even in the summer. That old Irish guy who wore his golf cap, even in bed, to cover the metal plate in his head where the skin wouldn't graft. Sometimes the wound was in a place where clothes couldn't do any good. Like the patient last month who'd lost part of his tongue to cancer. He couldn't wear anything to hide his tongue; the best he could do was place his hand over his mouth when he spoke, like a shy oriental girl. What with the tongue and the hand, Iris never understood a word he'd said.

So what was wrong with the man in the hat and scarf? It

must have been pretty bad, that he had to wrap and cover himself like the Invisible Man. She swallowed and looked around at the shadows of the night. Now there was a creepy thought: maybe he *was* the Invisible Man. She didn't remember seeing his hands or anything. No. His eyes. How could she have forgotten them? She'd looked right into them. The Invisible Man didn't have eyes; he always wore sunglasses. The man in the car looked like he wanted to be invisible, though. He didn't get out much, she was pretty sure of that. The way he scrunched down in his seat when she asked him about the funeral and that rusty, unused sound to his voice. She'd heard voices like that before, people who'd been in comas for days or weeks and then awakened, they always sounded dry and a little lost.

His voice was unused, maybe, but not his eyes. He lived through his eyes, she could tell. Like the paralyzed patients she'd worked with, those imprisoned bodies with the eyes that were everywhere. Their sight was almost a palpable thing. She could feel it on her skin when she entered the room, when she bathed them, and turned them. They were so hungry for something new to look at. They used their eyes to look, and to smell, too, and to touch and taste. It was very strange for her to be so appreciated for her physical presence. She, Iris, who had not one thing of beauty to offer, was practically devoured by the eyes of her paralyzed patients. She'd felt something like that when the man in the hat and scarf lifted his eyes to her.

Iris began to feel a little funny. She tried to blame it on the beer, but that wasn't it. And she was very tired, but that wasn't it either. She hadn't eaten a proper meal since breakfast—too many Pepsis and candy bars. Maybe her blood sugar was screwy; she was certainly fat enough for it to be a problem. She shook her head to clear the dizziness, then stared into the darkness. The night surrounded her, and she forgot that Arnie and Duke were nearby. She was alone. A sound, a faint sound, and lights, too. The crickets, that's what she heard, and the shimmering lights came from the fireflies. She lifted her hand and placed it softly on her chest, felt the rising and falling there. The sound of the crickets became the voice of the man in the hat and scarf, and in the light of the fireflies she saw his eyes.

He had the voice of a man in a coma, just roused from his sleep. His voice was the sound of crickets. And his eyes were the eyes of a paralyzed man that touched and tasted everything before him. His eyes shone with the light of fireflies.

She had never imagined such words, and she had to listen to them over and over to get their meaning. His voice was, his eyes were, over and over, until at last the words clarified themselves in a simple and unbelievable sentence, which she spoke quietly into the darkness before her.

"I'm thinking of a man."

Arnie, just behind her on the front steps, had been watching her closely. When she spoke, the words went in his left ear, his bad one.

"What? What's that?"

Iris hardly heard him. I'm thinking of a man. She'd never, ever thought of a man before. Of *men,* yes, faceless men in daydreams, men who didn't exist and never would. But the actual eyes of a specific man, and his voice—she'd never dared. What would have been the point? Why ponder eyes that would never turn in her direction, or imagine a voice that would not speak her name? Had the man in the hat and scarf spoken her name? No. No, of course not. Or had he? When she tried to remember what they had said to each other in the cemetery parking lot, it seemed now that he might have said her name several times, as if calling to her. And he looked at her, in a way no man had ever looked at her. His eyes had called her name, too, hadn't they? Something moved from him to her, left his eyes or mouth, and came to her.

"Iris," said Arnie.

But the voice she heard belonged to the man in the hat and scarf. "Hello, Iris." A coma patient coming to, the sound of crickets. I am thinking of a man.

"You okay?" said Arnie.

Iris turned to him and brought him into focus. She found her own voice, and said too loudly, as if overcoming the rasp and chirp of the crickets, "Sure I am. Of course I am." She smiled.

The smile made Arnie nervous. He scratched his hook back and forth over the wooden porch step. "You been changing shifts too often. You look a little dazed, girl."

She turned her face again to the dark. What if, she thought, what if there is nothing at all wrong with the man in the hat and scarf? Be careful, Iris, it can't be true, she warned herself. Don't go too far with this. But she couldn't stop. Maybe, she giggled and grew warm beneath her nurse's uniform, maybe it's just the opposite, maybe he's so good looking he has to hide himself so that women won't bother him. She imagined then the face of Peter O'Toole as Lawrence of Arabia, obscured by his turban and flowing sash. Peter O'Toole's voice spoke her name. "Iris," he said with a wearied relief, as if he had crossed an interminable desert to find her, to place her name on his tongue like water from an oasis. He chooses me, because of all the women in the world I expect it least. And I will be the only one who ever gets to see his face. Each night, before we get into bed, he'll bend down and I'll remove his hat, and then his scarf, and kiss his sweet pale hidden skin.

She jumped when Arnie's hook touched her own skin, the cold metal pulling her out of an Arabian bedroom and away from sweet kisses. She looked at Arnie's hook, and thought again of the face behind the hat and scarf. Peter

O'Toole's features melted away in the wavy heat of the desert. She knew better. She knew it was really a world of hooks instead of hands, where secret injuries were protected by baseball hats and bandaged by purple scarves. She was a nurse, and she knew when she was in the presence of a wound. She had a thought then, as she looked out into the night. She tugged at her white uniform, and chewed on her lip. Am I drawn to the man, or his wound? She pictured the wedding night, saw herself dressed in a bridal veil and nursing cap. The big moment would not involve lovemaking, but a different experience of the flesh. Late into the night, and on into the morning, she'd dress and redress his face, expertly applying antibiotic salves, experiencing his wounds until they became her own.

That was about as far as she could go. "Iris," she said out loud, "you're a real sicko."

Arnie still touched her lightly with his hook. "What?" He turned his good ear toward her. "What are you saying?"

She sucked down the remainder of her beer. "Nothing, Arnie. I'm not saying anything."

"You were. Don't say you weren't. Whispering all the time so I can't hear you. I might as well be conversing with Duke here. Least when he barks I can understand what the hell he's saying."

Iris closed her eyes in fatigue and took comfort in her father's exasperating talk. His words were welcome after listening to her own crazy thoughts. "You ever consider a hearing aid?"

"A what?"

Iris smiled. "A hearing—"

"Aid," he said triumphantly, and loud enough to cause Duke to hop up out of his sleep. "See? I heard you. You health people are always trying to push some goddamn device. Bifocals, and pacemakers, and super wee-wee pads for dribblers." He waved his hook at her, to no great effect since her eyes were still closed. "Well, I got my device. This is it. This is all I'm getting, and I'm never getting a hearing aid even if you have to shout at me through a bullhorn."

"The neighbors should enjoy that," said Iris.

"Ah, the hell with the neighbors. We ought to move out of this town, you know," said Arnie. "I'm getting the old itch again," he said sleepily.

Iris stiffened. "No," she said suddenly.

But Arnie didn't hear her. He was nodding off against the porch column. "No," she said again to the still figure, as if trying to plant the word in his subconscious. She didn't want to leave Waverly. I'm thinking of a man, and he lives in Waverly.

"Oh my God, Iris," she whispered. "It's time to get your fat ass into bed."

VII

A week later the Tube Man died. He died on night shift, when Iris wasn't there. She came in for day shift, chewing her morning Three Musketeers bar, and walked past his room on her way to the staff refrigerator to store her two Pepsis. She walked by his room again on her way to her locker, and it wasn't until she hung up her jacket that the Tube Man's absence registered in her sleepy brain. She poked her head around the corner and stared at his room. When the Tube Man had been alive, the curtains were always half-drawn and the lighting was dim. Now the curtains were open wide, the lights glared, and Lionel from Housekeeping was swabbing the walls with green antiseptic. They did total room cleanings after the death or departure of a infectious patient, or a patient who'd occupied the room for more than a month. The Tube Man had made it to six months.

Lionel, his disposable protective cap cocked jauntily on his head, saw Iris looking in, and waved to her through the

window. Then he mouthed the words "Two A.M." in anticipation of her question. Iris felt weak. When she'd taken care
of the Tube Man yesterday, he'd seemed stronger, or at least
less moribund. She should have known. They always did
that, veered in the opposite direction to throw you off the scent,
and then tricked you and died hours later. She'd taken care of
him every day for the last week, bathing and turning him,
performing all the rituals, and each time, at the end, she'd
speak to him. "Tell me," she'd whisper, keeping an eye on
the door to make sure no one would walk in on her. "*Is*. Tell
me who the man in the window is. Is who? Is who?" she'd
repeat, the rhythm of her urgent words falling into the rhythm
of all the Tube Man's machines, the beeps and blips, the
hisses and sighs that filled his interminable hours. But her
words seemed to penetrate no deeper than the sounds of his
machines, and mean no more to him. Nothing arose from his
breathing tube, other than the mechanical exhalations that
were a response to the breaths he received from the ventilator, 12 a minute, 720 an hour, 17,280 a day. If she'd had time,
she'd have listened between each of those breaths for the
word that would complete the Tube Man's sentence.

"Yeah, last night. How about that?" came a familiar
voice from behind her.

Iris turned away from the window and looked at Shelley,
the big charge nurse on night shift. "He's dead," Iris said.

"Yeah, hard to believe. I look at the room and still see
him lying there. A permanent fixture, you know? But they
finally beamed him up."

"Did you have him?" Iris could hardly stand the pounding in her chest.

Shelley gave her a look. "No. Paula had him." Shelley's
eyes suddenly moved past Iris to another room. "Oh shit."
She rushed past Iris. "Get back! Hold on there, Mr. Petrie,
you get back in that bed." Mr. Petrie, the patient in bed 5,
was half out of bed, having wiggled free from his wrist

restraints. He had a grip on the rubber Foley tube inserted in his penis, stretching it a foot or two, and tighter than a bowstring. Iris winced. Shelley slapped his hand away and the Foley twanged back into place. Then she lifted him off the floor and plunked him in bed. You didn't mess with Shelley, who, like most night nurses, was built big for trouble.

Iris found Paula in bed 8 setting up a nitroglycerin IV drip. The patient was stretched out, still as death, squinting in pain.

"Hey, Paula," said Iris.

"Hey, Iris." Paula shook her head. "Can you believe it? This guy's been having chest pain since five A.M., and I told the docs the sublingual nitro wasn't working, I told them then the morphine wasn't working. I must have called them six different times for orders, and it wasn't until just now they let me hang a drip. I mean, Jesus, this guy could have died before they got their asses in gear."

The patient squinted even more, and let out a frightened groan. Paula had a habit of talking too much in front of the patients. Iris patted his arm and he grabbed her hand in relief.

"What a night, I'm telling you," said Paula. A monitor beeped. "Mr. Bleary, lie still. You're setting the alarms off when you jiggle like that."

Mr. Bleary wasn't jiggling, he was trembling. Chest pain scared the shit out of patients. Nothing taught the mortality lesson like heart trouble.

"You feeling any better, Mr. Bleary?" said Iris. "The nitroglycerin should be kicking in."

"A little," he whispered. "Maybe just a little."

"You'll be fine," said Paula. "We'll be back in a few minutes to check on you, okay?"

They left the room. Paula said to Iris, "*You'll* be back to check on him. I'm going the fuck home to bed."

Iris stopped her. "You had the Tube Man last night?"

"Yeah, how about that? The Tube Man's finally gone up to the fifth floor." There were only four floors in Barnum Memorial, and the fifth floor was the nurses' slang for heaven.

"Were you there?" said Iris, trying to control the shakiness in her voice. "I mean, how did it go?"

"You getting a cold?" Paula said, stepping back. "You sound a little hoarse." Paula had been handling patients with hepatitis, rampant bacterial infections, and even an old guy with active TB. But a cold, now that was something else. "I don't need a cold, let me tell you. Not this weekend. Larry and I are going away. Poconos," she whispered confidentially.

"The Tube Man . . ."

"Oh, yeah, well. You know, nothing much to it. Cardiac, like we all knew it would be. He went from a brady into a complete heart block. Then from there basically into a flat line. It didn't take long after he started blocking down."

Iris stared at her, obviously wanting more.

Paula paused. "And then we wrapped him up, after we took all his tubes out. He was a mess. Leaked from about ten different places. And then we called the orderly, and—"

"Did he speak?" Iris said suddenly. "Did he say anything?"

Paula brightened. "Yeah, you mean like he'd been doing? I never believed any of that, you know. Shelley said she heard him once, and a couple of the others, but I never did, so I wasn't paying that much attention and all. And I was busy all shift, so it wasn't like I could stand around waiting for him to speak. But . . ."

"But?"

"Jeez, Iris, I didn't know you were so into it." Paula stepped back again, because Iris had moved too close. "But anyway, maybe he said something, but I think I'm stretching it. It was probably just a *sound* he made, not a word, but you guys said he was speaking, so I listened for a word, too. But

I'm not sure it was. Probably just air leaking around his tube." Paula tilted her head like she was listening again for the sound. Then she spoke. "It was just before he went flat line. I went in there to check on him, like you do, and I was leaning over him fiddling with one of his monitor leads . . ." She hesitated, then went on. "Now this is weird, but I was leaning over him and the room went real quiet. There was this moment between all the little noises the machines make, the beeps and the ventilator breaths and stuff, like everything in the room paused for a second . . . and that's when I heard him."

Iris held her breath and squeezed hard on the Three Musketeers bar she'd been holding in the palm of her hand.

"It's kind of disappointing, really," said Paula, "if it really was a word. But this is what the Tube Man said: 'loose.' "

Iris looked down at the Three Musketeers bar she'd mashed between her fingers, then back up at Paula. "Loose?"

"Loose," said Paula, heading for her locker. "If it was a word at all, which I'm not betting it was. Loose."

Iris turned and stared into the Tube Man's old room. *"The man in the window is loose."* Lionel scrubbed the floor as Iris watched blankly. That was the Tube Man's sentence? What did it mean? Loose? *What* man in the window? Loose where? Was the man in the window some kind of escaped crazy? She'd waited so long, and now the Tube Man's final word meant nothing. The whole sentence meant nothing. If it was a sentence, if they really were words the Tube Man had been speaking. Maybe Paula was right. Maybe it was all sounds, meaningless noises misinterpreted by a bunch of tired, overimaginative nurses. She was suddenly angry—at the Tube Man, at herself for going so far on so little, at Paula for not hearing a magical final word. She glared at Lionel, who was standing with his mop, waving her into the room.

"Come here. Hey, Iris, come on in here," he called out to her.

Iris didn't want to go into the Tube Man's room, but she did.

"Hey. Look down there." He pointed at a square of linoleum with a red splotch in the center of it. Blood. Nothing unusual on a hospital floor.

"Blood. They pulled out his tubes. He leaked. So what?"

"You're a pain in my ass, girl," Lionel said. "Bend down, take a look at that. That's some funny spot of blood."

Iris squinted at the spot. She saw it then. The blood was in the shape of a heart, an almost perfect valentine heart.

Lionel nodded. "How about that shit?"

Widows
and
Widowers

I

THE WIDOW GRACIE MALONE. WIDOW MALONE. OLD
Widow Malone. Gracie walked alone in her yard on a late
December day, trying on names like hats. A silly thing to be
doing, just as it was silly to try on hats, as if there were such
a thing as a perfect hat, one that truly suited and defined her
above all the others. She rarely wore a hat, and she would
never call herself the Widow Malone, though she'd been
trying it on for months. No one was called the Widow
anything anymore. When she was young, every other house
seemed to be occupied by a widow—Widow Bunting, Widow
Dalton, Widow Pitts. These were women who wore their
widowhood well, who seemed, almost, to be born to it. As a
child, that's what Gracie assumed, that just as there were
parents, or brothers and sisters, there were widows, women
who had always been as they were, alone, white-haired, and
possessors of some undefined, scary, and magnificent secret.
The secret, Gracie knew now, was grief, which was indeed
scary, but in no way magnificent.

Why hadn't the grief, the missing, shown on the faces of Widows Bunting, Dalton, and Pitts? How had they concealed it? Or was it that she'd been too young to see it? She saw it now, on her own face in the medicine cabinet mirror each morning, and each night before she went to bed. She had stood before that mirror a thousand thousand times, and often Atlas had stood behind her, brushing his teeth as she brushed hers. The mirror seemed out of whack now, capable of revealing only half the team of Gracie and Atlas, and Gracie often whirled around in the bathroom, hoping to suddenly see her other unreflected half, Atlas, absently flossing his teeth, or combing his hair behind her.

Had Widow Bunting whirled in her own bathroom, sixty years ago when Gracie was only ten? Gracie imagined herself as a child, standing at night at her open bedroom window, listening to a faint rustling sound coming from a small window on the second floor of the house next door. It was Widow Bunting, in her dry petticoats, whirling round and round in her bathroom, trying to catch a glimpse of her long-dead husband.

Gracie walked in her yard and wondered what hidden child was observing her at this moment, the Widow Malone, the strange new widow of Waverly. Well, guaranteed at least one child watched, her own, Louis, just behind some curtain or shade. She looked back at the house, scanned each of the windows, but didn't see anything. Which only convinced her he was there, crafting the unnaturally perfect stillness that revealed nothing. She waved, then began to walk the yard again. Louis would be watching only in the sense of watching over her; he didn't spy. His was a protective gaze, she knew. He cleared the way for her with his eyes.

He protects me now, Atlas, but do you remember when it was you and I who protected him? It was a lovely time, wasn't it, the years when we thought we could protect him. Gracie looked around her, and for just an instant the winter brown gave way to a shimmering green, the green of a summer in the backyard. Atlas was there, young, holding tiny Louis in his arms.

Gracie saw herself, her brown hair in a ponytail, rushing toward Atlas. "Don't drop him!"

Atlas grinned and dipped his arms as if he were about to toss Louis into the branches of the horse chestnut tree.

Gracie froze. "Atlas."

But Atlas only lifted Louis high enough to bring him to his lips. He kissed Louis's cheeks once, and then again, before surrendering him to Gracie. "Don't you drop him either," he said.

Gracie looked down at Louis. He gave her a drooling smile. "Mothers don't drop their babies," she said.

"That a fact?" said Atlas. "I guess mothers are about the most perfect thing there is."

"No. Babies, then mothers."

"Doesn't leave much room for fathers."

Gracie didn't answer him. She moved closer and leaned against him, felt Atlas against her, and Louis in her arms, immersed herself in the loveliness. "This is it," she said after a long moment.

"Yes," said Atlas, pulling her closer still, and Louis with her, so that Gracie was unsure where she stopped and Atlas began, whether the rapid beating within her chest was her own heart, or Louis's.

"Oh Atlas," she whispered. "What will we do?"

Atlas was very still. Then he said, "Remember as best we can, Gracie. Remember that on a summer day, the three of us stood a minute beneath a tree."

Gracie remembered, then returned again to the late winter afternoon. She walked the backyard. She paused beside the garage where bits of morning frost still whitened the bottoms of the leaves that had blown up against its shaded brick side. She stooped and picked one up, and touched the white crystals. She traced her finger along the back of the leaf until the ice melted, then she brought the leaf to her mouth and tasted the water. It tasted of fall, just as July raindrops on a green leaf taste of summer. She stooped again and carefully returned the leaf to its spot against the garage. Then she picked up a horse chestnut burr. She squeezed it too hard and felt the sharp points digging into her palm. One of the points pierced her skin, and a drop of blood emerged, like a single tear. She tasted it, too, then turned and looked at the horse chestnut tree.

I could cut the tree down, she thought, then I wouldn't see Atlas lying under it. And have the stump dug up, and then I could fill the hole with dirt and plant new grass in the spring. But she knew how it would go. The new grass would never really blend with the old, and she would remember that the grass covered the dirt, and the dirt was used to fill the hole, and the hole was from the stump that was dug up, and the stump belonged to the horse chestnut tree under which, in one way or another, Atlas would always lie. She pictured him there in all seasons, with the green grass of spring around him and perhaps a purple crocus by his head, pictured him in the heavy shade of full summer, and in the fall with the dry leaves banked against one side of him, and pictured him surrounded by the winter snow, still lying there, still dressed in his gardening clothes as if he were only resting, just for a moment, and would rise again.

That's how it had been since the funeral. Atlas was either terribly present, so that she could actually feel the weight of him, as if she lay beneath him there under the horse chestnut tree, or he was terribly absent, less than a ghost or a memory, unreachable, even though she was surrounded by the facts of his existence, the reminders that beckoned and glittered, like the diamond on the ring that he had given her so many years ago.

She slowly peeled the spiny burr, picked and peeled until she reached the two perfect brown chestnuts hidden within it.

She lifted them out. They were slightly moist, like, she imagined, the surface of an eyeball, or the dampness left behind by a light kiss. She raised them to her mouth, and without really thinking about it, touched them to her lips, first the larger one, and then the smaller one. She thought she tasted something of Atlas in them. She smiled, remembering his kisses, specific kisses, so immediate she reddened and turned away from the window so Louis wouldn't be able to see her face. Really, Atlas, she thought, not in front of Louis.

Gracie approached the horse chestnut tree. She had not gone near it since the summer, since the day she had come around the house from mulching the tulip bed and seen Atlas drop slowly to his knees, then down into the grass. The grass had been mowed and raked since then, but she still thought she could see the shape of his body, outlined in broken blades. She dropped to her knees, as he had, and touched the spot. Then she began to pluck at the brown blades of grass, to clear a small area. When she reached dirt, she started to dig with her fingers. A dot of blood appeared again where she had pierced herself with the burr. She held her palm over the small hole she had dug, and watched as the blood made a thin rivulet through the dirt on her hand, swelled into a drop that trembled slightly, then fell. She picked up the larger of the two chestnuts and fingered its smooth surface, then dropped it into the hole and pushed the dirt over it. She kept the smaller chestnut for herself. She held it in her closed hand as she walked back to the house in the weakening light of the cold afternoon.

Louis, of course, had been watching. When Gracie began to scratch at the earth like a squirrel, he looked away, so that she could have her moment. He had looked away often over the last few months.

Early the next morning, before Gracie was awake, he slipped out the back door and went to the spot where she had buried the chestnut. The frost covered the grass, the leaves, and even the handle of a misplaced trowel that lay half-hidden in the brown remains of the daylily bed. But the spot where Gracie had dug remained untouched; the frost bordered the fresh dirt and then stopped abruptly. Louis placed the palm of his hand on the dirt and it felt warm, as if it had absorbed the heat of a long summer day. He kept his hand there and slowly closed his eyes. He felt a rustling beneath the dirt, then a small pressure against his palm. He moved his hand away and saw a tiny nub of green poking between small chunks of moist dirt. The nub became a stem, grew an inch, then two, and began to sprout tiny translucent green leaves. When it grew to be a foot, which happened in moments, Louis saw that it was a small horse chestnut tree. He stepped back as the tree continued to grow and grow, until soon he was looking up into its thickening branches. He grabbed a passing branch and hauled himself into a sitting position, his back against the swelling trunk. His house appeared below him, and then his neighborhood, and then all of Waverly. When he couldn't make out the streets of Waverly any longer, he was almost to the clouds. The tree continued to grow, silently, as silent as the clouds through which Louis now passed. When he was just above the clouds, the tree stopped growing. The white stretched out before him, like the white of the frost that covered the grass in his backyard. He slid off the branch and onto the cloud, turning slowly when someone said his name.

"Louis."

"Atlas."

They stood face-to-face but did not touch. Louis looked down and saw that his feet had sunk into the cloud. Atlas, in his old Hush Puppies, hovered an inch or two above the misty white, kept aloft by the gentle movement of his wings.

"I'm pleased to see you, Louis, but you shouldn't be here."

"I couldn't help it."

Atlas nodded, because he knew Louis.

And then he said, already turning to go, "Tell your

mother, tell Gracie to get on with her life. I'm gone now. Tell her that planting chestnuts won't do any good.''

Louis closed his eyes against the words, and when he opened them again, he saw that he'd been nowhere, that he still knelt in the frosty grass of his backyard, his hand on the spot where Gracie had dug. When he looked up into the early morning sky he saw that it was cloudless.

Two yards over, Francine Koessler opened her back door to let out her cat, Minky. Louis dropped down into a crouch. Francine stood on her back porch, resplendent in her pink curlers and orange bathrobe, gazing vaguely in his direction. Minky made an immediate beeline for him, even though he was almost entirely hidden by a clump of bushes.

"Minky," Francine called. "Minky. Don't you go in that yard."

That yard. Meaning where he, Louis, lived. Francine was a widow (though she was not referred to as the Widow Koessler), and things tended to make her nervous. She went up on her toes and stared into the dark twist of bushes where Minky had discovered Louis.

"Minky. No, no, Minky. Come on back." She clapped her hands anxiously.

Minky walked up to Louis, stared at him, then began to bat at the end of the purple scarf that hung loosely around Louis's neck. Louis flicked his hand at Minky, trying to shoo her away. Minky thought it was a great game.

Louis looked up and saw Francine crunching through the frost and brown grass, coming his way.

"Minky. Mommy's had enough of this now," she said in a wheedling voice.

Louis looked at Minky, and Minky looked at Louis. Then Minky gave Louis the cat equivalent of a devilish grin, took the corner of Louis's scarf into his mouth, and gave it a yank. It was a very doglike maneuver, and Louis was so surprised he didn't react. But he was not half as surprised as

Francine, who let out a piercing yelp when Minky shot out of the bushes dragging the scarf like it was a big dead rat. Francine instantly recognized that scarf, although she had never actually seen it before. Louis's purple scarf (and baseball hat) was the stuff of legend, everyone in Waverly knew about it, though few had seen it.

Francine yelped, then dashed across the yard, curlers bouncing off her head as she went. When she reached her kitchen door she was so upset, she pushed when she should have pulled, which upset her even more because she thought somehow Louis, or Louis's scarf (for who knew, maybe the scarf possessed evil powers, that's how scared she was), had gotten into the house and was blocking her way. At last she jerked the door open, scurried inside, and banged the door shut with her shoulder. Francine's frantic efforts frightened Minky, who dropped the scarf and took off at high speed through several backyards, finally coming to a stop midway up a dogwood tree. Louis made his move then, taking a quick look around to make sure the coast was clear. He sprinted around the bushes with one hand over the exposed part of his face, and rescued his scarf, which he tied around himself as he ran back to his house, wondering whether the moisture he felt on the scarf was melting frost or Minky spit.

Gracie came into the kitchen just as he burst panting in the door. At first she was alarmed, but then she saw the smile in his eyes.

"Well," she said, cocking her head. "Out for a bit of a stroll, were we?"

"I was attacked," he said, "by Francine Koessler's precious Minky."

"Attacked?"

"Well, not exactly attacked," said Louis, dropping into a chair, "but she did steal my scarf, which was worth it, because of the show Francine put on."

Gracie imagined the show, smiling as she reached into

the refrigerator for an egg. Then she frowned. She didn't much care for Francine, but her sympathies had changed. "Poor Francine," she said. "She's a widow. You shouldn't be out there scaring the widows. We widows have to stick together, you know." She spoke distinctly, emphasizing the word *widow* each time, trying to get a feel for the continued foreignness of it.

They ate their breakfast silently for a time, then Gracie spoke, as if continuing out loud a conversation she'd been having with herself. "She is an old cluck, though. Francine, I mean. Atlas could not abide that woman. She was a flutterer, he said. He was always telling how he'd be having a nice peaceful day at the hardware store, then in fluttered Francine Koessler to ruin it."

Louis remembered, too, those peaceful Saturdays at the store, he and Yank Spiller stocking shelves or helping customers, Atlas at the cash register, when suddenly there'd be an alteration in the quality of the air. Everyone felt it, all the regular Saturday customers, Joe Turner in for his paint thinner, Jake Lucas bringing in his screens to be fixed, Fred Werther browsing in the toilet fixture section. Louis, Yank, and Atlas all felt the change even before Francine touched the doorknob to let herself into the store, felt the commotion that always preceded her, like the smell of ozone and electricity before the first flash of lightning and clap of thunder of an approaching storm. Then Francine would burst into the store like she was running from thieves, waving her arms, her voice all charged up. The men would look at her, their faces neutral, trying not to let their shared sense of grief and disapproval show, not that it mattered since Francine, so distracted by her own performance, hardly noticed them. The men didn't disapprove of women in their store (*their* store, even though Atlas was the owner, because a hardware store is a shared institution, like a church, and for a certain type of person just as sacred)—most of the women acted with dignity and restraint, if not always decisiveness, when shopping in the store. But the atmosphere of the place was most definitely male, a church run by and catering to the needs of monks, not nuns.

Before she was five feet inside the store, Francine had pulled half a dozen things off the Peg-Board display, and scooped up a handful of stuff off the shelves, and was already pressing Atlas with a run of exasperating and unrelated questions, while simultaneously sending Yank and Louis in search of any number of vaguely described items. Francine knew she was in need, and she must have instinctively sensed, like Mrs. Meem and Harvey Mastuzek, that the hardware store, with its curative potential, was the place to satisfy that need. She searched hard, turning the store, and everyone in it, upside down in the process.

"Atlas," she'd say, dumping a can of glazing compound, a tube of naval jelly, two C clamps, and a spool of solder on the counter, "ring these up for me, will you please?"

Atlas would eye the stuff, while a couple of the men customers stood behind Francine shaking their heads. He'd start to say, framing his words carefully so as not to hurt her, "Um, Francine, now what sort of project is it you have in mind?"

"Various projects, Atlas. I am a widow, you know, and have to maintain my house on my own." (Archie Koessler, who'd died thirty years into the marriage, had met his end maintaining the house, a bizarre death involving a stepladder, a bucket of paint, and 120 volts from a power drill—none of which, it should be noted, was purchased from Atlas's store.)

"Of course, yes, Francine," Atlas would say, knowing in fact that Francine's house was maintained by a number of Waverly handymen, plumbers, and electricians, and that even he, as her neighbor living two houses down, had been called upon in times of household emergency. Francine, Atlas had long ago decided, needed the illusion of competence and self-reliance, a defense mechanism of widows. "Is it," he said, searching for clues among the items before him on the counter, "some sort of plumbing problem you have?" Naval jelly, C clamps . . . who knew?

"Could be," Francine said, waving her arms, and handing a crumpled list to Louis, then nudging him down the aisle. Louis tried to make sense of it; it looked like a list of objects you were sent in search of in a scavenger hunt at a children's birthday party. "Could be," said Francine, "now that you mention it. There's been a kind of gurgle in the pipes lately. I hear it at night, you know, Atlas, and it is not a comforting sound for a widow to have to listen to."

"No, ma'am. But the C clamps . . ."

"C clamps?"

Atlas picked them up and Francine eyed them. "These aren't for fixing gurgles," he said gently.

She snatched them from Atlas and crooked a finger at Yank. He approached reluctantly. She handed him the C clamps. "Here," she said. "Find me the other kind of clamps."

"The other kind," said Yank slowly.

"Yes," she said evenly. "The other kind."

Yank looked to Atlas for help, but Atlas only shrugged. Yank started off down aisle three.

"Try aisle two!" she shouted after him. "I think I see some way in the back there, against the wall."

Yank wandered lost in aisle two, his hand hesitating before monkey wrenches, and pipe cutters, and all the other things that Francine Koessler might have thought were clamps.

Atlas tried the easy way out. "Shall I ring the rest of this up for you, Francine?"

"Yes," she said. "No, wait." She picked up the tube of naval jelly. "Is this good for pilot lights that sputter?"

Atlas scratched his head and tried to look as if she had asked a reasonable question. "Gee, Francine. That's a tough one. That's a real stumper. But really, I think naval jelly is better for—"

Francine cut in. "Well, Archie, my husband, he used to use something on the pilot lights, I remember. Something in a tube."

Which helped explain to Atlas how Archie had met his untimely end via the stepladder, the electric drill, and the paint bucket. If they hadn't gotten him first, surely the pilot light and the naval jelly would have.

Louis came back from his searches empty-handed. "Mrs. Koessler, are you sure this is the right list?" Atlas took it from him and read it to himself. "Belts. Supporters. Inserters. Pads." God only knew what she meant. It seemed, though, that she might have better luck in the personal hygiene section of Berret's Drugstore. He handed the list back to her, and she stuffed it into her pocketbook as she drew in a great indignant breath.

"Well!" she huffed. "Well, as usual, this store has been absolutely no help to me, no help whatsoever. They ought to call this place the Just Out Shop, as badly stocked as it is." She waved her arms and popped her eyes wide. "If I die from gas leaking from my pilot light, or drown when my pipes burst, I'll know who to blame, I can tell you that!"

The men customers pressed against the wall as she stormed by on her way to the door, which in her highly emotional state she pushed when she should have pulled. She at last made her way through it after a great struggle and more unkind words for the Just Out Shop and its treatment of widows.

And just as everyone let out a communal sigh, Yank appeared with an armful of things, any one of which, he figured, might have been the clamp Francine Koessler imagined she wanted.

Gracie looked up from her poached egg, which she'd been staring at, lost in her own thoughts of Francine. "Louis," she began, then hesitated.

Louis fingered the side of his coffee cup.

She started again. "Louis, the thing is, you see, I don't

want to be a widow. It's not going to be . . . my kind of thing, something I can settle into. I'll never be very good at it." She shrugged and gave him a worried smile.

"No one's ever very good at it, do you think, Gracie?"

"Kitty is. And so is Francine, in her own way. She's gathered her widowhood up around her, has learned how to use it for her own purposes. Her own fluttery purposes, Atlas would say. And when I was a young girl, too—the widows I knew all seemed born to it, seemed to use it as a source of power, even sustenance." She got up and reached for his empty coffee cup. "But not me. The whole business is unnatural. It doesn't fit me. It's ten sizes too big." She touched his arm. "And this sounds awful, but I don't mean for it to. I'm tired of missing him. I've been tired of missing him since the day he died."

She was at the sink now, rinsing dishes. "He came to me last night, Louis." She turned to face him. "I hadn't dreamed of him, not once, since the summer. Isn't that strange? But last night he showed up, just for a moment in the corner of a dream, like he didn't want to intrude. He was sitting in a chair, jiggling his leg slightly, in that way he had when he was nervous about having to say something he didn't really want to say. I bit my lip and waited, I was so eager to hear his voice again. And then the words came out, left him and came to me, although I don't think he actually spoke. He said, 'Gracie, you're seventy years old. Don't waste a minute missing me.' And then I woke up, full awake, and there was not one tear on my pillow. Just the opposite: I was smiling in the dark. I thought to myself, Imagine a man loving me so much he'd say a thing like that."

Wasn't it just like him, thought Louis, thinking of his own encounter with Atlas in the clouds, to make doubly sure his message would be conveyed to Gracie. He had always been like that, putting two locks on the door, having one umbrella at home and one at the hardware store. Even in death he wanted to be sure of a thing, to cover himself twice over. There was no need, Louis decided, to describe to Gracie his own encounter with Atlas. The redundancy in this case had been an unnecessary effort on Atlas's part—he had gotten through to Gracie.

Don't grieve for me—there's no time. Louis looked at Gracie as she turned back to the sink to rinse her hands. Those were generous words, but what was it exactly Atlas expected her to do with her remaining time? Don't waste it beneath the horse chestnut tree, don't kneel at his grave plucking weeds from around his tombstone? How did she move beyond him when the chair where he always sat for breakfast, lunch, and dinner stood ready to bear the sudden weight of him; when the indentation on the other half of her mattress was so distinctly his, spoke so clearly of his thereness, was even, it seemed, still warm (for Louis had touched the spot more than once), as if he had just risen to brush his teeth and greet the day? If he, Louis, still felt Atlas's warmth, what on earth did Gracie feel? How far did that kind of love go? he wondered, knowing that all the beds that he would ever sleep in would be warmed only by himself.

Then Gracie said, "Of course, I'm not sure what it is he wants me to do." She was up on her toes, watering the violets and spider plants that crowded the sunny windowsill in front of the sink. "I mean, I'm not twenty-five years old. It's not like I can go out and do it all over again. Or want to. I mean"—and she let out a curious laugh—"it's not like I'm going to remarry or anything."

Louis took the watering can from her, and held it up to the hanging rabbit's-foot fern. Atlas had always watered the fern for Gracie. Would Gracie's next husband be tall enough to water it? That Gracie should marry again, even at seventy, did not seem impossible or absurd to Louis, who measured the question against his own possibilities. Even on her death-bed Gracie would be much more likely to elicit a marriage proposal than he.

"It's okay, you know. If you do get married again," said Louis, not looking at her. "I'm thirty-two years old. I could get a place."

Gracie touched him. "Louis. It's just talk. I'm just saying things."

"No, but really. If something like that should ever happen. I could . . ."

Get a place, get married, start a family? Hi honey, I'm home. Louis looked around the kitchen, now a kitchen in a different house, his own. Hi honey, I'm home. In he walks wearing a suit, briefcase in one hand, his other hand raised in greeting. His wife, who'd been reaching for something in the refrigerator, closes the refrigerator door, and he sees that she is holding his baby son. Both are wearing baseball hats and scarves, identical to his own. Of course they are—who else would have married him, and what other child could he have possibly sired? He goes to them, and they lean together, the three of them, the bills on their hats lightly touching, the tassels on the ends of their purple scarves interlacing.

And then he was back in the kitchen with Gracie, remembering another encounter, one that had taken place just before the fire in the hardware store. He slid his hand under his scarf and touched what remained of his lips. They were wet and coarse at the same time; he could not pucker them into a kiss now if he wanted to. Even if someone showed him how. Ariel Nesmith had shown him how. Ariel had liked him, and he had liked her, and after a high school party a week before the fire, she became the first and last person to touch his cheek in that way, to press her lips to his. Sometimes in the hospital, when the nurses laid their fingers on the gauze that wrapped his face, he mistook their touch for Ariel's. She came to the hospital several times, and even to the house, but he refused to see her. He watched her go that last time, from the edge of a curtained window, watched as she turned when she reached the end of the sidewalk and looked back at the house, the afternoon sun lighting her perfect skin and making diamonds of the moisture on her perfect lips.

II

Most people his age felt the winter in their bones, but Arnie felt it in his hook. The damn thing sucked the chill right out of the air, then shot it into his stump all the way up his right arm. You couldn't put a mitten on it, although LuLu once offered to make him one. That sure would have been a swell sight. Besides, he needed it exposed so he could grab on to things. It was hard enough as it was, without a violet and orange mitten, the colors LuLu surely would have chosen, wrapped around it. Even with his frozen hook, though, sliding up and down the handle of his snow shovel, he still managed to finish his walk before old Krupmeyer across the street. Krupmeyer started to gain at the end, so Arnie really had to gun it across the finish line. He leaned against his shovel, panting, seeing spots before his eyes from the effort. When he'd caught enough of his breath to speak, he called across the street to his rival.

"Yo, Krupmeyer! Could you use a hand?" He waved his hook at him. "I sure could."

Krupmeyer hadn't thought it funny the first five times he'd heard it, and he didn't think it was funny now. There was something downright indecent about a handicapped man making fun of his own handicap, especially when the handicap didn't stop him from finishing his walk first.

"My walk's a good thirty feet longer than yours," Krupmeyer shouted to Arnie.

"The hell it is. Every lot on the street's the same size."

"So you think."

"So I know."

"I got five years on you," Krupmeyer grunted.

Arnie could almost feel the heat coming off his neighbor's fat red face. "It's not the five years, it's the fifty pounds you got on me," Arnie called.

Krupmeyer didn't say anything.

Arnie watched him happily. "You're slowing down, Kruppie. It's taking you a half hour longer this year. What are you using over there, a trowel?"

The two old men spoke to one another only during snow season. Both of them seemed to relish the animosity and competition. They went at it five or six times a year, which was how often it snowed in Waverly. Neither man remembered how it got started, but it had gradually evolved to the point of becoming a spectator sport, the neighbors watching the excitement from their windows. No one dared go outside while the two cantankerous old bastards went at it. The unspoken rules were simple: one man, one shovel, and you couldn't start until the last flake hit the ground. Once that had been at three in the morning. Arnie awoke to the sound of Krupmeyer scraping away at his walk in the dark. He shot out of bed and started shoveling in his pajamas and bedroom slippers, and he might even have caught up with Krupmeyer if LuLu hadn't latched on to his good arm and tried to drag him back inside.

Today, though, victory was his. "Hey Krupster," called Arnie, "you're sounding a little wheezy. You sure you can't use an extra pair of hands? Well, don't look at me, kid." He laughed, waving his hook at Krupmeyer again.

Krupmeyer lifted his own hand and made a gesture at Arnie, presumably giving him the finger, but since he was wearing a mitten Arnie couldn't quite tell. "Hey, Arnie. I let you beat me, okay? Since what I did to you last time was so pathetic. Christ, I went inside and had two cups of coffee before you even got close to finishing. It was almost goddamn spring before you got done shoveling."

"Yeah, well, you look like you could use a cup of coffee

now. And last time, as if you goddamn didn't well know, the snowplow jumped my curb and dumped an extra two feet of snow on my walk.''

"So you say."

"So I know, Krapski."

Krupmeyer bent over his shovel again, redder than before, and more wheezy. Arnie tried to think of something else to say, but he couldn't come up with anything good. Besides, his hook sucked in so much of the cold, the right side of his body was going numb. He started up the front walk to his house, after taking a last look at Krupmeyer and smiling. Iris opened the front door just as he got there, and he expected, from the way she looked, that she was about to rag him for being such a fool and for causing so much commotion on the public streets. Then he saw she wasn't looking at him but past him, and he saw, too, that up and down the block his neighbors were starting to come out of their doors, were running in fact, like Iris was suddenly doing. They'd seen from their windows where they'd been watching the snow-shoveling battle, what he had not as he walked to his front door with his back to Krupmeyer: that Krupmeyer had dropped his shovel, clutched his chest, and fallen face forward into the foot or so of snow that remained on his unfinished walk.

The ambulance came and went, an effort that was a mere formality since in Iris's judgment Krupmeyer was probably dead before he hit the ground, and could just as well have made the trip in one of Big Bill Rose's two hearses—which is what she whispered to Arnie when the ambulance swerved off down the snow-slick street. The neighbors thinned out, and Iris left Arnie to go back inside, patting his good arm as she reassured him for the fifth time that Krupmeyer's death wasn't his fault, that Krupie would have keeled over and died no matter where he was or what he might have been doing at the fatal moment, because it was obvious to Iris, who knew a thing or two about the manner in which people go, that the Krupster had had one of those time-bomb hearts, tick tick tick, and if he had just lifted his finger to pick his nose, let alone lifting a shovel full of wet snow, he still would have gone, any effort at all would have killed him. Hell, blinking too hard would have killed poor old Krupso. He was due to go, tick tick tick, ka-boom.

Yeah, well, thought Arnie, after Iris left him to go back inside, maybe so, maybe not. It sure didn't do Krupmeyer any good digging through the snow like a maniac, like he was a teenager with a thousand healthy years ahead of him. Arnie removed his knitted cap, and surveyed Krupmeyer's unfinished walk. Krupmeyer, he said to himself silently, I didn't much care for you, but I mourn your death because you were a fellow warrior. We had us some great battles. Christ, remember two years ago, when it snowed nineteen inches and we finished our walks in a dead heat? And the ice storm—when was that?—both of us sliding all over the place, hacking at the ice with the handles of our shovels, falling on our asses. I creamed my wrist that day, and you were sure you broke your hip, but we kept going, didn't we? Arnie tasted salt in the back of his throat, and felt a thickness behind his eyes. He cleared his throat and blinked. You went down on the field of battle, Kruppie, there's no dishonor in that. You went down with your sword in your hands. Arnie leaned over and picked up Krupmeyer's sword, an aluminum snow shovel Krupmeyer bought ten years ago for $2.98 from Malone's Hardware.

Shit, thought Arnie. We're all dropping like flies. LuLu, Krupmeyer. He slowly turned his head, squinting at the bright white that surrounded him. And me, he wondered, how much longer have I got? He slid his hand inside his coat and felt the strong even beat of his heart, and was not reassured.

He shook his head and clutched Krupmeyer's shovel with his hook, and made an adjustment with his good hand.

You went the good way, Krupso, you bastard. You went down hard and fast, but you went down all in one piece. Me, I got one hand gone, my left ear's shot, and I'm going soft in the brain. You beat me, Krupmeyer—in the big contest, the one that really counts—you left this world in one piece, not like me. They'll tie me in a chair in some nursing home, I'll be drooling on myself, I'll have goddamn pee-pee stains on my pajamas. And a brain as soft as Cheez-Whiz. Krupster, you won.

Arnie walked to the end of Krupmeyer's walk, to the last unfinished stretch, the foot of snow Krupmeyer died trying to clear. Arnie bent low, leaned into Krupmeyer's battle-scarred shovel, and began to clear it. He moved slowly, meticulously, in a final snow-shoveling tribute. When he finished, he redid parts of the walk where the ambulance crew and the gawking neighbors had trampled. At last, he looked up and down, satisfied: it was the way Krupmeyer would have done it. Then he walked up the path to Krupmeyer's front porch, and leaned the shovel beside the door to the empty house, empty because Krupmeyer lived alone, with no one to mourn him but Arnie. Arnie was about to go, was halfway down the steps, when he suddenly turned and reached for Krupmeyer's shovel, his sword, lifted it, and brought it down hard across his knee. Then he carefully laid the two pieces side by side on the steps.

God, his hook ached. He felt the winter's cold again. Everything ached. He was old. Old. He walked slowly across the street to his own house. When he reached the front door, he lightly touched his chest again, then pushed the door open, and quietly entered the dark.

Through the Looking Glass

I

IN THE SPRING OF THE FIRST YEAR FOLLOWING ATLAS'S
death, Louis fell out of his second-floor bedroom window.
He landed, one bright early May afternoon, in full view of
the neighborhood (which for Louis might as well have been
in full view of the whole world), in a small bed of yellow
and red tulips which bordered the front walk. For Kitty
Wilson, passing by the Malone house, her aqua-lined eyes
as always trained on its windows in hope of catching a
glimpse of Louis, it was a fantasy come true. She would
have been satisfied with just a hint of a shadowy movement
at the edge of a curtain, which is what she sometimes got if
she was very lucky. But suddenly there he was, Louis in his
baseball hat and scarf, sailing headfirst out of a second-
floor window.

Kitty was not the only person on the block to witness
Louis's abrupt defenestration. Bev and Bert Howard saw it
too, as they stood across the street from the Malones',
chatting with Carl Lerner, enjoying a bit of afternoon gossip

in the warm May sun. And Francine Koessler saw Louis, and so did Minky. Francine had been walking Minky on a leash, was no more than ten feet from Kitty Wilson when she saw Kitty turn pale and let out a whoop. Francine and Minky both turned when Kitty whooped, in time to catch the last half of Louis's downward flight. Francine whooped too, and Minky puffed out her fur and hissed—the scarf in particular attracted Francine's attention, and probably also Minky's, who had held that very scarf in her feline jaws some five months earlier.

Louis saw all of these people very distinctly, saw Minky, and even the three or four neighborhood kids playing kickball in the street, during his rapid descent. For sixteen years he had avoided all human contact, and now, he thought as the tulip bed fast approached, here I am about to land right smack-dab in the middle of a not unsizable group of them.

It must have occurred to him, just before he hit the tulips, that perhaps this sudden and accidental return to the world was not quite as accidental as it seemed. Since the summer, since his brief exposure to humanity on the afternoon of Atlas's funeral, Louis had been experiencing an uncomfortable longing. He'd assumed he longed for his father, since the feeling had begun almost from the moment Louis had stepped out of Jim Rose's funeral limousine and walked back into the house with Gracie. When the door had closed behind him, he felt a great wash of sadness. When would he walk through that door again? For Gracie's funeral? Is that what it would take to get him out into the world again? Though he watched from his windows, and still made secret night trips into the neighborhood, it no longer seemed enough. With Atlas gone, he'd lost half his contact with Waverly, lost one ear, and one eye. That's how he felt the loss of Atlas, as something physical, a part of himself missing. And when Gracie died, he would be left deaf and blind, and mute too, for who would he talk to?

He had been thinking like that at the moment of his fall from the window. A moment of panic, a sense of absolute and overwhelming confinement, caused him to lean far out of his bedroom window, in full daylight, in front of people, caused him to extend himself beyond all the boundaries he'd known for sixteen years, to attempt to perceive a farther distance, to view what could not ordinarily be viewed from the window frame with its white wooden ledge worn from the countless secret hours he pressed against it year after year, seeing, seeing, seeing, but not being seen.

Louis's eyes remained open even as he tore through the red and yellow petals of the tulips and hit the soft earth. The soft earth is what saved him, and he had Gracie to thank for that. She was a relentless mulcher, her flower beds were as light and yielding as a kiss. Louis might have jumped right up and run back inside the house, might have hidden there for another sixteen years, because hiding was always his first impulse, was what he knew how to do, but despite all that good soft Gracie mulch, he broke his right arm. It was the impulse to hide that had caused his injury: even as he was tumbling out of the window, he had thrashed about trying to keep his hat on his head and his scarf around his face. And so he landed, hat and scarf in place, but with his right arm twisted beneath him. He heard the arm go, the gristly pop of bone. The pain kept him on the ground, kept him from doing anything more than staring at the front door, the front door he never thought he'd walk through again, except for Gracie's funeral. And now here he was on the other side of it, on the outside looking in, back in the world of Waverly.

Kitty Wilson was the first to react. "He's gone and killed himself!" It must have looked that way to her, Louis suddenly at the window, and then out of it, launching himself into thin air. The air did seem thin, like you always say but never really think about. For some reason this crossed Kitty's mind even in all the excitement—with a body hurtling through it, the air was as thin as thin gets. And Louis didn't utter a word, a cry, a sound even, so it had to be suicide, his silence an act of will, connected to the act of will that caused him to leap out of the window. That's where it had already gotten to in Kitty's mind, from accident to intention, falling to leaping. She went even farther with it. She thought, He waited until he saw me to do it. All these years he was playing, keeping my interest up, appearing and disappearing at his windows, because he knew it would keep me looking, that my eyes would be right there, open and ready, primed for the occasion. He chose me to be his witness. Kitty stared at Louis, his body motionless, his face turned away toward the front of the house, his hat askew but on his head, his scarf flowing straight out behind him as if he were falling still, Kitty stared and thought, And he wants me to be the first to look at him.

Five seconds after Louis landed, Francine Koessler's panicked brain began to function. That horrible deformed thing, that monster who has terrorized this neighborhood for sixteen years, he was trying to get me, me and my Minky, because of what happened last fall with the scarf—poor Minky getting all tangled up, trying to run away from him. Why hadn't she called the police, that creature loose in the neighborhood, trying to strangle pussycats with a scarf? He saw us walking by...Francine licked her lips, imagining Louis's inflamed berserk lunge through the second-floor window, as he spotted his victims and something snapped. Whatever thin thread that had kept him fettered indoors snapped, and he took the quickest route, right out the window, thinking he could actually reach them, thinking it even as he was falling straight down to his death, because she saw him struggling with that hideous scarf, trying to pull it off so he'd be ready when he hit the ground, ready to get my pussy, and get me too. Francine's legs wobbled, and she dropped down to one knee, pulling Minky close to her.

Bert Howard watched the whole thing, his mouth rounded to a perfect empty O. Bert was not a quick thinker, even under the best of circumstances. His mouth remained open, even as Louis lay across the street in the flower bed. Finally, as the seconds ticked by, a first thought trickled into Bert's head. Bert was a very meticulous gardener, what with his bear and elephant topiaries, and his rows of prized dahlias, and his two beds of Waverly Festival first-prize-winner John F. Kennedy roses, so when he looked over at Louis, he thought, Why would a man want to do that to a stand of tulips, jump out of a window and land right on top of them?

Even as Louis tumbled from the window, before he even hit the ground, Bev Howard had him dead, in the back of Bill Rose's hearse, and on his way to the grave at Waverly Cemetery freshly dug, the mourners assembled. When Louis actually hit the tulip bed, that was merely dotting the *i* and crossing the *t* as far as Bev was concerned. No, she saw him start out of that window and her mind raced ahead to recipes, or more specifically, to food for the bereaved. Poor Gracie would be especially bereaved, losing her husband, then her son, both in the space of a year. Well, I'll definitely do the sweet potato casserole with the marshmallow glaze again, and maybe a ham. Or maybe potato salad—no, that was probably too picnicky. And then, as Louis, tumbling, hit the ground—I know, a pineapple upside-down cake.

Carl Lerner, who had moved onto the street only a few months ago, was the only one of that group of on-lookers, excluding the kickball-playing neighborhood kids who'd scattered when Louis fell, as if, being kids, they somehow might end up being blamed—Carl was the only one to spring into action. When Louis began his descent, Carl, not being weighted down by sixteen years of having pondered his terrible presence, took off across the street with his arms outstretched as if he truly believed he might catch Louis before Louis smacked into the ground. Carl wasn't being entirely absurd: he had an actual record of catching human beings who were falling out of windows. Once, on a high school field trip to see Independence Hall and the Liberty Bell, he was standing at a street corner when a city bus pulled up beside him. A woman suddenly cried, "My baby!" and the next thing Carl knew, a toddler, who'd been allowed to lean too far out of the hot bus, suddenly fell into his arms. The reason Carl's arms had been in position for the catch was that he and a classmate were snickering about a chesty woman who'd just passed by. Carl had had both of his hands cupped and his arms out, and had just finished saying, "Did you see those big bazooms?"

So Carl ran, fleet of foot even though he was forty years old and sixty pounds overweight, his arms out and ready. He was not afraid of the person he hoped to catch, and even if he had been, hell, he still would've run across the street to help, because that was the kind of person he was. Somebody falls out a window, you catch him, who cares if he's got something wrong with him, who cares if he don't ever come out of the house, isn't that his business, after all? Carl was gaining speed like a great racehorse with a quarter lap to go. My God, I'm going to make it, he thought, but then just as he'd crossed the street he caught his foot on third base, the third base the kids in the neighborhood had been using for generations, first was the telephone pole, second was the manhole cover, and third was the funny hump of asphalt the size of a grapefruit next to the curb, God knew what the street department of Waverly had tarred over—the boys always said it was a rat or a Chihuahua or some such thing—but anyway it was third base, and Carl caught his toe on it and went crashing into the gutter, arms outstretched, arms that most definitely would not be rescuing Louis.

Louis was dead, Kitty knew it, Francine and Minky knew it, Bert and Bev knew it, and Carl Lerner, sprawled and despairing in the gutter, knew it. Everybody but Louis knew it. Which is why they all nearly jumped out of their skins when Louis slowly lifted his head and turned his eyes toward them.

II

Fucking ER. It was Iris's turn to be pulled to the Emergency Room, and she was definitely not in the mood. The patient census in the Intensive Care Unit was low, had been all week, and the Unit nurses were getting pulled to work on floors all over the hospital, wherever staffing was short. Iris knew she was in line for the next hit, and she'd been hoping for a regular medical-surgical floor, or maybe Rehab. Not that either was much to hope for. On a med-surg floor she'd have eight patients, not one or two like in the Unit, and though they weren't as sick, you still ended up running your ass off all shift. Everything was too spread out, you spent your time traipsing up and down the long hall getting nickeled and dimed to death. Rarely a real emergency—unlike the often incessant flow of emergencies in the Unit—mostly handing out pills, changing soiled beds, feeding patients, turning and wiping, then more pills. It didn't take a lot of brains, but it was still hard work. By the end of a shift, answering the endless call lights that blinked on above the patients' doors, Iris felt like she was one of those metal balls inside a pinball machine, bonging from light to light. Rehab, where the amputees and stroke victims recuperated, was a little better, but still not what you'd call a winner. Rehab required a nurse who could move slowly and patiently, which Unit nurses were psychologically incapable of doing. Iris liked to go, to move, to get things done; to stand there, barely assisting as a Rehab patient learned to put on a brace by himself, or to use a knife and fork again, was a unique form of torture. Iris wished them well, she truly did, but the fact was she liked the patients better when they were in the Unit, very ill, and dependent on her skills and speedy interventions.

She had walked into Barnum Memorial Hospital feeling almost good, the warmth of the May afternoon still in her when she approached Herb, the security guard, and punched in to work. In fact, she felt so good she made the mistake of smiling at him.

Herb's wrinkled face lit up, and he smiled back at her, which put a severe strain on his dentures. His uppers popped forward, which threw his alignment out and caused his lowers to list to the right, which shifted his tongue up and to the left, which forced his uppers to be pushed even further forward until at last they shot out of his mouth altogether, and unfortunately for Iris, her natural reaction was to reach out and catch them before they hit the linoleum and shattered.

"Atta irl," Herb shouted, meaning "Thatta girl," reaching out to claim his teeth.

Iris made a face as he took them and began, with a great many juicy sounds, to force them back into his mouth. "Herb," she said, "I've handled some pretty disgusting dentures in my time, but those things take the cake."

"A little fuzz on the molars never hurt a man," he said. "Iris, girl, that was quite a catch. You're a marvelous woman, you're my Georgia peach." He smiled at her again, but more cautiously. "Quite a catch. You sure do know how to use your hands." His smile became a leer and he gave his eyebrows a wiggle.

"You got a twitch, Herb? You got a problem with your eyebrows?"

He leaned his face toward her. "Think I do, Iris. How about taking a closer look?"

Iris stepped back and stared at him for several moments. "Herb, practically every female employee of this hospital is better looking than me. I don't get it. Not once, never have I seen you come on to any one of them. Only me. Why is that?

Because I'm such a joke, you think you might actually have a chance?''

It was Herb's turn to stare back at her. He shook his head, then spoke to her in his wheezy asthmatic voice. ''You think I'm a crazy old fart, don't you? Don't you? Well, I'll tell you something, I know a thing or two. I got no teeth, and I got hardly no wind left in my lungs, and I got the arthritis bad—hell, there's something wrong with practically everything I do got. But my brain works, Iris girl, and my eyes are cloudy but they can still see. I watch you coming here to this time clock every day, and I see something I don't see in any other of those female employees you was talking about.'' He stopped to catch his breath, placed a gnarled hand on the wall to brace himself.

Iris whispered, ''What? What is it you see?''

Herb took a white handkerchief from his back pocket, lifted his hat, and wiped his brow. At last he said, ''I see love. I see pure, one hundred percent untapped love. You call yourself ugly. Well, you're just looking *at* the package, girl, and me, I'm looking *in* the package. So there. That's what causes old Herb to kick up a fuss every time he sees his Iris. He gets all excited 'cause it's Christmas Eve and he knows what's in the package.''

They stood there in the hall, eyeing each other as several nurses walked past them, punching in for evening shift. Iris turned to go, started off down the hall.

Herb's voice reached her just before she disappeared. ''Hey. You're a peach.''

She stopped, and shouted back at him. ''Don't be thinking about taking no bites out of this peach until you get those dentures fixed.''

He laughed. ''So long, bye-bye, I'm off to the dentist now.''

So when she walked into the Unit, Iris was thinking about Herb's words, or rather, she didn't know what to think about his words, so that when her head nurse, Gloria, said, "Iris, sorry, but you're pulled to the ER tonight," Iris only half heard her. After Gloria repeated herself, "Earth to Iris, you're working in the ER tonight," Iris came to and heard twice, which was two more times than she wanted to hear that she'd be working in ER.

"Shit," said Iris. "Pardon my French, please."

"Oh, come on," said Gloria, with the eternal pep that so grated on her staff's nerves, "ER's not so bad. It'll be a break from this place."

Iris looked at her. "All them damn fingers. Who needs it?"

"Fingers?"

"You know, people coming in with broken fingers, jammed fingers, lacerated fingers, infected fingers. I had a shift there once where all I did was fingers, I'm telling you. I even had a lady who managed to put a crochet hook through one of her fingers."

"Ouch," said Gloria.

"Tell me about it," said Iris. She rooted around in her locker, found her stethoscope and scissors, and headed off down the back way to the ER.

"Maybe it'll be toes instead tonight," Gloria called cheerfully after her.

It would sure be something. Maybe ears. Or eyes. ER always seemed to be having a special: knee night, "sprain two and we'll wrap the second one for free." Sometimes, though, the ER was a variety store: in room 1 there'd be an OD, in room 2 an allergic reaction to a bee sting, in 3 pulmonary edema, in 4 a psych case, in 5 a laceration of the chin, and in 6 an MI. Mix and match. Some of this, some of that. It got on Iris's nerves waiting to see what was going to walk through the ER doors. Or crawl. Or come in on a stretcher. The news was overwhelming and it depressed her: human beings just did not have the slightest idea how to take care of themselves. The things they do—take the wrong medication, or the right one but too much of it, or too little. Cut off the tip of a finger with a steak knife or a carrot peeler. Break a hand in a baseball game, or by dropping a log on it, or in a fight with a goldfish. Yes, Iris once had a patient who got mad at his pet goldfish and smacked the side of the aquarium hard enough to break his index finger and dislocate his thumb.

Iris had another feeling about ER. The people who came in with all their cuts and dog bites and broken ankles and sudden fevers and unusual discharges were practicing for death. This of course didn't include the people who were delivered to the ER dead, or dying—people who had already passed the final exam. Iris believed that every so often, a person just had to taste mortality, just a nibble and a lick, succumb to a few stitches, or a strain requiring an Ace bandage and a trip down the hall to X-ray, but not all the way down the hall, not down there to the white door at the end, the unmarked door to the morgue, not yet. Maybe they thought by practicing, by their slow accumulations of little wounds and illnesses, they'd acquire a knowledge and a readiness, so that when the time came, they'd know how to open the door. But Iris was a nurse. She understood about the door, how it was loose on its hinges, liable to swing open at any time, sometimes with a terrible suddenness and force. Or ease open, creaking, which was just as terrible, like with the Tube Man, for whom the door remained ajar for months, before it finally closed behind him.

Oh great, Iris said to herself, rounding the corner to ER, Inez and Winnie. Looks like I'll be working my ass off tonight. Inez and Winnie, two of the regular ER staff nurses, stood over by the narcotics box giggling and talking in low whispers. When crunch time came, usually from five to eight P.M., they'd still be standing there, giggling and gossiping. Then Dr. Gunther walked out of room 3, and Iris's night, which hadn't even started yet, went from bad to worse. Dr. Gunther admitted practically every patient who came into the ER. Admissions, with all the paperwork and tests, tripled the work of a nurse. Iris had been hoping Dr. Lords would be on. Dr. Lords's motto was "Patch 'em and pitch 'em." He knew how to clear out an ER, how to keep the traffic flowing. With Dr. Gunther, the traffic backed up for hours.

Iris walked over to Inez and Winnie. Inez looked up and snapped her bubble gum by way of greeting. Iris had once seen Inez blow a large pink bubble during a code, a telling example of Inez's reverence for human life. Winnie was even worse. During a code, at least Inez and her bubble gum would show up, while Winnie would simply disappear to that mysterious place where coworkers always seem to hide when you need them. Home in bed? Iris wondered. Shopping at the mall?

"So they pulled you here," said Winnie.

"Looks like it," said Iris.

"You pissed?"

"No more than you'd be if you got pulled to Intensive Care."

"Then you must be really pissed," said Winnie with a pleased smile.

"Work is work," said Iris.

"Yeah," said Winnie, as if she had any idea in hell what Iris was talking about.

Iris checked out the patient information clipboards, numbered one through six, to correspond to each of the ER examination rooms. All the clipboards were in use, so all the rooms were full. Three rooms had lacerations in them. Two fingers and a nose. A nose? Iris read the clipboard. The Accident/Illness Description box read, "Patient states was feeding pet cockatoo, ran out of peanuts, cockatoo bit nose. Laceration two cm's, on right nostril. No active bleeding at present." So, Iris thought, looks like the ER will be having a special on lacerations tonight. Oh well, at least Gunther couldn't admit those.

Inez said, "Yeah, ain't that a bitch. We're full already. You want to take whatever's in rooms 1 and 2, I'll take 3 and 4, and Winnie'll take 5 and 6."

Iris gave her a look and picked up her clipboards without a word. "Whatever's in 1 and 2," as if Inez didn't damn well know. The patients were either going to be real sick, so Gunther would admit them, or so repugnant, like an alcoholic in DTs or a GI bleed, that nobody would want to take care of them. Sure enough, Iris read her clipboards, a patient from a nursing home in room 1. That almost definitely meant a Code Brown, nursing lingo for a patient covered in shit, which nursing home patients usually were. This one suffered from dehydration and syncope, fainting spells. In room 2 there was an asthmatic, a Pink Puffer. Another admission, but no big deal. Give her some IV aminophylline and clear her right up. Iris eyed the waiting room as she went into room 1. Half-full, with the usual mothers yelling at kids, people holding home-made bandages to their small injuries, some lady in the corner mumbling earnestly to herself—people practicing for death. Iris sighed and went in to check her first patient.

"Hello, Mr. Toofer," said Iris to a long wad of sheets and blankets which covered a stretcher that was pushed against the wall. Presumably, somewhere underneath those sheets and blankets, there was a Mr. Toofer. Nursing home patients often completely hid themselves deep within their bed linens, for reasons Iris did not wish to contemplate.

"Mr. Toofer, you in there, sir?" said Iris again, lightly touching the sheets. She also sniffed the air around the stretcher, a reflex of nurses with potentially incontinent patients. Hmm, maybe no Code Brown after all. Things were looking up. Now if she could just find Mr. Toofer.

A slight rustling sound from the stretcher. Iris realized the sound was Mr. Toofer speaking.

"What's that, sir?" Iris said, going up on her toes and leaning close.

"You're mighty tiny," came the voice of Mr. Toofer from beneath the sheets.

"How do you know that? You can't even see me from under there."

Mr. Toofer's head popped up from the other end of the stretcher. Iris had been conversing with his feet. Mr. Toofer, for all his dehydration and syncope, had managed to turn himself around on the stretcher when no one was in the room.

"What are you, a foot doctor?" Mr. Toofer let out a few raspy heh-heh-hehs. Then his head dropped back down on the stretcher. Iris moved down to address the head, which he hid again beneath the sheets.

"Mr. Toofer, why'd you turn around on the stretcher?" said Iris, who, in spite of her negative feelings about ER, felt a growing fondness for this particular patient.

"To face the door, young lady. Why else?"

"Why do you have to face the door?"

"Them what don't face the door get shot in the back. Don't you know nothing about the Wild West? I just told you rule one. Want to know rule two?"

"What's rule two?"

"Don't trust nurses whose noses don't come up to the stretcher."

Iris slowly peeled the sheet back from Mr. Toofer's face. "I'm short, Mr. Toofer, but you can trust me."

"Well, if you ever do tell a lie, at least it won't be a big one," he said, letting loose with another string of heh-hehs.

Mr. Toofer was one wrinkly old man. When they got some fluids in him, though, some of those wrinkles would disappear.

"Sir, you got a face that tells me you've done some living. How old are you?"

"In dog years or people years? In dog years I've been

dead since 1950. In people years I'm ninety-three." Mr. Toofer lifted his white head a little higher off the stretcher and looked around. "Say. Say. I'm not in my room, am I?"

Mr. Toofer was not as with it as he'd sounded. Iris touched his arm. "No, you're at the hospital. You're in the Emergency Room of Barnum Memorial Hospital."

"Did I do something wrong?" He tried to pull the sheet back over his head. Iris stopped him. He looked at her vaguely. "Say. Do I know you? Weren't you just in here?"

"I'm Iris, Mr. Toofer, your nurse. And you're in the hospital because you're sick."

Mr. Toofer brightened. "Oh yeah? Sick? Is it fatal, what I got? I'm waiting for something fatal. At ninety-three you'd think I wouldn't have so long to wait."

"Nothing fatal. You just need some fluids and a little medicine."

Mr. Toofer lifted a thin white arm off the stretcher and crooked his finger at her. "Come a little closer. That's it. Say," he whispered, "how about we forget about all this? Why don't you take me out to my Oldsmobile, and I'll just kind of slip out of the parking lot. That sound reasonable to you?"

It sounded very reasonable to Iris. She could almost picture it, Mr. Toofer looking natty in a white suit, behind the wheel of the Oldsmobile of his dreams, driving off into whatever sunset was waiting for him.

"I can't," Iris whispered back to him. "I can't, I'm sorry."

"Well," Mr. Toofer sighed. "You looked like a sensible young woman, so I thought I'd ask. Here's an easier one. How about finding me a urinal? I got to piss so bad, I could fill a bathtub."

When Iris went in to check on Mrs. Horner, the acute asthmatic in room 2, she was sitting bolt upright on the stretcher, puffing into an oxygen mask. Like many chronic lungers, her personality was on the low end of pleasant, which Iris immediately discovered when Mrs. Horner whipped off her mask and snapped, "It's about goddamn time. I coulda died in here." She pushed her mask back onto her face and took three or four dramatic breaths.

Iris kicked into her neutral professional gear. It didn't pay to be genial; that just made the lungers crankier. Iris understood, and didn't take their moods personally, or at least tried not to. She imagined that to be chronically short of breath was akin to spending twenty or thirty years half-drowning in high waves, while the rest of the beachgoers frolicked blithely on shore.

"Hello, Mrs. Horner," Iris said. "I'm Iris, I'm your nurse, and I'll—"

Mrs. Horner whipped off her mask. "Hold it. Hold it right there," she gasped. "You're not my nurse. There was someone in here, Candy, Mandy..."

"Sandy," said Iris. "Her shift ended. Now I'm assigned—"

"Oh, you are? Assigned? Is that it? I have no choice, of course. They just assign you somebody, whether you like it or not."

Iris could hear Winnie and Inez cheerfully chattering out at the nurse's desk. She said, "Mrs. Horner, you're making yourself more short of breath. Why don't you lie back on the stretcher, and let me—"

Mrs. Horner suddenly pushed Iris's hand away. Iris had been about to take Mrs. Horner's blood pressure.

"Get that thing away from me. You're not doing that."

Iris heard something snap. Her own mood, perhaps? No. Just Inez's bubble gum out in the hallway. "Mrs. Horner, this is only a blood-pressure cuff. It's not going to hurt you."

Mrs. Horner's bulging Pekingese eyes glared at her. "You're right. Because it's not going on me." She took some breaths. "That thing cuts off my circulation. Cuts off my oxygen."

"It goes on your arm, not around your throat." Although in your case, thought Iris, I might make an exception.

"I don't care. Leave me alone."

"Okay, Mrs. Horner. I'll start your IV then. Get some medication in you." Iris began to assemble things from the IV tray.

"Oh no you don't. I get my medication by mouth."

"You're too sick for that now."

"I got my rights, Shorty. You're not—"

With that, Iris marched over to the door, closed it, then turned around to face Mrs. Horner. She raised a finger and pointed it like a loaded gun, directly at Mrs. Horner's nose. "Mrs. Horner, I'm sorry. But you caught me at the wrong hour of the wrong day of the wrong fucking year." Mrs. Horner held her breath, not an easy thing for a chronic lunger. Iris continued. "Now, in my opinion, you're a sick lady. But if you don't want us to treat you, that's your choice. Like you said, you got rights. But it's pretty warm out there for May, Mrs. Horner, and in that heat, and breathing the way you are, I bet you last under an hour. Then we get you back, by ambulance this time, and we might even be able to save you. I doubt it, though, from looking at you. Now, if you don't want me to help you, then there's the door. There are plenty of sick people out there who do need my help. And one more thing. My name's not Shorty. It's Iris. It's not a great name, but it's the one I got and you sure as hell better use it."

Mrs. Horner looked at Iris, remembered to breathe again, then fell back against the elevated head of the stretcher with her arm straight out. "Here," she whispered. "For my blood pressure. Not too tight though, okay. . . Iris?"

"No sweat, Mrs. Horner," Iris said, wrapping the cuff. "You won't even feel me pump it up."

III

Was it like being born, looking up from your bassinet and seeing those curious and strangely disconcerted faces, or was it more like dying, lying in your open coffin, eyes wide, gazing upon those same disconcerted faces, disconcerted by the newness of you and the unexpectedness of your act, by the sudden alteration in the norm of the neighborhood, and in the rules that placed you, Louis, in your house, hidden, and your hiddenness contemplated from a known distance, an inviolable distance, you in there, us out here, so what in God's name—Louis saw in every pair of eyes that now blinked from the middle of every pale face that stared down at him—do you think you're doing sprawled here in this tulip bed out in the world of blue May skies and a beaming sun that's shining on every good citizen of Waverly, a term which has not, for sixteen years and up to this precise moment, included you?

Louis couldn't decide, being born or dying, but it was something like that. His eyes moved from Kitty to Francine to Bev and Bert, and then to Carl. Then he did something the newborn and the dead never do: he spoke. If a dead man were to speak, he might just say the word that passed in a whisper from behind Louis's scarf.

"Boo," Louis said.

Wasn't that what they expected from the monster of Waverly? Certainly Francine Koessler expected it. No one else could understand him, but she'd been listening so hard her ears about popped off, so when Louis went "Boo," she jumped back behind the others with a little scream. "Get back, everybody. He's crazy dangerous!"

They'd been standing in a circle around Louis, but they drew back, because this was not a normal man in a normal kind of accident. But Louis didn't do anything except lie there, so they looked at each other, and positioned themselves around him again.

"He'll attack. I seen him do it," said Francine behind them, clutching her Minky.

Carl Lerner went down on his knees beside Louis. Kitty hunkered above Carl, because if Carl was going to do anything with Louis's hat or scarf, Kitty wanted to be the first to see.

"Hey buddy. Can you speak? Where you hurt?" said Carl.

And then, in a simple, ordinary gesture of human concern, Carl did something that no one, beyond Atlas and Gracie, had done for sixteen years. Carl, who had no memories or imaginings. Carl, who saw him as the recluse, but not the monster, because who has it in him, thought Louis watching in wonder, to do to a monster the thing that Carl now did. Which was to reach out across sixteen years and touch him with a hand that was lighter and more lovely than the teenage kiss of Ariel Nesmith.

"Hey buddy. Where you hurt?" said Carl, touching Louis lightly on the shoulder.

Louis stared at Carl's hand. For a moment, under Carl's touch, Louis wasn't sure that he was hurt, that his broken arm hadn't suddenly healed. And if his arm had healed, if a painless knitting of bones had taken place, what then had occurred under his scarf and beneath the lowered rim of his baseball hat? Had he grown a nose, did he have his eyebrows back, if he licked his lips would they be smooth and full again, had Carl's touch regenerated to pinkness and health the skin on his forehead and cheeks? But when Louis shifted the arm that lay twisted beneath his body, the pain was instantly there, sharp and terrible, and it caused him to involuntarily speak out the answer to Carl's question.

"My arm."

"It's a trick," Francine called out from beyond the

perimeter of neighbors who surrounded Louis. "He'll get you close, then strangle you with his scarf."

The entire group, including Louis, turned their eyes to Francine. She hugged Minky to her. "Well," she said, "I mean, he might."

Kitty looked again at Louis. The moment was escaping her, she knew. Her chance, the years she'd spent waiting for him to reveal himself. She began to reach for his scarf, slowly, to inch herself toward the complete knowledge of his wounds, to unwrap his mystery.

Louis smelled her oversweet wine breath, then saw the hand coming. He felt no comfort in its approach, nothing of what Carl in his innocence had given to him.

Kitty said hoarsely, "We better . . . we better get the scarf off . . . loosen his collar. He needs air. I think he needs . . ."

Louis said, "No," and at the same moment, another hand stopped Kitty. Not Carl, but Bert, reached down and plucked Kitty's hand from Louis's scarf, plucked it as he might pluck a weed from amongst his winning roses. At first Louis couldn't decide whether it was the compelling force of decency which induced Bert to intervene or simply his fussy ways. Yes, most likely Bert couldn't tolerate the incongruous sight of Kitty's hand on Louis's scarf, because nothing was so out of order as that, no two things belonged less in conjunction, like the weed and the flower. For an odd moment Louis wondered which was which; in Bert's mind, was Louis and his scarf the flower, and Kitty's hand the weed, or was it the other way around?

Kitty turned red with anger and disappointment, and just as quickly Louis saw the relief on her face, on all their faces, because really, wasn't it enough just to have him out here among us, let's get used to the miraculous idea of that first, one thing at a time, whoa Nelly. In the interest of self-preservation, because that's what it really was, let's do this thing in degrees, who knows what will be unleashed upon us, and all of Waverly, if we get to tinkering with that hat and scarf?

That settled, Louis could concentrate on the mounting pain in his arm. Was it really pain? The flames had given him his definition of pain, and what could compare to the agony of flame, the fundamental force of energy, heat and light, reshaping the soft flesh of his sixteen-year-old face? He tried to move, but the arm stopped him, provided him with another definition of pain.

Carl said, "Hold on, buddy, let me help you up." Carl caught Louis under his good arm, his left one, and Bert provided support from behind. "Easy now. That's it, you're almost there. Okay, that's it."

He sat up in the bed of battered tulips. He supported his arm, and looked up at his window, the window from which he had descended. There was no getting back to it, no rolling the film backwards—neighbors running in reverse, broken tulips snapping themselves upright, and he himself flying upward toward the window, ass first, and then a hesitation at the windowsill before he was suddenly gone from view. He turned and looked at his neighbors, one by one. So this is my welcoming committee, as ordinary a group of Earthlings as a monster from outer space could want. Of course, he hadn't imagined it would go this way, when after Atlas's death, he began to have thoughts about how he might join the world again. Or if not actually join, at least get out the front door and sniff around a little. If he did do it, and he never really thought he would, he had imagined it would be a matter of increments, step by microscopic step. He might actually get outside, in the full daylight, in a matter of a few short years. And now here he'd gone and thrown open his window and just hurled himself, because whether he jumped or fell it was still an act of force, the bonds were broken and you were going down, there could be no further debate, except for a brief second when he was uncertain whether he was plummeting toward the tulips or the tulips were plummeting up toward him. Maybe, he thought in that one second before he hit, maybe the world, the actual solid daylight earth, is tired of waiting, and it's coming up to the window to meet me, since I haven't in sixteen years exhibited any inclination to jump down and meet it. But when he hit, he got his sense back, and he understood that at long last he had made his move. Who would have ever thought it possible?

Bev filed away her condolence recipes, and spoke softly to Louis. Louis appreciated her consideration, and Carl's, even if they didn't know they were being considerate. He needed lowered decibels, muted voices.

She said, "Gracie's not home, is she, Louis?" That was obvious to them all now. Gracie wasn't home, or she'd have appeared. One or two of them wondered if having his momma gone might have caused Louis to panic, for who knew the delicate condition of a mind like his, what minor alteration in the regularity of his day might cause him to fling himself from a window? With Gracie gone, their commitment to Louis, whose very existence had been something of a question five minutes earlier, continued to grow.

"She's out with a friend," he said. "Gracie's with Donna Hodges." He attempted to stand. "If you could just, kind of, help me back inside."

Carl wouldn't let Louis get up. "You got to go to the hospital. I can see the break in that arm."

Hospital. That's how it would go, that's how it would go. Louis let out a little moan and closed his eyes. He sank to his knees, still clutching his injured arm, and began to moan louder and sway from side to side. Hospital. He should have known. The weeks in the hospital as they worked on his face, as they struggled with the fire on his skin, igniting it and extinguishing it, hour after hour, as they dressed his skin, and applied ointments, and scraped at his wounds, igniting and extinguishing. And now I go back, I have waited sixteen years and they have waited too, at the hospital, they knew I would be back, that sooner or later I'd jump, as if the house where I imagined I was safe had actually been smoldering, sixteen years smoldering, and then it burst into flame. Trapped, I ran to the window and jumped, only it's no good. Louis swayed and moaned, and though they didn't realize it all the neighbors began to sway with him, to pick up his rhythms. I jumped but it's no good, and now Louis opened his eyes wide and saw that the flames had come with him, that he was surrounded by the heat, and the burning orange light.

"Flames!" he shouted.

All the neighbors looked where he looked, and in the mounting madness of Louis falling from the window, Louis in the tulips, Louis speaking to them, in the accumulation of so much Louis where for all that hidden time there had been no Louis, in the agitation of the moment they gave themselves over to him. Not even Carl was immune. Louis swept over them, his vision became their vision, his flames became their flames.

"Flames," shouted Louis, pointing to the pavement where Bev and Kitty were standing. Instantly their feet went down, then again and again, stamping at the flames that sprang up from cracks in the sidewalk.

"Flames." And Louis pointed to the grass, and Bert ran over, and his foot went down, as he tried to smother the orange licks of fire that spread along the green of the front lawn.

"Flames!" Only this time it wasn't Louis but Francine who shouted, because if there ever was someone waiting to leap into a hysterical episode, it was Francine. She dropped Minky and ran over to Bev and Kitty on the sidewalk, hopping up and down on the little bursts of fire, her eyes ablaze and happy, her open mouth emitting grunts of effort.

Carl leaned over Louis, to shield him, his hand out, fluttering in the air like a butterfly to keep the sparks and embers from landing on Louis. The fire fighters whirled and jumped and stamped their feet. Their faces flowed red with sweat and exertion, and they made excited noises because at last they could see that they were winning, not one lick of flame had reached Louis or would now, Louis saw that from beneath Carl where he had cowered, watching in amazement as his neighbors beat back the fire. How was such a thing possible? Fire could be beaten. It had never occurred to him. Why should it have, when the evidence of its casual malevolence was there before him in his dresser mirror every night as he unwrapped himself before bed? And yet, each time his neighbors brought down their feet, the fire withdrew, lacking the energy even to blacken the soles of their shoes. At last their movements slowed to a kind of dance of victory, as they snuffed out the scattered flarings on the lawn.

When it was over a calm passed through the little group, and they felt full and empty at the same time. Louis saw something move through their eyes, a question forming, and they exchanged looks because it was beginning to dawn on them that they didn't quite know what the hell was going on, or what exactly they'd just been up to. Francine thought she'd just been holding Minky, yet Minky was over by that dogwood sharpening her claws on its trunk. And Bev and Kitty couldn't figure out why they were so sweaty, and how their underwear had gotten all hiked up and uncomfortable in their crevices. Bert's legs were about to fall off, he felt like he'd run a mile, and Carl had the notion he'd been shooing away bees, because why else was he flapping his hand around in the air?

Now they were less afraid of Louis. They'd danced away their panic, passed through the ring of fire which had surrounded him, and sensed that his terrible misfortune was not infectious. What had burned him would not burn them. And Louis, from within the ring, had felt the fire's heat but had not been scorched. If he'd survived a fire, then surely he could manage a trip to the hospital, where in fact they had not been waiting sixteen years to torture him again. I must remember that, he told himself, and besides, what choice do I have, as the shooting pain in his right arm reminded him.

He thought, If these good neighbors extinguished the fire that threatened me, I can rely on them to get me to the hospital. Even Francine, for the moment, seems competent. Besides, the matter was really out of his hands. Bev and Kitty had gone off to fetch Bev's car, and Bert and Carl were starting to help him down the front walk to the curb, and Francine was doing her arms up and down in that maestro way Louis recalled from the days she used to burst helter-skelter into the hardware store thinking she was being purposeful, which was how she thought of herself at that moment, directing Carl and Bert down the walk and to the curb as if she thought that without her orchestration such a move might not be possible. Louis felt himself being pulled forward, under the influence of the same forces that had hurled him out of the window. The trip down the walk became an extension of that original event, the sense of plummeting, leaving his window, his bedroom, his house of self-confinement, farther and farther behind.

Bev drove up, doing at least forty, a feat since her driveway was only four houses down from the Malones', and jumped the curb. Who could blame her, they were all excited, because the magnitude of the event had begun to dawn on them. Louis Malone had leapt out of his window and into their arms.

After Carl and Bert, under Francine's careful direction, got Louis situated between them in the backseat of the Chevy wagon, Francine ran around to the front and shoved in alongside of Kitty and Bev. They were crazy if they thought they were going to leave her behind.

Bev started off, then braked to a lurching stop. "What

about Gracie? Shouldn't one of us stay behind in case she comes home?''

It was the right thing to do, of course, but no one volunteered. Miss going to the hospital? A silence, with everybody starting to feel bad, especially Carl because he was somewhat more morally inclined than the others, though he sure did want to make the trip to the hospital himself. They sat there squirming, thinking about how it would be for Gracie to come home to a house which Louis had occupied steadily for twenty-four hours of every day for sixteen years, what the awful silence of that might feel like. She'd think he was dead, as in suicide dead, dead in the bathtub, or hanging dead in the stairwell, some just awful kind of dead, and Gracie didn't deserve that. So just as they were all about to volunteer simultaneously, as a disappointed but dutiful throat-clearing sound began to rise out of everyone in the car, Louis came up with a plan that satisfied them.

"We can drive by Donna Hodges's and get Gracie. It's on the way," he said softly.

Of course. Yes. Perfect. Bev shifted the Chevy into drive, which wasn't easy since they were all crammed in there tighter than a rosebud.

"Donna lives on Oakley Crossing, doesn't she?" said Francine after they'd gone a block.

"Yes," said Bev. "And she has the most amazing hydrangeas, isn't that right, Bert?"

"That's right," Bert called from the backseat.

"Of course, it's not hydrangea season," said Bev, for the benefit of those passengers who were not as up on their gardening as she and Bert.

Francine thought about Oakley Crossing. She didn't want to say it, but she hoped everyone knew the Waverly police station was also at the end of Oakley Crossing, and they'd have to pass it before they took a left on Spring Street. Given the unusual circumstances, she felt that some sort of a police escort was called for. A motorcade was what she really had in mind. Francine Koessler riding in the main car right smack in the middle of a motorcade with flashing red lights. And flags would be good too, little ones flapping on the antennas. Wouldn't that be something, going through the center of town like that?

Kitty, between Bev and Francine, sneaked looks at the rearview mirror, in which she could just see Louis's covered face. He was sitting perfectly still, cradling his arm, Carl and Bert on either side of him. Bert rolled his window partway down and a puff of wind blew back a part of Louis's scarf. Kitty caught a glimpse, and she winced and made a small sound. Louis's eyes met hers in the rearview mirror. Both of them looked away.

"How you doing there, buddy?" Carl said to him. "How's that arm doing?"

"Okay," Louis said in a quiet voice. He could see everyone in the car lean slightly toward him: the women up front tilted their heads back, just a little, the men next to him tilted theirs sideways. No one wanted to miss what he said.

"Hey Bev, watch the bumps," Bert said to her. He'd seen Louis's eyes squint when the car jostled.

"I'm trying to, honey. This isn't a Mercedes."

"Weren't they the ones who had that commercial?" said Francine. "The one with the fellow shaving in the backseat while the chauffeur hit all kinds of potholes?"

"I think it was Chrysler," said Kitty, looking at Francine. She was glad to look at Francine. She didn't want to look in the rearview mirror anymore. Her chest still felt fluttery. She needed a cigarette. What was that she saw? Part of his nose? He could breathe through that? She thought she could hear him snuffling behind her, his breath warm and wet on her neck. "Yes," she said again to Francine, her voice too loud, "definitely Chrysler."

Everyone in the car nodded, and then Louis, seeing

them, nodded too. Carl and Bert, seeing Louis, tacked on a few more nods. It went back and forth that way, nod for nod, until they all felt foolish and loose in the neck and brought the nodding to a close.

"That arm doing okay?" Carl said again.

"Maybe we could kind of put some sort of sling on it or something," said Bert. He did a quick scan of the interior of the Chevrolet for something suitable, and then his eyes came to rest on Louis's scarf, which was, of course, the most suitable potential sling in the car. Bert swallowed once or twice, the spit suddenly thick and tenacious in his throat. "Really, I guess, though, they say you shouldn't fiddle with an injury before you get to the hospital. Really should let the professionals take care of it. You're holding on all right, aren't you, son?"

"I'm fine," Louis said, everyone in the car tilting toward him again as he spoke, listening hard. There was too much coming at him. He was out among them, among them but not one of them. Their essence swelled his brain against the confining contours of his skull. Kitty's aqua eyeliner, glittering sharply in the sun. Bev's hair, sprayed with something unendurably redolent. Carl's thigh against his own. When Louis looked, though, he saw a thin space, a knife-blade-thin distance between them, so he and Carl weren't really touching. But Louis's skin was so alert to the nearness of Carl that his nerve endings jumped the distance, sparked through his pants and across the thin gap, and then moved through Carl's pants to Carl's skin, so that in Louis's mind the shock was more intense than actual touching. A lovely feeling, and dreadful. On his right, Bert swallowed. He could practically hear the thick spit tumbling down Bert's throat. Francine belched surreptitiously. Louis knew it was Francine, he'd seen her cheeks bulge slightly as she tried to keep it in. But she had to release it, which she did with a deflating hiss between her slightly pursed lips. The sharp fumes wafted back to Louis and landed not in his nostril, of which he had only one, but on his tongue where her partly digested grilled cheese sandwich and Diet Pepsi lived a second life among Louis's quivering tastebuds.

Louis's senses were filled with his five neighbors—and if they were already brimming in the first two minutes of a car ride with five very ordinary citizens of the ordinary town of Waverly, how in God's name would he survive when they opened the car door and released him into the world? Bev swerved to avoid a boy on a tricycle, and a jolt of pain flashed down Louis's arm, dominating and clearing his sensory overload. He sucked his breath through his teeth, focused on his pain, and was calm. When Francine belched again he barely noticed, and when Carl shifted and brushed his thigh, Louis felt a surge, but it passed. For a few blocks he was almost normal, centered by his pain. He was not the recluse, the monster among five normal people. He was one of six neighbors out for a May car ride along the uneventful streets of their small town.

The ride was a little too uneventful for Francine. She'd been reaching her arm out the window and waving to the crowds as she passed by in the lead car of the motorcade of her imagination. The crowds consisted of two old men gabbing on the corner of Rutledge and Park, a woman pushing a stroller down Yale, the child on the tricycle Bev nearly ran over, and a dubious-looking teenager fingering his ear as he rested against the handle of a lawn mower. The two old men waved back, but that was it for crowd response. The Chevy definitely needed a police escort. She decided to broach the subject.

"You think maybe," she said to no one in particular, "we should stop by the police station after we pick up Gracie?"

"Whatever for, Francine?" said Kitty.

"Well, to report the accident," she said. "Aren't you supposed to report accidents?"

"Car accidents," said Bert.

"Oh," said Francine, her hopes for police motorcades and flags on antennas fading.

"Or suspicious accidents," said Carl, although he wasn't quite sure what he meant by that. "And there wasn't nothing suspicious about this accident, was there?" Carl had intended the question to be rhetorical, but then everybody got to thinking, and a quiet fell over the interior of the car.

Louis looked down at his knees. Of course the accident was suspicious, he knew that better than any of the five witnesses. Would they bypass the hospital now, take him directly to the police station for interrogation? Under the bright lights, asking him a question, then pressing their fat thumbs on his broken arm if he hesitated. . . .

"So talk to us, buddy. What were you doing climbing in the window of the Malones' house?"

"I wasn't climbing in, I was—"

"Don't give me that bull, you were breaking into that house."

"That's not true!"

They tugged at his scarf. "Oh yeah? If you're not a burglar, whatcha doing hiding your face? What do you say we get a good look at you, creep." The hands reaching for him . . .

Bert brought him back. "Say, Louis," he said gently. "How is it you fell out that window?"

Louis still looked at his knees. Bert used the word *fell*. But he meant it to cover all sorts of words, including the suspicious ones, like *push* or *jump*. Did someone push you, Louis? Gracie, even, did she finally break after all these years, suddenly and irrevocably tire of your unending eccentric presence and come up behind you as you stood before your bedroom window, and give you the shove you probably deserved? Or did someone else push you, a citizen of Waverly who'd cracked under the strain of your hidden thereness, who wanted to see you, damn it, after all these years, who wanted your ass out of the house and in the daylight where we can keep an eye on you, because who knows what you've been up to all this time, there's such a thing as too much privacy, so if you're going to be among us, then be among us, out the window you go, neighbor, enough is enough. Or did you jump, Mr. Louis Monster Malone? That's probably what happened, isn't it, because who among us, if for one terrible moment we became you, lived within your skin, the unimaginable skin beneath your hat and behind your scarf, who among us would not run to the nearest window and hurl ourselves out of it?

Louis felt the intensity of their wild surmises build around him. They had to know, but what could he tell them, since he didn't know himself. He'd been at the window, watching, content to watch, even. He had not been predisposed to go out the window, but the moment had suddenly changed, as it does when you are pushed, as it does when you are standing at the edge of a cliff and you are overwhelmed by a thought you had not had a second before: I could jump, you think. Or perhaps he had merely stood by the window and, of its own accord, the house shifted all of its molecules for him, moved itself back a foot or two but did not take him with it, so that where there had been a floor and a wall with a window, there was only air, everything that was in front of Louis was suddenly behind him. Down he went, reentering the world through no effort of his own. But would they understand this? Louis lightly touched his broken arm, and the whisper of pain cleared his head so that he might answer the looming question.

He said, "The storm window, you see. The screens." His listeners craned toward him. "The one in my bedroom always sticks, you know." His listeners nodded as if they did know, as if they'd watched him every year during the window-changing seasons, struggling with the screens. They were rooting for him, they wanted his answer to succeed, to be within the realm of ordinary experience and not be some strange, complicated reclusive mishap. "I put my knee on the windowsill," said Louis, "which I shouldn't have." They were behind him now, they'd all done foolish, dangerous things within the household, hadn't they? "And I wasn't paying attention . . ." Who among us has not been guilty of that sin of omission? "And I gave the screen a yank, and the next thing I know I'm out the window."

Hooray! Not jump or push. He fell. Bert almost clapped him on the back. Up front, the ladies released a collective sigh of relief. He's one of us, sort of. He fell.

Carl said, "My Aunt Ruth fell out her window about ten years ago. Did something funny to one of her eyes. Knocked it loose or something, so it doesn't quite sit right, like those walleyed people where you never know where they're looking."

"Soupy Billings had a cat like that," Francine joined in.

"Fell out a window?" said Bev.

"No, had eyes that looked every way but straight ahead. Think they were different colors, too."

"I fell off my back porch landing one time," said Kitty. She hadn't meant to bring it up, but then she didn't want to hear Francine start in on cats, or next thing you knew it would be Minky this and Minky that.

"Falls can be dangerous," said Bev.

"Sure can," said Carl.

But boy oh boy, they'd all take falling over pushing and jumping any day.

Bev turned off of Spain Street and onto Oakley Crossing. "Which one's Donna's? Blue with white shutters, or white with blue shutters?"

"Green with no shutters," said Louis. This caused everyone to look at him again. How did he know, if he'd been inside for sixteen years? They didn't want to ponder the question, having just survived his falling out the window. It was exhausting if you had to think about the implications of every little thing he said. But he answered it. "Least it was sixteen years ago." *Of course,* they all thought. "I see Donna's Honda up ahead on the left," he said.

Gracie was walking out of the house with Donna, and when she turned slightly she noticed the Chevy wagon weaving up the street, with a disembodied arm hanging out of the passenger-side window, and the hand attached to it waving slowly up and down. A moment or two went by before she recognized the car as Bev's, and the hand as Francine Koessler's, and in those moments she and Donna reacted to the hand and responded in turn, wiggling their fingers in a sort of generic, noncommittal greeting.

Gracie said, "Isn't that Bev's car?"

Donna said, "That's Francine waving, isn't it?"

The Chevrolet approached, full of people, but the sun and shadows playing off the window glass made it hard to see them. When it pulled to a stop beside the curb, Donna took a step or two forward on her chubby legs and began to call out names to Gracie, her voice rising excitedly as if the car were a mobile surprise party in her honor. "That's Kitty next to Francine, and there's Bev," said Donna to Gracie. "And Bert! And I think the new fellow who moved in across from you, isn't that Carl?" Donna's voice stopped with a squeak, as if an invisible hand had reached up and plunked a large cork in her open startled mouth.

Gracie's hand, too, was moving, toward her own mouth. *They have Louis.* Not, Louis was *with* them, but, they *have* Louis. Words that Atlas had once spoken came to her suddenly: "His covered face is like the monster . . . sound the alarm, let the citizens light their torches and brandish their clubs and pitchforks." While she had had tuna and egg-salad sandwiches and iced tea, the citizens had broken into her home with their clubs and taken Louis. They had waited all these years to do it, for Atlas to die, for me to let down my guard, and then they lit their torches. She saw them breaking down her door, heard Louis's pitiful sounds as they clambered up the stairs and into his room where he slumped in the corner cowering, his hands before his face not to protect himself, which is what they thought, but to protect them. Even as they came after him, he sought to protect them from the burning deformity of his face. Oh, Atlas. Gracie's eyes went blurry with frightened tears.

She started to move toward the car but her legs went weak. She could hardly see, and the air pressed in on her. Bert opened the back door. Then she saw Louis clearly, and he called to her. "Gracie, I'm hurt..." Words continued to come out from behind his scarf, but she failed to comprehend them because all she heard was "Gracie, I'm hurt," and his voice turned into the frightened bleating of a lamb for its mother, or some other animal child calling, and the maternal force surged within her. She could see again and her legs were strong, and she ran with her head down right straight for Bert's soft belly. Bert's eyes bugged as he waited to be gored by the horns that he imagined sprouting from Gracie's white head. Francine, who'd started to open her door, shut it again quickly, but even a steel door didn't look like it was going to stop Gracie.

Francine was about to scream, when a voice unknown thundered, "Duke, get your ass back here!" From nowhere, a reddish-brown blur of beast leapt between Gracie and Bert. Duke gone squirrel crazy, one moment leashed and walking down the block with Arnie, the next, loose and crashing across the sidewalk, Arnie in pursuit, pursuing more than just Duke, because the leash had been looped over the end of his hook, something he didn't ordinarily do and which he sure shouldn't have done this time because he'd experienced Duke and squirrels on too many occasions. Duke and one squirrel was bad enough, but this was three squirrels which they'd both spotted in the same instant. Arnie had been distracted by the sight of an elderly woman running down the front walk with her head lowered like a bull, and he hadn't got the leash off his hook in time, not that he'd have had much time even if he hadn't been distracted, Duke took off so fast. So Arnie's hook was jerked free of its straps by the force of Duke's interest in the squirrels, and the hook, still attached to the leash, bounced along behind Duke. That's what saved Bert and Francine from being attacked by Gracie—the combination of the total surprise of Duke's big reddish-brown body, the leash with Arnie's hook, and Arnie tearing after Duke. Gracie stopped short as Duke whooshed past her with such speed that sparks flew off the tip of Arnie's hook as it clattered along the sidewalk. Arnie followed, shouting at Duke. Then the two of them, preceded by three terrified squirrels, rounded the corner and were gone. Just like that.

Which gave Louis enough time to slide along the backseat and arrange himself before the open car door so Gracie could see him, see that he was safe and not a captive of a neighborhood mob.

"They came to my rescue, Gracie," he said. Everyone began to nod, yes, that's right, to his rescue, really, Gracie. Easy, now. Don't go charging the car again.

"He broke his arm, we think," said Bev, coming around the driver's side toward Gracie.

"He fell from his window," said Carl from beside Louis.

"The second-floor window," said Bert, watching Gracie carefully in case she should sprout horns again.

"We happened to be there. I was just walking by," said Kitty. She didn't mention that her eyes had been glued, as always, on Louis's window, and that there might have been some sort of cause and effect between her eyes and Louis's fall.

Francine twittered, "Why, he almost landed right on top of me and Minky," which she still believed might have been Louis's intent.

Gracie looked from one to another as they spoke, and then back to Louis for confirmation. "We're going to the hospital," he said. "Want to come?" His mouth made a movement behind his scarf, which she had come to know as his smile. She looked in his eyes as she started toward him, to make sure she saw nothing unstable there. Like everyone else, her first thought was that for a recluse, reentering the world was an act of madness. Then she was ashamed that she should think her son so out of place in the ordinary world. But it was dizzying to see him sitting there, surrounded by people, touching them even, for Carl sat beside Louis holding him upright. When she'd left him two hours earlier to have lunch with Donna, she hadn't given him a thought—that is, leaving her recluse son behind in the house was an act not worth thinking about because, she now knew seeing him there in the car among her neighbors, she had assumed that it would go on forever that way. Seeing him where she'd forgotten he'd once belonged, among people, she was ashamed and jealous, because she understood now that when he was hidden in her house he was hers completely. In her house he was within her, carried by her, nurtured by her, protected by her, and what mother gets a chance like that twice, to be so needed that the cord reappears? Louis didn't fly away at sixteen, as had all the other sons of all the other mothers in Waverly. A flaming moment reversed time, returned him to her arms. How very wide they had been opened for him, thought Gracie. Was this why I could look at Louis when Atlas could not, why I could dress his wounds which so tormented Atlas he couldn't bear to be in the house when I did it? Was it because I was so happy to have Louis with me again, my baby back, while Atlas mourned his return, the loss of manhood? Atlas mourned, but not me, thought Gracie. I was his mother. When he came back to me this second time, when he wore his scarf and hat, when I left him two hours ago so casually I thought nothing of it, I had assumed that he would stay within my house, and within me, forever.

Louis must have sensed it, how hard it was for Gracie to see him suddenly out, with no warning, pushed into the company of Francine and Kitty and the like. When she was close, he whispered, "Gracie, I want to go back home." He said the words for her, gave them to her, so she could participate in the event he'd begun on his own, so it would appear to her that she could influence his destiny, make the choice for him, so that what he'd started, she'd continue of her own free will.

She said next what he knew she'd have to say. "Not home, Louis. We have to get you to the hospital." And when she said it, they both felt better. Gracie had given her approval for a further step into the world, allowed for the reemergence of the possibilities that had been taken away from Louis sixteen years before.

Bev touched Gracie's arm. "You okay now, Gracie?"

Gracie turned and touched Bev's hand. "I'm fine now. I was just..."

"Shocked?" Francine offered from the front seat. Kitty nudged her in the ribs.

"I guess, yes, Francine, surprised anyway. Really surprised." She looked at Bert sheepishly. "I'm so sorry, Bert. Reacting that way. You must have thought I was, well..."

"Crazy?" said Francine, who'd certainly thought so.

"Francine," said Kitty, giving her an elbow again.

"Well, sure, crazy," said Gracie, trying a smile.

Bert shrugged. "Upset," he said. "You were just upset. Things coming at you so sudden and all." Bert was being exceedingly gracious. He still wasn't quite sure she wouldn't charge at him again.

"It's certainly not the kind of day I thought I'd be having," said Gracie.

"Me neither," said Donna Hodges, peering at Louis over Gracie's shoulder.

Carl said, "We better get going."

Francine did a silent head count. Eight. How were all eight of them going to fit in the Chevrolet? Well, she wasn't staying behind, that's for sure. She slid a secret hand up the car door and locked herself in.

Francine wasn't the only one who'd pondered the situation. "Hmm," Bert said. "Looks like we'll be needing another car."

"Another car?" said Gracie.

"For all these people," said Bev.

And then Gracie understood. She looked at her neighbors and imagined what such an event must have meant to them. Of course they'd all want to be in on it. Louis gave his approval with a tiny nod. This was his way of thanking them, though they could not know what it must be like for him to be so overwhelmed by the continued nearness of them.

"Yes," she said. "I want you all to come. Louis and I would appreciate it."

"We would," said Louis.

"We'll take my car, too," said Donna, who'd felt insecure about joining the original rescuers. But with her car, she had suddenly become integral to the effort. "It's only a little Honda, but you'd be surprised how many people can squeeze in there. Last week, after the Rotary barbecue, I gave five of the girls rides home, including Bea Hoaster. As much as I love Bea, she is not petite, especially after three helpings of braised chicken, which I know for a fact is the number she had because I was in line behind her every time."

Up in the front seat Kitty rolled her eyes at Francine, and Francine rolled her eyes back at Kitty. For once the two women were in perfect agreement: Donna Hodges was a silly old bird.

"So," said Donna, "who wants to come with me?" She smiled expectantly at the group.

Well, nobody, of course. Francine checked the lock on her car door; she sure wasn't going. Kitty settled firmly in her seat. Bev slowly made her way back around to the driver's seat; she'd decided her role was too important to relinquish. Carl held on to Louis, so he certainly wasn't going. Louis was definitely staying put, and that meant Gracie should be sitting beside him. Bert glanced around and realized he'd been outmaneuvered. He shot a look at his wife as she slid in behind the steering wheel.

Donna's smile faded. Bert shrugged and said, "How about I go with you, Donna? That should be enough. Gracie'll take my place in the Chevy."

Donna perked right up. "Great," she said, already hurrying up her front walk toward her house. "Let me get my keys. I won't be a minute."

In that manner they made their way through town and on to Barnum Memorial Hospital. Bev's Chevy wagon led and Donna's Honda brought up the rear. It was good enough for Francine Koessler, who held her hand out the window again waving to the citizens of Waverly. For Francine, smiling ear to ear, two cars were a motorcade.

IV

Of course Iris's shift was going horribly, she was working in ER, wasn't she? Mr. Toofer and Mrs. Horner both turned out to be keepers, so Iris spent an hour getting beds for them through Admissions, contacting their attending doctors for orders, having Lab draw bloods and X-ray do their chest films. Plus all the admission paperwork. And it wasn't like the ER was quiet. The waiting room was full, so she still had to pick up the patients with lacerations, and sprains, and bloody noses. Even Inez and Winnie were working. Inez was blowing quick little bubbles and popping them angrily as she moved in and out of the ER treatment rooms.

"Looks like you're having fun," Iris said to her as Inez rifled through the supply cart in search of sterile gloves.

Inez snapped her gum. "I mean, does this place suck, or what?" she growled.

Iris noticed the wet stain on the front of Inez's uniform.

Inez shook her head. "Guy in room 5 puked on me, can you believe it? We're just sewing up his thumb, and all of a sudden he turns his head and loses it all over me. I mean, why didn't he turn his head the other way and puke on Dr. Gunther? I'm telling you, the nurses get the shit end of the stick every time."

Can't think of a nurse who deserves a shittier stick, thought Iris, breaking into a grin as she walked out of the supply room.

The ward clerk, Dotty, waved her over as she walked by the front desk. "Iris, call for you on line two."

Iris picked up the phone, expecting to hear from Lab or X-ray. "Iris Shula," she said.

"That you, girl?" came Arnie's voice over the phone. He didn't sound right.

"Arnie, what's wrong?"

"I want to speak to Iris Shula," said Arnie in a loud voice.

"Arnie, this is Iris. Put the phone to your good ear!" Heads turned as she shouted into the phone.

There were crackling noises, then a loud crash as Arnie presumably dropped the phone at his end. Oh Christ, he's had a heart attack. He's keeled over in the kitchen with a massive MI. Iris almost hung up to go to him when she heard his voice again.

"Iris, you there, girl?"

"Arnie, this is Iris." She drew a grateful breath.

"Iris. I don't mean to bother you at work—"

"It's okay. It's all right, Arnie." She looked around at the ER waiting room, filled to overflowing. "Things aren't too busy here."

"Good. That's good. I'm not calling just to chat, though." There was a pause.

"Yes?" said Iris.

He cleared his throat into the phone. "You see, well, something came up. Something kind of happened." He paused again.

"Arnie, you there?"

Arnie started up again, his voice sounding a little vague. "See, what happened is, well, the thing is . . ."

"The thing is . . . ?"

"The thing is, my hook kind of disappeared."

Iris closed her eyes, squinted, then slowly opened them again. The nurse in her was fast at work: Arnie had suffered a small stroke. His hook was right there on the end of his arm, but he wasn't able to see it. Some tiny part of his brain had ceased to function, and he'd gone partially blind, or perhaps he was experiencing some sort of aphasia which rendered him unable to recognize things. Or maybe he'd just snapped, maybe he'd lost it. She'd noticed he was getting a little wifty these last months; Krupmeyer dying in the snow had shaken him.

"Arnie," she said carefully. "How do you mean 'disappeared'?"

"Not so much disappeared as gone, I guess you'd say."

Gone? Misplaced gone? Stolen gone? Who steals hooks? "Gone in what way, Arnie?" Then she said, "You want I should come on home, Arnie?"

"Just listen, I'll tell you how it's gone. Duke. Duke's got hold of it."

Rabies? Duke went crazy and turned on Arnie and he fought the dog off with his hook. "Duke attacked you? Do you have any wounds, Arnie? You should come in to the ER. No, wait, I'll borrow a car and—''

"Hold on, girl, did I say attack? You ain't getting me in there, poking rabies needles in my belly. Fourteen of 'em. That's how many they give you, isn't that right?''

"You're not bit?''

"No, I'm not bit. So put your needles away and listen. I was walking Duke and he saw a bunch of squirrels, and that's all it took.''

She waited. "Took for what?'' she said finally.

His exasperated voice jumped through the phone. "Hell, girl. Took to get him going! He saw them squirrels and went off like a rocket. I was holding the leash with my hook, and when Duke went, so did my hook. I'm telling you, it hurt. And now he's gone, dragging my hook all over town. Jesus, girl, I feel terrible, don't you know?''

There was a commotion at the entrance to the ER—the ambulance crew bringing in a noisy one. Iris looked at the guy's face as they wheeled him by. Shit shit shit. Harvey Mastuzek was back. Mr. GI Bleed himself. "Arnie,'' she said. "I'm not sure what I can do. Things are kind of picking up here.''

"I'm falling apart. Your old dad's falling apart.''

Arnie, Arnie. "I'm sure we'll find it, I'm sure it'll turn up.''

Arnie suddenly shouted excitedly into the phone. "Holy hell! It's turned up right now! I see that goddamn Duke out the window.'' Iris heard a rhythmic banging. Arnie pounding on the window? He was suddenly back on the line again. "He's trying to bury my hook in the hole I dug for the azalea. Gotta go, Iris! Christ, he's got a foot of dirt over it already.''

Arnie hung up on her so hard she jumped. She stood looking blankly at the phone, then handed it back over to Dotty. Dotty gave her a hopeful stare. She'd been trying hard to listen in on the conversation.

"You don't want to know,'' Iris said to her.

"Yeah, I do," said Dotty. "Tell you something you don't want to know. Guess who the crew just brought in?"

"I saw. Harvey Mastuzek. Mr. Congeniality himself."

"Funny," said Dotty, looking this way and that. "I don't seem to see Inez and Winnie anywheres. Poof, they vanished just like smoke."

"Like dust in the wind," said Iris.

"Like turds down the toilet," said Dotty, shaking her head.

"Dotty, I'm shocked."

"They a bunch of lazy asses, them two. You been getting all the hard patients."

"My reward's waiting for me in heaven, I guess, Dotty."

"Yeah, well, it ain't waiting for you in room 5. That's where they got Harvey." Then she said, "You taking him?"

"Who else?" Iris said, starting off for room 5. She bumped into Winnie as Winnie was coming out of the med room.

"Oh, sorry, Iris," she said. "What's in 5? You taking him?"

Iris looked up at her. She had a lot to say, and was just revving up to say it when a more fitting punishment for Winnie suddenly appeared at the ER entrance. Another ambulance crew was coming in with what looked like a code, a big fat guy with a blue face. "Yeah, I'm taking 5"—Iris nodded in the direction of the advancing chaos—"and you're taking that. Paybacks are a bitch, huh, Winnie?"

Iris left Winnie and went to check on Harvey Mastuzek. She would let Winnie dangle for a bit, but then she'd come out to help with the code. The ambulance crew was there to cover in the interim.

Iris expected the worst, walking into room 5, expected blood on the walls, Harvey thrashing around trying to land punches on whoever came within striking distance, but what she saw when she walked through the doorway was much more alarming than that. Harvey sat upright on the stretcher, absolutely motionless, his hands folded on his lap. His skin was very pale, she could see his thin dark veins through it, and his eyes were open. Whatever he was looking at was not in the room.

The two members of the crew who brought him in shrugged at Iris. The tall one said, "We picked him up in Waverly. In the alley behind the hardware store. Drunk. Rowdy. Threw up some blood, that's why they called us."

The short one, who was very short but still a good five inches taller than Iris, said, "I'm telling you, he was fighting us all the way. Even coming in here, all the way till we got in this room."

"Then his eyes kind of bugged open and he just stopped. Froze like."

Iris nodded, then she went over to the stretcher. Was Harvey fixing to have the Big One? Patients did that, wild one second, then going weird and quiet the next, before stroking out or going flat line. In fact, Harvey looked dead already, pale and still as he was.

Iris turned to the ambulance crew. "Thanks, guys. I got it from here."

The short one said, "You sure?"

"Yeah, finish your paperwork. I'll yell if I need you."

When they left, Iris turned back to the stretcher. "Harvey. You there?" She wiggled her fingers in front of his eyes. "Anybody home?"

Harvey blinked slowly, like an owl.

"Hey Harv, it's me. Iris from down in the Unit. The little troll. You remember calling me that?"

Harvey began to turn his head toward her, in imperceptible increments. Iris had seen many strange things in her years as a a nurse, but this was definitely spooky.

She began to wrap a blood pressure cuff around one of his thin arms. "You with me, Harvey? I'm taking your pressure now. Your belly feel okay? You know how it usually hurts when you come in here? How's your breathing been?" He looked at her. His pressure was normal. Harvey never had a normal pressure; the times he'd come in bleeding, his pressure had always been low. Even when they'd straightened out his fluid levels, his pressure was below normal. He looked at her. She listened to his lungs. Clear. He smoked at least a pack a day. They were never clear. His heart sounds were good. Harvey looked at her, and then his mouth began to move.

He did nothing more than speak softly, but Iris still jumped when the words left Harvey's mouth. "He's loose," he said.

Iris fiddled with her stethoscope. It was hard to meet Harvey's eyes. "Loose?" she said. "Who's loose?"

"The man," said Harvey.

Iris cocked her head. "What man? What man is loose?"

"He's coming here."

"Harvey, who? What are you telling me? I don't get it." Did she want to? Did she want to get it? She looked at his hands. He was doing something with his fingers, playing with something small and round and black, passing it back and forth between his fingers.

Then Harvey spoke, and his words made Iris clutch the side of the stretcher for support. "The man in the window," he said. "The man in the window is coming here."

The Tube Man's words.

Someone yelled for her. "Iris, you got a curved blade in here?" Inez ran in. "For the code. They can't get an airway in the guy. Straight blade's not working."

Harvey closed his eyes, then Iris gathered herself and turned away from him. She grabbed a curved laryngoscope blade out of the extra code cart and followed Inez out of the room to the code.

All sorts of people crowded the hall outside the room, including four or five gloomy-looking men in dark suits. Iris squeezed past them, then she whispered to Inez, "Boy, those guys look like undertakers. Kind of early, aren't they?" She closed the door behind her.

"Those guys *are* undertakers," Inez said. She pointed to

the fat man whose face was still blue, and who was almost totally obscured by busy hospital staff who were jabbing him with needles, shooting drugs into him, hooking him up to IVs and monitors and oxygen. "Don't you know him? That's Big Bill Rose, the funeral director from Waverly."

Now Iris recognized him, despite his increasingly darkening color. From LuLu's funeral. The guy who kept pushing Arnie to include a ride in the Lincoln limousine as part of the funeral deal. Arnie practically had to toss Big Bill and his son out of the house, and after he slammed the front door he had called him a "nickel-sucking son of a bitch." Looked like Big Bill's nickel-sucking days were fast coming to a close.

Iris helped prepare meds from the code cart. As she worked, one of the blood techs whispered to her that Jim Rose had found Big Bill on his living room floor. Big Bill had been making terrible choking sounds, and Jim Rose Heimliched him but nothing came out. The ambulance arrived, but they couldn't get anything out either. Iris could see Dr. Gunther struggling to slide an airway down Big Bill's throat; obviously there was an obstruction. Big Bill was not doing well. He was staying in V-fib now. They couldn't shock him out of it.

"Hey, I see it," Dr. Gunther suddenly said, from the head of the stretcher where he was bent over working the laryngoscope blade in Big Bill's wide-open mouth. Big Bill's tongue was the color of liver. "Give me a pair of forceps." He worked at it. "It's something shiny. Almost . . . almost. Got it."

Everyone craned forward to see. A golden ring. Winnie did the logical thing: she lifted Big Bill's meaty left hand. "Not his. He's still wearing his wedding band."

Dr. Gunther dropped the ring on an instrument tray, and they all went back to work on Big Bill. But Big Bill had been too long without a good flow of oxygen. If he'd been young, he might have had some kind of chance. But he was old, and carrying too much weight, and he'd been a heavy smoker, Iris could see from the stains on his fingers. He had nothing going for him, had had no chance from the moment he put that wedding band in his mouth. Put it in his mouth? Who sticks wedding bands in their mouth? The code was almost over, they were just going through the motions now, dragging things out a little so the people gathered outside the door would think they had engaged in a magnificent struggle for Big Bill's life, had done everything possible, although nothing they'd done in this crowded room had altered Big Bill's fate in the least. Iris eased over to the instrument tray where the ring shone golden among the silver scalpels and hemostats. She held it up to the bright examination light hanging above Big Bill's stretcher. There was an inscription. She squinted, then read it aloud:

"Norman Keeston. May 10, 1886."

Silence in the room.

"Anybody ever heard of him?"

Everyone shrugged and looked blank.

Dr. Gunther said, "Maybe he was some sort of relative."

Gerald from Respiratory said, "Yeah. Maybe Big Bill was going through a bunch of old family jewelry."

Inez said, "And he bit the ring to see if it was real gold."

They all smiled and averted their eyes. What Inez said had a definite logic to it. Big Bill's love of the holy buck was well known. That he should sink his teeth into a golden ring and then accidentally choke on it certainly seemed within the realm of possibility (and fitting, though no one would dare suggest it).

"It's been a big year for choking deaths. That guy a month ago who choked on a Pepsi bottle cap," said Dr. Gunther.

"Mrs. Framingham, who choked on a grape," said Winnie.

"And the Ping-Pong ball guy from Maryland. We never did figure out why he put a Ping-Pong ball in his mouth," said Inez.

"I guess a wedding band isn't so strange," said Gerald.

Truly, to the hospital personnel gathered around Big Bill's large and discolored form, choking on a wedding band was not so strange as to be unbelievable. It might not have even seemed so strange to Big Bill, who, at the moment of his death, must have recalled the unfortunate incident of the ice and understood that although his punishment was harsh, it was not unforeseen.

Far stranger for Iris were the whispered words of Harvey Mastuzek, words that had vibrated within her brain throughout the code, as if Harvey had been standing near, his hand cupped to her ear, words that she heard now as she left the code room, made her way past the dark-suited undertakers, and aimed her small thick body toward the room in which Harvey waited. Distracted, therefore, Iris was the only human being in the Emergency Room who didn't hear the screeching words of the tall, elderly woman who suddenly burst into the ER followed by a veritable parade of people.

"Someone get this boy a doctor!" Francine Koessler's voice did something electrical and unpleasant to people's nervous systems. Lab techs, Dotty the ward clerk, the four undertakers, and all of the patients in the waiting area jerked their heads in Francine's direction and regarded her with open mouths.

"You there," Francine shouted again, to the one person not paying attention to her. "Nurse, we need you here this instant!" Now Francine entered Iris's head—that's what Francine seemed to do, jump right inside Iris's head. Iris, well past the overload stage, who wouldn't have been in the mood for someone like Francine on the best of days, and who you certainly did not yell at as if she were a dog, not if you valued your life, whirled around and lowered her head, so that Francine was threatened for the second time in less than twenty minutes by a woman transformed into a bull. Francine realized in an instant that Iris made a far more dangerous bull than had Gracie.

"Easy now, girl." Dotty tried to calm Iris from the side. "You know how family members get."

Heedless, Iris advanced toward Francine, accelerating as she moved down the hallway. Francine hurriedly positioned herself behind the only thing capable of stopping Iris, and that was Louis, in his baseball hat and purple scarf, who indeed stopped Iris dead in her tracks. He took a step forward, supported on one side by Carl, and on the other by Bert, and nodded to Iris, because he recognized her. How could he not, for she had been the first woman, aside from Gracie, to whom he had spoken in sixteen years. And Iris recognized him, how could she not, the man in the scarf and hat, who had spoken as if he'd emerged from a coma, rusty and reborn, who had the urgent all-seeing eyes of a paralyzed man. He was here, her Lawrence of Arabia. He had crossed his desert for her.

"Oh, my, my," said Dotty in a low voice, because she recognized Louis too. She lived in Waverly, as did the undertakers and many of the hospital employees and patients in the waiting area. They all knew of Louis, knew of his scarf and hat, his sixteen hidden years. Their eyes were upon him. They were so intent, so excited and dismayed by his presence, they forgot to breathe. Louis could actually feel it, the oxygen around him that went unused, that entered his own lungs and made him dizzy with its richness. They stared at him. Dotty tried to speak again but could bring no sound to her words, not that she even knew what words she had meant to say. The undertakers momentarily forgot that Big Bill lay dying or dead in the next room. A lab tech who had been shaking a vial of newly drawn blood was shaking it still but didn't know it, didn't see as Louis did that her arm going up and down, up and down, was the only thing moving in the Emergency Room. The patients back in the waiting area, with their bruised knees, and their stove burns, and infected ears, and sprained tendons, the patients stared at Louis, too, unbreathing, and forgot their own injuries, for they either knew in fact from the legend of Louis, or if they'd never heard of Louis they knew instinctively from his overwhelming presence, that neither their individual pains, nor the collective mass of their pains, were equal to whatever lay beneath that hat, behind that scarf, and within those frightened eyes.

A short, high-pitched scream broke the spell that Louis had cast over the Emergency Room. It came from behind the closed door of room 3, the code room. Inez, not known for her personal courage or her tact, appeared wide-eyed in the doorway and practically shouted into the faces of Jim Rose and his fellow undertakers:

"He moved!"

"Daddy's alive?" Jim Rose pressed forward.

Inez shook her head. "No, he's dead. But he still moved." She rushed past the undertakers and into the locker room to find a piece of bubble gum to calm her nerves. Big Bill had not just twitched a little, as many corpses do, which probably wouldn't have sent Inez skittering out of the room; no, Big Bill had momentarily emerged from the realm of the dead and moved as purposefully, it had appeared to the code team, as a living man. He had suddenly reached his big hand, the fingernails purple in death, out from under the sheet which Winnie had just pulled over him, and slapped it stiffly down on top of the instrument tray that lay on the rolling table beside his stretcher, the instrument tray that held scalpels, hemostats, syringes, and, of course, Norman Keeston's ring. As if the condition of rigor mortis were occurring before their eyes, Big Bill's fingers curled and closed around the ring. Even in death, it seemed, Big Bill sensed the nearness of gold, and sought to acquire it.

Inez's performance took the focus temporarily off of Louis, and everyone in the room breathed again. The lab tech stopped shaking her vial, the patients remembered their injuries and cradled them, and Dotty the ward clerk was able to speak.

She shook her head and said to no one in particular, "Somebody please tell me what in hell is going on in my ER this afternoon?" Then she called over to Iris. "Supposed to be a full moon tonight? Must be an extra full moon coming tonight."

Gracie emerged from the group that surrounded Louis and took a tentative step or two toward Iris, hesitated, then continued forward.

"Excuse me," Gracie said, looking down at Iris.

Iris looked back up at her, somewhat vaguely, and then she slowly cleared. She glanced again at Louis, then returned to Gracie. "He's hurt?" Iris said. Then she realized that was a foolish question. "I mean of course he is, or you wouldn't have brought him here, right?"

"That's right," Gracie said. "He had an accident."

Iris peered around Gracie again. "His arm, huh?"

"Yes we think"—Gracie gestured at her neighbors—"that it's probably broken."

"That's a lot of people come with him. You're his mom?"

Gracie nodded.

"And all those people . . . relatives?"

"No," said Gracie. "Neighbors. Involved in his rescue. Who felt they should accompany him."

"Jeez, that's a lot of people."

Francine had broken off from the group and was already relating, in excited detail, the story of Louis to a friend she had spotted in the waiting area. Her arms flapped as she spoke.

Iris, with Gracie at her side, approached Louis. She was unable to look at him from so close a distance. She looked instead at his arm. "I'm Iris Shula," she said softly. She gently lifted Louis's shirtsleeve.

"I'm Louis Malone," Louis managed through his teeth. Even her whisper touch caused crackles of pain.

"Definitely broken. Definitely," Iris said. "Okay, you want to come back with me to room 4?"

"But these other patients, in the waiting room, aren't they before me?"

"We treat you according to the severity of your injury. Mostly that room's full of bug bites and little cuts. You got a good-size break, and you're trembling and your skin's kind of cool, all symptoms of early shock. You need to be seen." It was easier for Iris to talk to him when she adopted her no-nonsense nurse tone.

Carl and Bert, on either side of Louis, and Gracie, Bev, Donna, and Kitty, took a step or two forward. Francine saw them and hurried over. Iris put her hand out. "No, no. I'm afraid you people will have to wait here."

That was it? You mean we have to hand him over? Disappointment swept through the group. Francine said in a little voice, not wanting to rile Iris, "But, you know, we were the ones rescued him."

Iris hesitated, then said, "I'm sure you did, ma'am. But you see, he's here now. You've done your part, and now we have to do our part." She waited, as if for a group of children to relinquish the treasure they deeply desired but knew they could not keep.

Carl, whose lead the others had followed since Louis had landed in the tulip bed, took the first step away from Louis, slowly released his arm. Louis felt the sudden absence of Carl's touch, and missed it terribly. On his other side, Bert let go. For a brief instant Louis felt lighter than air, adrift, as he had been at the moment he left his window and gravity had not yet found him, so that he was unsure whether he would fall or rise. Gravity found him now in the form of Iris, solid and low to the ground. She reached up and took hold of him. When she touched him Louis knew at once that he was earthbound, that in her grasp he would not be allowed to drift.

"I got you," she said. "You hold on to me, and I'll hold on to you."

Everyone in the Emergency Room watched. They had

never seen anything like it, such a fit. A pair mismatched to all but each other. That's what Louis and Iris looked like, briefly, as they moved slowly down the hall together toward room 4—a pair, a couple enwrapped in one another's arms, on a stroll. What a couple. Iris, whose physical limitations were utterly apparent, low and slightly stooped Iris. And at her side, looming above her, Louis, his misfortunes unapparent, and therefore dreadful because of what was not revealed but only hinted at by the scarf that adhered to the misshapen contours of his hidden face.

Someone, it didn't matter who because it might have come from any one of the watchers, let out a high sharp laugh, like the bark of a seal. Several people put their hands to their mouths thinking the sound had come from them. Iris and Louis kept moving; they had not heard, or heard and knew, as only such a pair of people would know, that in that laughter there was no joy, or approval. That laughter was like a dog's smile that is not a smile at all, but a frightened show of teeth. Gracie turned and looked at the watchers in the waiting room, and they all wore dog smiles. Then she turned again and opened her mouth as if to call out a warning to Louis and Iris, but they had disappeared into room 4.

Someone touched Gracie's elbow and said, "They'll be all right. You take it from ol' Herb, they'll be just fine."

Gracie stared at the old security guard smiling up at her with his gappy dentures. There was nothing dangerous in his smile, and she felt comforted for a brief moment. She was about to thank him but he was suddenly off, tipping his hat to her before he stepped through a door beside the Coke machine and vanished.

Iris helped Louis up onto the stretcher in room 4. She stepped back and hesitated before she spoke. She glanced at him, and he glanced at her, then they both stared down at the linoleum floor.

"I'm going to have to take a look now," she said.

When he lifted his good arm and pressed his hand against the scarf that hid his face, she shook her head and said, "No, no, I didn't mean that. Not there. Your arm. I'm going to have to get a good look at your arm. I'll have to cut off part of your shirt. Okay? So I don't have to move your arm around. Okay?"

Louis slowly nodded. "Okay."

Iris worked carefully with a pair of bandage scissors, cutting the shirtsleeve well above the break in Louis's forearm. He watched her, sitting erect and still on the edge of the stretcher as she worked on him.

He said, "Were you here sixteen years ago?"

She finished with his sleeve and bent close to look at his arm. "Seems to be a clean break. Big bump, but clean. I'll have to get Dr. Gunther to look at it, and we'll have to get you to X-ray for some films." She wrapped a blood-pressure cuff around his good arm. "Sixteen years ago. No. I just been here a couple years. What was sixteen years ago?"

"Just wondering," Louis said.

"Oh," said Iris. "Well, no, I wasn't here then."

"But it was you I saw?"

"Sixteen years ago?" said Iris.

"No, at the end of last summer. In the parking lot. The cemetery."

"That was me, yeah. You remember that?"

"I remember everything. Most everything, anyway. I don't get out much, you see, so it's important I remember." Louis shifted on the stretcher and felt a warmth growing on the part of his face that was not numb. What was he saying?

Iris said, "Why don't you get out much?"

"Because," Louis said after a minute, "because I stay inside a lot." Then he added, "More than most people, I guess."

"Oh." She inflated the blood pressure cuff. "You keep to yourself, then, is what you're saying."

"Yes," said Louis. "That's it exactly. I keep to my-self." For sixteen years. But he didn't say it.

"Sometimes that's best," Iris said, writing his pressure on the ER sheet. Her hand was trembling slightly, and she had trouble fitting the numbers in the correct column.

Neither of them spoke. Iris pretended to write more numbers in columns. Louis crossed, then uncrossed his legs. Iris heard herself suddenly say, "I don't get out all that much either, really."

Louis watched his legs crossing and uncrossing. "So that when you do," he said, "when you finally do, it becomes . . . it becomes . . ." He stopped. Unbearable, he did not say. It becomes almost unbearable to be amidst what you have gazed upon season after season, to touch what you have only seen for sixteen years, to speak not sentences in a dream where the words have always been from me to me, but in ordinary tones, in sounds that rise from my chest and pass between what is left of my scarred lips and reach you, you there inches before my face, you there in pure white whom I must not mistake for a white vision, another vision in the endless visions that have filled my hours.

Iris looked at him and frowned. She was not having any of this. This . . . this what, she didn't understand, but whatever this feeling was, she wasn't having any of it, not about this patient, one of the endless patients who filled her hours. Iris, so firmly of the world, who slept dreamlessly, had no time to wonder about this patient, who would pass before her and be healed, or not be healed, but either way would be gone.

She said, all business now, "I have to ask you a few more questions. Do you have any food or medication allergies?"

"No," said Louis.

"Are you taking any medication at this time?"

"No," said Louis.

"Have you had a tetanus shot within the last five years?"

"No. No, I haven't."

"We'll have to give you one then." Iris made notes on her clipboard sheet. "Okay." She looked up at him again. "One more thing. How did you break your arm?"

Louis tried to meet her eyes. "I was at my window." He paused.

"Your window," Iris prompted. "At your window and . . . ?"

"And then I was out of it."

"Out of it?" She tilted her head.

"By accident. Onto the ground," Louis said quickly.

"First-floor window? Second-floor window?"

"Second floor."

"Did you hurt yourself anywhere else? Your back? Your head?"

"Oh no, just my arm. I landed in a flower bed. Where it was soft. And I wouldn't have even broken my arm if . . ." He didn't go on. If I hadn't twisted and turned trying to keep my hat and scarf in place.

"If?"

"Oh, I don't know. If I was luckier, I guess."

Iris started for the door, picturing in her mind Louis at the window, and then out of it, falling and falling. "I'd say you were pretty lucky. I'm going to talk with Dr. Gunther and set you up for an X-ray, and get you a couple of pain pills. If you need anything press the call light, that button there above the stretcher."

She pointed, then closed the door behind her and took a long breath. She kept seeing it, Louis at the window. She closed her eyes, opened them, and began to move down the hallway. She went three steps and stopped short, and made a sound, which Inez heard as she hurried out of room 1 blowing a large bubble.

"You say something, Iris?" Inez called down the hall to her.

Iris didn't answer, couldn't answer, so Inez shrugged and walked off.

Louis. The Tube Man had said *"Louis,"* not *"loose."* Paula, the night nurse, hadn't gotten the Tube Man's final word right. Now the Tube Man's words made sense, were brought to sense by the man in room 4. He fell from a window because he is the man in the window. She heard the Tube Man once more, as if she were again in his room, and he was speaking to her in his whispering ventilated voice, his machine-breath coma voice. The Tube Man, the valentine-shaped dot of blood on his floor, his Cupid words like arrows piercing her heart. *The man in the window is Louis*. Iris pressed against the wall. And he has left his window, he has crossed his interminable lonely desert for me. My wounded Lawrence, whose eyes have endlessly searched the horizon, has found me. These unimaginable words came to Iris as she moved unsteadily up the hall toward the ER nurses' station, touching the green wall for support.

Unnoticed by Iris who was in the nurses' station trying to compose herself, unnoticed by Winnie and Inez who were busy with Big Bill Rose and the rest of the ER, unnoticed by anyone, the door to room 5 opened just a crack and an eyeball peered through it. Then the door opened a little more and Harvey Mastuzek craned his scraggy neck and peered up and down the empty hallway. Coast clear, he thrust open the door and hopped out into the hallway, his skinny butt hanging out of the open back of his hospital gown. He lifted his nose to the air as if picking up a scent, then pointed his right index finger like a divining rod at the doors of each of the six ER examination rooms, settling at last on the one to the left of him, room 4. Soundlessly, he turned the handle to the door and hopped inside.

Louis, who'd been watching the door since Iris walked out of it, did not recognize the bedraggled man who skittered into his room and who now placed a pale trembling hand on his stretcher and peered up at him with intent eyes.

"Louis," the man said.

The man spoke his name so sadly and so quietly. Louis leaned forward instinctively, to hear more, when the man opened his mouth to speak again. But instead of speaking, the man suddenly lifted his hand and laid it on Louis's scarf-enshrouded cheek. Then he let his hand drop.

"Louis. Do you forgive me?"

Louis placed the voice then, and the eyes. The body had changed so, like his own, though the ravaging of it had been slower, an eating away.

"Mr. Mastuzek," Louis said, as if he were ten years old again and addressing Harvey Mastuzek as a Saturday customer in Malone's Hardware. How long had it been since he had waited on Mr. Mastuzek, that single time he had entered the store? It had been an entire life ago. "Mr. Mastuzek. Forgive you? Forgive you for what?"

"It was so beautiful, you see," said Harvey, looking away.

"What was, Mr. Mastuzek?"

Harvey glanced around the examination room as if he were in another place. His eyes had softened, become hopeful. "The store. Your father's store."

"Yes," said Louis.

"It was such a tidy place. It was a place of such clarity. Does that make sense, that things were clear there? You could see immediately, just by looking at all the supplies, that something could be done about everything."

"Yes."

Harvey's voice took on the slow rhythm of remembrance. "You thought," he said, walking up and down the examination room as if he were perusing the aisles of his remembered vision of Malone's Hardware, "you thought, entering the place, that anything could be fixed. Not just the actual thing you sought to fix, the leaky pipe or the torn

screen or the clogged drain, but all things, you know? It was
a place that let you know that . . . that things could be held
together, that if *this* happens, then you do *that*. Solutions,
answers! Right there on the shelf, and all you had to know
was what you needed, because if you needed it, Malone's had
it.'' Harvey whirled around and looked wide-eyed at Louis.
''And if Malone's had it, if a simple hardware store in the
middle of a nothing town like Waverly had it, then it was all
around you, outside the store and everywhere. Life, is what
I'm saying, Louis, life didn't have to be such a goddamn
hardship and a puzzle. Life was a fixable thing. If a thing
goes wrong for you, and you know where to look and how to
look, then you need not be hobbled by your calamities. You
just reach right out, get the thing you need, and fix your leak
and your torn screen, and yourself, most of all yourself,
because it can be done, don't you see?''

Louis nodded.

''Well it's true, Louis, or it was true when I walked into
Malone's Hardware that day. That's what I believed, looking
around me and watching you and listening to you, it's what I
believed when you found me this.'' Harvey reached out and
placed a small black washer on the stretcher beside Louis.

''You handed me that washer and Jesus Christ, it came
right to me, the idea of the washer almost dropped me to the
floor. You see, when I walked into Malone's Hardware and
said, 'I need me a washer,' I wasn't asking for a washer at
all; and when you found me the washer, and handed it to me,
and I paid my thirteen cents, that's not the transaction that
really transpired. The transaction, I knew suddenly, was this:
I was actually saying, 'Louis, boy, I got me a host of
calamities that I need not specify. Maybe I beat my wife and
maybe I don't, maybe I'm a drinker and maybe not, maybe I
have the cancer eating through my bowels and maybe I don't,
and maybe I need a washer for the torturous dripping of my

faucet and maybe not—what I need to know is, if a thing is broke, can it be fixed?'

"And you took me all over that store pointing out all the possibilities, the ways to mend a thing, the tape, the screws, the caulk, the hammers and nails, and in that small drawer at the back of the store, the washers. Harvey, I said to myself when you handed me that perfect washer, you see how easy it is? Solutions, answers, alternatives. I floated out of the store. And I said, Harvey, it's going to be okay. A sorrow had been eased, lifted, Louis, by what I believed I learned in my brief encounter with you in that store. I was, for the first time in years, a happy man, a man with hope. I was going to be fixed."

Harvey's face was very near Louis's now. "So I hurried home, and I went down to the basement and found me a screwdriver and a pipe wrench, then I bounded back upstairs to the bathroom on the second floor, all the while clutching my little washer like it was gold. I took off the faucet handle, and I removed the valve stem and scraped out the old washer, then slipped in my new one—the first nervous step along what I thought to be the road to my rehabilitation, the restoration of my luck in life. Then I put everything back together and turned on the faucet, and the water flowed as sweetly as a waterfall, and when I turned it off, no drips!

"Hallelujah, my fortunes had turned! I danced a jig right there in the bathroom, I hugged my dog who I had treated wretchedly only an hour before, I made plans to bust up every gin and vodka bottle that I had hidden in shoe boxes and closets in every room of my house. Louis, if I had been struck deaf and blind at that very moment, at the height of my elation, I would still be a happy man—and you would not be wearing the scarf and hat you do today."

Louis tried to stand. "Mr. Mastuzek..."

"Wait." Harvey held up his hand. "Because had I been deaf and blind, I would never have heard the sound that was to me catastrophe, seen the sight that dashed my faith and hope. The faucet, you see, began to drip again. It was not fixed, could not be fixed no matter how I tried. And I did try, again and again, hour after hour. No solutions, no remedies, no answers. 'That which breaks remains broken' —those are the words that should have been painted under MALONE'S HARDWARE. Or maybe, MALONE'S HARDWARE— WE SELL ILLUSIONS.''

Louis said, ''But you should have come back, Mr. Mastuzek. I sold you the wrong size washer by mistake, that's all.''

''It was the perfect washer.'' He fingered the washer that lay on the stretcher beside Louis's leg. ''You sold me the right washer, but even that wasn't enough.''

''Then you needed a new valve stem, or something else.''

''You expected me to come back?'' said Harvey, finger- ing the washer and not looking at Louis. ''You expected me to come back and go through it all over again? To buy the perfect valve stem, or whatever other perfect part you had there on the shelves of your store?''

''Sometimes it takes a while before—''

Harvey snatched the washer off the stretcher. ''A while! I didn't have a while. A while didn't have anything to do with it. I never had a prayer. That washer, the idea of the washer, would've worked for anyone else but me. I watched that faucet drip for a day and a night so that my soul would be filled to overflowing with the black truth, the certain knowl- edge that sometimes a thing that breaks is supposed to remain broken. Ruination is my natural state. I've come to accept it, but they can't accept that here''—Harvey gestured at the walls of the examination room—''this hospital is as bad as your father's store. They find me and bring me here and I bleed all over them and they patch me up for a while, but before too long, I feel the drip beginning inside me all over again, the burning drip, the unrelenting drip, the unstoppable drip of my life's blood, which will continue unabated until I'm dry and dead.

"But"—and now Harvey's voice dropped low—"just because ruination was to be my fate did not mean it had to be yours, and that's why I've come to you, Louis, to confess, and to ask for your forgiveness. You see, I blamed your father's store for the brief light that made darker the blackness that surrounded me. The bitter taste of hope. Louis: enraged and drunk, I lit the match and started the fire that burned you. It was me." Harvey could hardly speak now, and he grasped Louis's leg. "I didn't know you were there, though, boy. I had no idea. I tried to burn down the store, but instead I burned you." Harvey's agitation had opened the old diseased wound in his stomach again, and the first of the flow of blood had reached the corner of his mouth.

Louis said, "You're bleeding."

"I've been bleeding for sixteen years, boy."

"Mr. Mastuzek, please. It wasn't you."

"Forgive me." Harvey touched his tongue to the corner of his mouth where the blood welled up, and the spot was clean for a moment, then a new drop appeared almost immediately.

"It was an accident," said Louis. "A frayed cord touched some oily rags. I tried to put it out. A spark..." Louis closed his eyes, his voice a whisper. "A spark rose."

"No, I was drunk, drunk in the alley behind the store and I lit a match, Louis, forgive me, I lit a match..." Harvey dragged his arm across his red mouth.

"And the spark rose, like, like a firefly," said Louis. "Then it fell, into a jar of paint thinner, clearer than water, and when it flashed, I thought I'd been splashed with ice water, it was so cold on my face."

"And Louis, I pushed open the door to the back of the store, tossed the match into the darkness, and ran. I never saw you. I just ran and ran."

"After the cold, there was heat. And flames. Everywhere flames. Heat," said Louis, opening his eyes and looking at Harvey, "and flames." He looked through the flames at Harvey, at the blood running now, dripping from Harvey's stubbled chin and onto his hospital gown. He looked at Harvey and understood that Harvey's version of the fire at Malone's Hardware was true. And he understood, too, that his own version was true. Who knew how many true versions there were? How many people sat quietly in their houses, bleeding? How many linked their calamities and pains to his own?

Louis reached out with the end of his purple scarf and wiped the blood from Harvey's chin. "Mr. Mastuzek," he said softly.

Whether it was Louis's kind act or the natural ebb and flow of Harvey's seeping wound, the blood did not rise again where Louis had cleaned it away. Harvey stared at Louis for a long moment, then nodded once and turned for the door. He opened it a crack, peered out, then pulled it all the way. He waved once to Louis, and took off down the hallway like a man who wasn't coming back.

Less than a minute later Dr. Gunther walked into the room, followed by Iris. Iris held two pain pills out to Louis, which he took, brushing her fingers with his own. Both were trembling slightly and the exchange was not easy. Iris helped him hold the cup of water steady as he swallowed the pills. She stepped behind Dr. Gunther, who looked up from Louis's ER chart.

"Hello Louis," he said, looking at Louis's arm as he spoke, as if it were the injury that went by the name of Louis. "I'm Dr. Gunther. Looks like a good break, probably your radius with a little ulnar involvement. X-ray'll tell, then we put you in a cast and you'll be on your way." Dr. Gunther's eyes moved up to Louis's face. "I took a look at your old records. You were here before, sixteen years ago, was it? You were burned in an accident."

Iris's head peeked out around Dr. Gunther's back. "Let me ask you," Dr. Gunther said. "You underwent a lot of reconstruction. How did it work out?"

Louis looked at him.

"You know, reconstruction. They fixed you up."

Louis looked down at the linoleum. Beside Dr. Gunther's right foot lay Harvey Mastuzek's black washer. "Fixed," Louis repeated softly.

"Mind if I have a look?" Whether Louis minded or not, Dr. Gunther reached for Louis's scarf, as if it were the right of his profession to have unlimited access to wounds, new or old. At that moment Iris fell against Dr. Gunther from behind and emptied the remaining cup of pill water down the back of his pants.

He yelped, startled by the cold water and Iris clutching at his legs and backside.

"Oh Dr. Gunther, I'm so sorry," Iris exclaimed. "I—I lost my balance."

"I'm drenched! How could you lose your balance just standing there?" He slapped at the back of his pants.

"I think my blood sugar's low or something. I kind of just tipped over."

Dr. Gunther made a disgusted sound, and started out the door. "Excuse me, Louis. Iris will take you to X-ray now—if she's steady enough for the trip, that is—and I'll see you again in the cast room." He glared at Iris and went out the door.

When Iris turned to Louis, she saw his shoulders shaking. Then she heard, rising from behind his scarf, the sound of muffled laughter.

She tried not to smile. "I slipped."

"Yes," Louis said.

"It's none of his business what you got behind there," she said quickly, gesturing at his scarf. "That's not what you're here for."

"Yes."

"Doctors think they own you when you come in here."

"Yes," said Louis. "I remember when the doctors owned me. The nurses, though, were very good to me."

"There's nothing better than a good nurse when you need one." Iris flushed red when she thought about what she'd said. "I'll get a wheelchair, and we'll get you down to X-ray."

In an hour they had finished with him. Dr. Gunther didn't mention Louis's accident again. He hardly spoke at all as he wrapped Louis's arm and positioned it as the cast hardened; indeed, he paid more attention to Iris's activities in the cast room than to Louis's arm, keeping an eye on her in case she decided to fall on him again.

Iris wheeled Louis back down the hall to the waiting area where Gracie sat with Donna Hodges. The others had returned home after much coaxing by Gracie. Getting Francine back in the car had not been easy; Bert and Carl had ended up stuffing her, still squawking, in the backseat.

Iris paused just before turning the corner to the waiting area. She looked down at Louis's Pirates hat and at the scarf coiled around his neck. It was coming loose, slipping down from Louis's face. He tried to fix it, but with one arm in a cast he was having a difficult time. Iris reached down from behind and readjusted it for him. Her fingers touched the coarsened skin of his cheeks. She did not flinch.

"Thank you," said Louis. "I guess it will be a little awkward for a while."

"Wearing a cast is not as easy as people think."

Louis said, "I remember when I was small, I longed to have one. I was jealous of other boys who got them—I used to crave their injuries. Crave their injuries . . . can you imagine?"

Iris stood behind Louis's wheelchair, gazing down at the back of his head. A loose curl of brown hair poked through his purple scarf. "Mr. Malone," she said.

Louis turned his head partway around. "No, not Mr. Malone. My father was Mr. Malone. Louis."

"Yes. Well, Louis," said Iris, adjusting his scarf again, and just brushing with the tip of her finger that single brown curl, "you said . . . you said you don't get out much."

Louis shifted in the wheelchair.

"And I was thinking," said Iris, "you know, as your nurse and everything, being your nurse and all, maybe it would be a good idea if I looked in on you. If you want, that is. If it would be a help." Iris started pushing the wheelchair forward again, toward the glass doors to the waiting room.

Louis could see Gracie give a little wave as she rose from her chair. In the reflection of the doors he also saw Iris standing behind him and slightly to one side, so short she stood level with him even though he was sitting in the wheelchair. For a moment, in the reflection, they were together, cheek to cheek, and it was a strange and lovely sight for the man in the window who for sixteen years had seen only himself mirrored in the glass, standing alone.

"How soon," Louis said softly. "How soon before you could come?"

Flames

I

Now wait a minute, just where in hell was he? Arnie tugged the leash to stop Duke, the leash he held firmly in his good hand because he'd never, ever make the mistake of wrapping it around his hook again. Arnie tugged, and after passing two or three more houses, Duke, propelled forward by weight, motion, and intensity of purpose, finally came to a reluctant halt. Duke lifted his nose to the warm May night air and sniffed the redolence of an overturned garbage can in a nearby backyard, then let out a disappointed sigh.

Arnie immediately started up again, giving the leash a jerk, and Duke was not amused, this being the third time in two minutes Arnie had stopped and started. Duke stiffened and twisted his head, sending a jerk of his own back up the leash to Arnie. Arnie didn't really notice. He was squinting into the dark at a brightly lit bay window, hoping to see someone he recognized, because he sure didn't recognize any of the houses around him. They looked like the houses on his street, but then again they didn't. A figure suddenly appeared at the bay window, fiddled with a curtain, and disappeared again. Arnie's heart thumped against his chest, like a fist banging. Krupmeyer? Jesus, that was the Krupster himself, he wasn't dead at all, he'd just moved to another part of town. No—Arnie's heart thumped again—he'd just seen Krupmeyer's ghost. Krupso come back to haunt him. Arnie looked up and down the street, then, dragging Duke with him, moved in a crouch up the side yard. Here he comes again. Arnie sucked in his breath. Krupster, I didn't mean to kill you, how in Christ's name was I supposed to know you had a bad ticker? But it wasn't Krupmeyer. It was an overweight woman in curlers and a pink housecoat. Arnie dropped to his knees when she came to the window again to peer into the darkness. Probably watching for her husband to come driving home from bowling. That's just what I need, thought Arnie, to be caught peeping by the husband. Big as she was, the guy was sure to be a whopper. When she moved from the window back to her TV set, Arnie skittered low across the lawn like a crab, Duke in tow. When he was safely on the sidewalk and several houses down the block, Arnie leaned against a tree to catch his breath. Duke looked up at him with a mixture of concern and exasperation. Okay, Arnie, the look said, you've got some explaining to do.

"Man oh man," said Arnie, shaking his head. "Man oh man oh man. I'm going crazy, Duke. I'm going crazy and senile. Krupmeyer—I saw him. I was sure of it. Didn't that look like Krupmeyer to you?"

Duke sat very still even when the leash slipped from Arnie's hand, as Arnie rubbed his eyes. It was not the time to leave his master's side, no matter how sweetly scented with garbage the night air happened to be.

"Well it sure looked like the Krupster to me. I swear I even saw him holding his snow shovel in his hand." Arnie scanned the street, dark except for bright pools from the streetlights that stood every five or six houses. Most of the people in these unknown houses had gone to bed, which was where Arnie longed to be. Why hadn't he just let Duke out in the backyard for his bedtime pee? No, he had to walk him; the strangely warm May air beckoned him, lured him out of his house, and up and down streets until the familiar slid into the unfamiliar. What scared Arnie was that he wasn't sure whether he was genuinely lost in a part of Waverly he'd never been in, or if he was on a street he'd traveled with Duke every day for the last six years and he just didn't recognize it because his brain had gone soft. He swallowed and rubbed his scalp—he'd thought of a worse possibility. What if he was in a neighborhood he'd never been in before *and* his brain had gone soft? Seeing the ghost of Krupmeyer indicated the condition of his brain. And as for where exactly he and Duke were . . . he hoped at least he was still in Waverly, but thinking about it, he had no idea how long he'd been wandering around.

He knelt down to Duke and pulled the dog close to him. "I've lost it, Duke. If I ever get back to Iris she'll put me in a nursing home for sure. And she'd be right to do it, too." He held the dog and glanced around at the alien landscape that surrounded him. The houses loomed, the shadows from the maple trees above him were dark and deep. The air was no longer warm, and he trembled. "Where am I?" he whispered into Duke's fur. Then he said, "LuLu?"

LuLu had been the one to show him the way home, walking or driving, always at his side.

"Jesus," he'd say, "where are we?"

And LuLu would say, "I told you, Arnie, take a left on Columbia and a right on Morton."

"I took a right."

"You took a left," she'd say, patting his knee.

"On Columbia."

"On Morton, dear, when you should have turned right."

"Now what'll we do?"

When LuLu was beside him, he was never lost. He knew she would put him on the road home once again.

But now, alone on these streets, he was lost, had been since the day she died. "I want to go home," he whispered into the dark. Which home? He'd moved too many times. LuLu was home, and she was nowhere he could get to on this night. Duke! Arnie pushed back and looked the dog in the eye. Of course. Duke probably knew the way home. Like Lassie. That's the one thing a dog knew how to do—find his way back.

Arnie straightened himself and brushed a piece of dog hair off his tongue. "Hey Lassie. Take us home. Come on now, you know the way."

Duke blinked at him. Lassie?

"You ain't lost like me, are you boy?" Arnie patted the dog encouragingly. "You been marking the trail, right? Hell, you pissed every thirty yards since we left the house."

Duke slowly lifted his ass off the sidewalk, then pushed his nose around in the air like a bloodhound; at least that's the kind of dog Arnie hoped Duke had become, a Lassie/bloodhound hybrid. In fact, Duke had absolutely no comprehension of his master's hopes and fears. He was not sniffing out the trail for home, which he could have done with ease since the bushes he'd soaked were the scent equivalent of blazing flares; rather, he concentrated on the other suburban night smells that tempted a dog, the lurking cats, the opossums and raccoons that rousted themselves from beneath back porches, the half-closed trash bags that released their perfumes. Why in God's name would Duke head for home with this circus of fragrances swirling before his nose? Duke set out in a determined trot and Arnie hurried along behind him, at first with confidence, then, after several blocks, with growing suspicion, and finally despair when Duke suddenly reared up on his hind legs like a pony and bolted forward into a darkened yard, leaving his open collar dangling on the end of the leash which Arnie clutched in his throbbing hand.

"Shhhiiit, Duke," Arnie cried out, then caught himself and hid in some rhododendrons. He didn't need somebody calling the cops on him. "Duke," he whispered hoarsely, "get back here." But Duke was gone, his happy barks sounding faintly from some distant street.

Arnie felt the tears rise. He had not cried since LuLu left him. He was lost and abandoned, doomed to wander the streets in the changing seasons, known to no one. He might make it until winter, living out of trash cans, and then one night he'd freeze to death, the ice forming first on the tip of his hook. Dead in winter like poor old Krupso. Arnie began to wander, keeping mostly to the sidewalk, but sometimes veering across front yards, sometimes into the street. He looked into the windows of the houses as he passed, but he saw few lights on now. And what would I do, knock on the door and say, Hi, I'm Arnie, I can't remember where I live, can't remember my phone number or my last name, won't you please take me in? I won't be any trouble. I hardly eat a thing—hell, at my age I hardly breathe.

Since his mind was in such disarray, Arnie assumed his eyes were going on him too. He paused before a blue frame and brick house and stared at a light blinking on and off in the large window on the left side of the front door. Cataracts, he thought. Or is it glaucoma where you see flashing lights? He turned and looked at the streetlights: they were shining steadily. When he turned back to the house the blinking light had switched to the right side of the door. Not a good sign. And the light didn't seem to be coming from a particular source, like a table lamp or something, but from the window glass itself. Arnie closed his eyes for a long moment. My name is Arnie, he thought to himself. I'm Arnie, Arnie, Arnie, he chanted, using his name as a life preserver upon which he hoped to cling. Don't lose that, hold on. When he opened his eyes again, he knew he was lost. The light, steady now, had moved from the windows to the front door, now open. A man was standing in the doorway, backlit, so that Arnie couldn't see his face. What he did see were the tips of a great pair of wings, protruding from either side and behind the man starting at about hip level. Arnie stood motionless in the street. He would have stood there all night and into the next day if the angel (because that's what he had to be) had not lifted his arm and beckoned. Arnie was certain of one thing: when an angel beckons, you go to the angel. As Arnie moved up the front walk, the angel stepped back into the house, out of view. Arnie followed him into the lighted doorway which dimmed to darkness as Arnie passed through. He was so intent on the angel he didn't notice that Duke had returned and was at his side as he entered the house.

Arnie walked slowly up the long front hallway, which was faintly illuminated in bluish-white light from the street-light which stood directly in front of the house. He didn't move a muscle. Deep in the center of his chest his heart danced crazily. When Duke shifted beside him, his knees buckled slightly, and then he recognized his companion.

"Duke," he whispered. "I've really fucked up."

Duke nodded affirmatively.

Arnie understood, with a sudden rocketing clarity, his absurd and dangerous predicament. The fog that had set him drifting along the streets of Waverly and into this house had lifted. You old fool. You crazy one-armed no-brain bastard. Ghosts! Angels! Get yourself out of this house before you get your tail shot off. He grabbed Duke by his neck fur and headed for the door. The floorboards creaked and Duke squirmed. Arnie bumped into a telephone table and set a flower vase wobbling. He watched the vase totter. If it goes over the edge, I'm dead. I can't grab it fast enough with my hook, and if I let go of Duke, who is itching to run amok, I'm just as dead. Or I can run for it, let the vase hit the floor, let Duke loose, and run. All of these thoughts flashed through Arnie's mind. But the vase did not fall, and he didn't have to release Duke, and it really looked as if he was going to make it out of the house without getting caught. All he had to do was walk a few more steps. Only a few steps, seconds away, hell, spitting distance—so that when the angel reappeared in the corner of his vision, Arnie almost smiled. Well, he thought, here we go. I'm in it now.

The angel stood in a dark room just off the entrance hall. The blue-white light from the streetlight dimly outlined his form. Arnie still couldn't make out his face. When Duke stiffened and growled at the figure in the dark room, Arnie was almost relieved: the angel was real.

The angel spoke in a muffled voice. "We don't have much. There's a little money in the drawer of the table by the door."

Arnie thought, We? He squinted into the dark for more angels. And then he thought, What do angels need money for?

When Arnie didn't move, the angel took a step or two forward, and it looked to Arnie like the angel was wielding something in his hand. A baseball bat? In the dimness Arnie could see now that the angel's face was covered, and that he wore a hat. It suddenly occurred to Arnie that he might not be looking at the angel at all, but at somebody else who had broken into the house. Yeah, where'd his wings go?

It just came out of him. "You're not the angel," Arnie said.

That stopped the approaching figure. "The angel," he whispered.

"This is an attack dog," Arnie said. "Put down your bat." Duke, ever helpful, had stopped growling and now wagged his tail. Arnie poked him with his foot.

A woman's voice called down from the top of the stairs. "Who is it, Louis? Who's down there?" A light came on. Arnie froze.

Louis called from the dining room where he stood watching Arnie. "It's a burglar, Gracie. And his dog."

There was a pause, then Gracie said, "I'll call the police. Louis, don't do anything—he might have a gun."

Arnie immediately held out his hand to show it was empty.

But Louis was eyeing Arnie's hook. "I think he's got a knife."

A frightened "Oh" from upstairs.

"No, no," Arnie said quickly. "I only got one hand. See, it's my hook. You know, artificial hand." Arnie stepped forward. "Look, hey. Don't call the police," he said to Louis, who still stood in the shadows. Then he said in a louder voice, aiming it up the stairwell, "Hey lady. Please don't call the police."

There was a long silence. Arnie looked back and forth, into the darkened room, then at the stairs, waiting for his fate to be decided by these hidden people. It never occurred to him to decide his own fate and run out the front door. He needed to know, as much as these people did, just what he was doing there.

"Hey bud, really," Arnie said. "You can put down your bat. I'm not going to do anything."

Louis looked at his arm, then at Arnie. "Not a bat. My arm's in a cast." He raised it slightly.

"Louis?" Gracie called.

"It's all right, Gracie," Louis called back.

"Is he gone?"

"Come see," said Louis.

"He's still there, isn't he?"

"Yes. But it's okay, Gracie."

Arnie had forgotten about Duke, who had made his ambling way into the room where Louis stood. Duke the attack dog sniffed Louis's foot, then licked his hand when Louis knelt and held it out to him. "I've seen you before,

haven't I, doggie?'' Louis said. Then he lifted his eyes to
Arnie. ''And I've seen you before too.''

Arnie shrugged and looked blank. Another light went on
above his head, turned on, he presumed, by the woman,
Gracie, starting down the stairs. The light revealed more of
the man, Louis, and Arnie saw now that he wore a Pirates
cap and a purple scarf pulled above his nose.

Gracie came around the stair landing and into partial
view, then stopped. ''Louis, I'm just in my robe. I'm barely
presentable.''

Louis said, ''I'm in my pajamas.''

''The new ones, or that old ratty pair I just mended?''

''The old ones.''

''Oh Louis.'' Then, ''Is he still there?''

''Come on down, Gracie.''

Gracie descended, her slippered feet soundless on the
stairs. When she reached the last step she stopped again,
looked quickly at Arnie, then above his head to Louis in the
next room. Duke barked a welcome. Gracie spoke to Arnie,
still not quite looking at him, as if she hoped that by not
giving him her full acknowledgment he might disappear.
''You go burglaring with a dog?''

''My partner,'' was Arnie's ready response. He'd turned
the thing over in his mind and decided that he would rather
these people believe he was a burglar than a senile old fool
who'd wandered into the wrong house. At least there was a
veneer of dignity to burglary.

''Your partner,'' Gracie repeated carefully. ''I see.''

Arnie went on, trying to inject some plausibility into it.
''Well, it's hard for me sometimes,'' he raised his hook and
Gracie's eyes widened, ''so he kind of helps me carry things.
You know, like silver candlesticks and such.''

''Oh yes,'' said Gracie. ''I guess that would be helpful.'' She added, ''We don't have any silver candlesticks.''

''Well, um, I wasn't really here to steal anything this

time. I was more like casing the joint. It's important to prepare." He took a breath. "Preparation is the key to success."

"Except in this case," Louis said.

"Yeah, well, right. Except in this case. I didn't do so good here."

Gracie pressed her fingers to her chin and studied Arnie more closely. "I think I've seen you before."

"I've seen him, too," said Louis.

"Probably in the post office. You know, mug shots." Arnie grimaced. He knew things weren't going too well.

Gracie didn't hear him. She looked back and forth, between his face and the dog's. It was coming to her, and it was coming to Arnie too. Last summer—the woman in the funeral procession whose car broke down. He remembered now, her smile. And he remembered the concealed figure who'd sat silently beside her.

"Wednesday," she said suddenly.

"What?" said Atlas.

Louis nodded in agreement. Unlike Gracie, Louis knew he'd seen Arnie, and Arnie's dog, twice. The first time almost a year ago on the way home from Atlas's funeral, and the second time just as Gracie said, on Wednesday.

"The man chasing the dog," Gracie said, pointing. "That dog."

Duke barked, cheerfully admitting his culpability.

Arnie hung his head. So he'd been seen. He'd been hoping that shameful episode had taken place unnoticed. But of course how could it have, Duke charging through those people like that, and him not far behind, waving his stump and howling like a madman. And now here he was going out of his way to shame himself before this woman again.

Louis stroked Duke, and the dog shuddered blissfully at his touch. I've been out in the daylight world twice in sixteen years, Louis thought, and I've seen this man both times. He looked at Arnie's hook. Do the wounded of Waverly naturally

seek one another out? Louis wondered who else would join
them should he brave the daylight again. But the man now
turned away from Louis, whom he'd been facing, and lifted
his eyes to Gracie. Louis, who knew how to look carefully at
a thing, saw something at the edge of those eyes, something
directed at Gracie and not at him at all. Louis realized then
that each time the man had appeared Gracie had been there,
just as she was here now. Was the connection, then, between
the man and Gracie? Louis heard the man's words again,
You're not the angel, and drew the dog close to him as he
stepped back into the shadows.

Arnie answered Gracie's charges. "Yes, ma'am, I'm
afraid that was me on Wednesday. Duke, my dog, gets a little
out of control sometimes. Goes squirrel crazy."

"Well," said Gracie in a soft voice, "it was a crazy day
for a number of us. Believe me, though, when I say I was
grateful for your sudden and opportune appearance."

From the shadows of the dining room Louis said, "His
second opportune appearance, Gracie. Remember when Jim
Rose's limousine broke down? This was the gentleman who
fixed the car, who rescued us from the heat and Jim Rose's
mechanical ineptitude."

Gracie stared at Arnie, a smile starting at the corners of
her mouth. "Why, it *was* you, wasn't it? Then, and Wednesday."

"I guess it was, ma'am. But really it was no—"

"You're a mighty peculiar burglar."

"Well in a way, ma'am, you see . . ."

"Is it your practice to rob the people you have helped a
few days before?"

"I didn't know I *had* helped. I thought—"

"Preying on widows and children?"

Children. Louis liked that one. He made a laughing
sound behind his scarf. The poor man winced as if Gracie
were having a go at him with a rolling pin. If she got too
worked up she might turn into a bull again, like she had on

Wednesday. Louis looked at her slippered feet to see if she'd begun to paw the floorboards. No, she was steady, and in her eyes there was a certain mischief. Gracie was enjoying her intruder a good deal more than he was enjoying her.

She said to Louis, "Do you think he's connected to that rash of break-ins that occurred two or three years ago, you remember, over on Michigan Avenue?"

Arnie squirmed.

"It was hardly a rash, Gracie. It was just Ruth Benson, who reported one break-in, which wasn't a break-in at all, the *Waverly Weekly* said, but her husband up on a ladder working on a second-floor storm window."

"Still," said Gracie, securing her bed jacket which had winked open, turning away from Arnie as she did so, "still it appeared to Ruth as if she had a burglar, which counts as something."

"Well it counted as something to Mr. Benson, I'm sure, when the police came and hauled him off that ladder."

Arnie cocked his head trying to catch all their words. Much of it bounced off his bad ear before his good ear had a chance to make sense of it. He was sure he'd heard the word *police* again, though.

"Look," he cut in. "I really should be going now." He began to back toward the door. "Come on, Duke, we've inconvenienced these folks enough."

"Wait." Gracie put her hand out. "You can't just go."

"Please," said Arnie. "There's no need to call the police."

"You're not really a burglar."

Arnie shook his head and sighed. "Lady, listen. I got this hook here, I got a bum ear, my left knee is stiffer than a dry cornstalk, I'm saddled with a dog who goes off half-cocked with a minimum of provocation, and to tell you the truth, I'm not the brightest guy in the world. I'm not saying I'm a dimwit, but I ain't always on the ball, and to be a burglar, it seems to me, you got to be on the ball. So, no, I'm not really a burglar. And if you're wondering how I ended up inside your house, the fact is I'm something scarier than a burglar. At least it's scarier to me: I'm old. Old is what made me walk in here. Old and senile. So if you want to be calling somebody, don't call the police. Call the nursing home squad, because I've about had it with myself. I'm ready. Take me away." Arnie's arms dropped to his side and he lowered his head.

Gracie walked over to him and took hold of his arm. "Now don't talk that way, Mr. . . . ?"

"Arnie," said Arnie in a barely audible voice. He looked where she held his arm. It was his right one, the one with the hook, and he'd never known anyone to voluntarily take hold of it before.

"Well, Arnie, I'm not going to let you talk that way. When you call yourself old, you're including me too. And I'm not ready for a nursing home. You're not dead, are you? They only put dead folks in the nursing home. Those places are nothing more than cemeteries where they got beds instead of graves. You ready to lie down yet?"

"I feel like it tonight," said Arnie slowly.

"If you're ready to lie down, then I don't know who it was I saw running by me on Wednesday afternoon. Arnie, if you'd've had wings you'd have flown. It was one of the most impressive displays of fitness I've ever seen, young or old."

"I don't know," Arnie said. "I can't keep things straight like I used to. That's how come I'm here. I was just wandering around, and I wandered right into a strange house. Hell, excuse me, but hell, if I walked into somebody else's house I might've got my tail shot off."

"Louis," she said, still gripping Arnie's arm, "tell him. Tell him what I did this morning."

"She sprinkled instant coffee on her scrambled eggs," said Louis.

"Thought that jar of coffee was a pepper mill. Have you ever mistaken a jar of coffee for a pepper mill?" she said to Arnie. "I bet not. So don't be surprised if tomorrow night I wander into *your* house by mistake."

Arnie tried to smile at Gracie. "Really, thank you. You're being very kind, especially since I'm practically a burglar and all."

Gracie cut in, her voice stern. "I'm not being kind, I'm watching out for myself. I'm as old as you are, so what goes for you goes for me. And I'm not sure forgetfulness is our problem. It's remembering. We have too much to remember. It gets in our way, distracts us, makes us believe we're there when we're really here. For the last year I've come down to breakfast every morning and fully expected my husband to be at the kitchen table eating his cereal and reading the paper. I give a little jump because he's not there. Next thing I know I have a plate of scrambled eggs before me and I'm sprinkling instant coffee on them. Whole minutes pass as I wander back and forth in time."

"That's just what I was doing," said Arnie. "Thinking about LuLu. She's gone, too. But I'm still talking to her, you know what I mean?"

Gracie gazed vaguely at him, traveling again in time. Then her eyes cleared to the present. "I know," she said. "I know what you mean."

A minute passed, then Louis spoke up from the dining room. "How about we go into the kitchen for cocoa? Anybody in the mood for cocoa?"

Duke barked, in the mood for anything. Gracie started for the kitchen, arm in arm with Arnie. "Sure," she said. "But I'm not making it. Lord knows what I might end up putting into it. Right, Arnie?" She gave him a little look.

Arnie just smiled and walked beside her, overcome by the novelty of human contact, and feeling safely grounded in the present.

II

Less than twelve hours later, Iris, like Arnie before her, found herself standing before the blue and white frame house that belonged to Gracie and Louis Malone. Iris didn't know that Arnie had preceded her with a chance visit of his own. She did know he'd come in mighty late last night from walking Duke, and that when he got up this morning he was in an alarmingly chipper mood, but wouldn't tell her why.

"Listen to you," she had said, when Arnie came whistling into the kitchen. "I didn't even know you knew how to whistle."

"Morning, Iris, my love." He leaned over and kissed her on the top of her head.

My God, Iris thought.

Arnie stood in the middle of the kitchen, eyes closed, and whistled a few more emphatic bars. "Jeepers," he said when he finished, "I haven't thought of that song for years."

"That was a song?" said Iris. "I thought a deranged canary had gotten loose in our house."

" 'Don't Sit under the Horse Chestnut Tree with Anyone Else but Me,' " sang Arnie. "Now that's when songs were songs."

"I believe it's 'Apple Tree,' not 'Horse Chestnut.' "

"Yeah? That right?" said Arnie, grinning at her. "Well, one of them damn trees, anyway. It's still a hell of a song."

"If you say so," said Iris, returning to her oatmeal.

Arnie peered over her shoulder. "What you got there? Oatmeal?"

Iris looked down at her bowl of oatmeal, which was about the most unmistakable and clear-cut bowl of oatmeal on the planet Earth, then up at her father. "Arnie, what is the only thing I have eaten for breakfast for the three years I've lived here with you?"

"I don't know, girl. I haven't paid much attention. It's either oatmeal or the stuff I feed Duke. Well, no oatmeal for me this morning." He began to open and close cabinet doors. "I'm in the mood for something different. You know how that strikes you sudden-like, the mood for something different?" He turned and looked at her, at her oatmeal, then back up at her. "Hmm. Maybe you aren't familiar with that mood."

"Don't make a mess in here," Iris warned him.

"Bac*O-cheese waffles!"

Iris grimaced. "What the hell's gotten into you this morning, Arnie?" She regarded him suspiciously, with her nurse's eye. When patients' behavior patterns suddenly changed it always meant trouble. Arnie was reminding her of the ones she'd seen lying there for weeks who one day snap awake with this crazy look on their faces, sit bolt upright in the bed, yell something incomprehensible, then fall back onto the mattress dead. Arnie had been moping around for months, since Krupmeyer; well, for years really, since LuLu died. But he'd been particularly mopey since Krupmeyer, and now this: whistling and Bac*O-cheese waffles. Contradictory behavior. Not good. She wouldn't be surprised to see him suddenly keel over on the linoleum floor.

"Arnie," she said, rising. "Why don't you sit down? You're making me nervous. I'll cook something for you."

"Not something. Waffles!"

"Okay, okay. Waffles."

"Bac*O-cheese."

"Right, right."

She assembled things while Arnie gave Duke a long scratching with his hook. He hummed "How Much Is That Doggie in the Window?" over and over as he worked.

"You came in pretty late last night," Iris called over to him.

He cocked his good ear in her direction. "How's that?"

"Late last night. When you came in."

Arnie smiled instantly. "Sure did," he said. "How about that? What do you know, eh, Duke?"

"I was getting kind of worried."

"I'm over sixteen, ain't I?"

"Way over. Which is why I was worried."

"There been some kind of problem with old men disappearing on the streets of Waverly?"

"No, but..."

"Thought I'd run off?"

"No."

"Or died?"

"Well..."

"Bingo!" said Arnie.

"Hey Arnie. I'm a nurse. All I see is people dying."

"It's tainted you, girl. I'm alive and well and expect to outlive you by forty years."

Iris looked him over as she held the waffle batter and stirred. "Didn't you tell me just yesterday how your body was going on you? How you were falling apart starting with your teeth and ending at your toes?"

"I come to life."

"Tell me about it."

Arnie rose from his chair and headed for the back door, ignoring her. "Come on, Duke. What are we doing in here wasting this May morning? Let's go."

"Hey Arnie. Hey," Iris called after him as he cut through the neighbor's hedge. "What about your waffles?"

"You eat 'em," he called back. "You're the one who needs a change."

That was it, that was what brought her across Waverly and plunked her down in front of Louis Malone's house—the need for a change. She'd fretted for four days about going to visit him. Visit him? she'd say to herself. Since when do I visit people? And not just people—a man. What moved me to suggest such a thing? Well I'm not going to do it, she decided for several nights running, tossing and turning, twisting herself in her nightgown and among the sheets, I'm not going to make a fool of myself, or of him. He doesn't want to be seen by anyone; he's stayed in that house for, what did he say, sixteen years? But he did say yes, didn't he? He said, When could you come? Maybe he felt sorry for me. Who does he think he is? she'd wonder, and frown into the dark. In the mornings, though, she knew. He doesn't feel sorry for me, and he knows I don't feel sorry for him. She would put her coat on and start for the door, ready to go to him, but something stopped her each time. She couldn't do it. She didn't know how. What's the matter with you, Iris? she'd think, her hand sweaty on the doorknob. He's a patient, you're the nurse, go attend to him. Iris, the visiting nurse. But she couldn't trick herself. Yeah, sure. Like I've ever visited a patient's house before. Well, it's what you got, Iris, and you better fly with it, or you'll stay the way you are forever.

She chickened out every time, though. Until this morning, standing in the kitchen with a bowl of waffle batter in her hands. She saw then how utterly pathetic she was. "You're the one who needs a change," Arnie said. That he understood eating a waffle would represent significant change in her life, that it was so simple and obvious to him, sent a rush of panic surging through her. She set the mixing bowl on the counter before she dropped it, and stared with moist eyes at the lumpy batter. I can do better than waffles, she thought, gulping back the sadness. She looked up and saw herself reflected in the window above the sink, saw the close-set eyes and the thin hair, the colorless cheeks, the chin that sank into the fat of her neck. You have nothing to offer, less than nothing, but he has seen you and he's asked you to come. So, go to him. Go now. Go.

She went. Right straight out of the kitchen, and when

she touched the doorknob on the front door she turned it, fast and hard, without considering the times she'd failed at this exact point. She got the door open and practically ran across the yard to the sidewalk, her hand outstretched before her like she was turning doorknobs to innumerable unseen doors, opening them and letting them close behind her as she rushed onward.

People moved out of the way as she approached, her stubby legs pumping up and down, her low body as intent as a bulldozer. Dogs barked and nipped at her heels, one or two kids called out names as she passed, ready to run if she gave chase, but she didn't hear a thing. On the corner of Park and Yale she stepped into the street without looking, and Jim Rose, driving the hearse that bore the body of Big Bill Rose, had to slam on his brakes, which set more brakes in motion, most not in time to avoid a fender bender, along the long line of cars in Big Bill's funeral procession. Iris didn't stop even then, although she did look over her shoulder briefly at the sudden commotion of darkly clothed mourners erupting from their cars, pouring out onto the street like agitated black ants.

She didn't slow down until she turned onto Amherst, the street where Louis lived. She knew where he lived because she'd looked on his chart in the Emergency Room. Thirty-seven Amherst Avenue. She paused at number Forty-five to catch her breath. She saw then what she hadn't seen before, as she dashed from her kitchen and along the streets of Waverly: she was still wearing the apron she'd put on to make Arnie's waffles, and her chubby arms were dusted with flour. Look at you, Iris, going out of your way to make yourself appear ridiculous, more ridiculous than you already are. She slapped at the flour on her arms, and quickly pulled off the apron. What'll I do with it? She checked up and down the street, then pushed the wadded apron between the branches of a lumpy hedge. Had Iris stepped back a few feet, she might have noticed that the lumpy hedge was actually a large green bear, one of Bev and Bert's cherished topiaries. Iris had pushed her apron into the bear's stomach, where it was to sit undigested until the early summer when it would be discovered by Bert, in a rage, during one of his periodic hedge inspections.

Iris's activities did not go unnoticed. Across the street from Bev and Bert's, standing behind a white column on her front porch, Francine Koessler stroked Minky's fur and watched. She didn't recognize Iris, because Iris wasn't wearing her nurse's uniform. This was not surprising, because as Iris had learned, out of uniform she was invisible, or at least transformed. She'd long ago decided this was a defense mechanism, that people needed to pretend that outside the hospital, nurses, and the often embarrassing medical details they knew, did not exist. So what Francine saw was an unknown short and toady-looking woman littering in one of Bert's silly animal hedges. Which suited Francine just fine. Ordinarily, she'd have gleefully leapt off her porch and rebuked, admonished, and upbraided the wrongdoer, because Francine was lonely and bored, and such a confrontation would have been a release for her, a chance for conversation, however one-sided. But this time she stayed put, happy to have the litterbug (and Iris really did look like a bug to Francine) spoil Bert's beautiful yard. Francine was still angry at Bert, in a snit because of the way he and Carl had hauled her out of the Emergency Room and away from the most exciting thing she'd been a part of in years: the materialization of Louis Malone, the recluse of Waverly.

Iris smoothed her dress and brushed at another dusting of flour she found on her sleeve. Jesus, I probably got it all in my hair, too, and boogers in my nose, and food stuck between my teeth. She fidgeted and arranged herself there on the sidewalk. Hidden, Francine watched, wondering if Iris had worms or something. Iris advanced a few steps, then stopped. Maybe she's retarded, thought Francine; she's sure something. It took Iris almost as much time to travel the final one hundred yards to Louis's house as it had to make the entire journey across Waverly to Amherst Avenue. At last, pacing her final steps to the rhythm of her powerfully beating heart, she found herself standing before the Malone house. She closed her eyes, and almost hoped that when she opened them again she'd be at home in her kitchen clutching her mixing bowl. She had been safe there, with her oatmeal and the routine of her days. Not once in her life, never had she offered herself, in full friendship or love, to another human being. It had never occurred to her to do so. She opened her eyes now and saw where she was, and what she was doing. She stood very still for a moment, then took a deep breath and started up the front walk, gave herself this one chance, prepared to make her offer.

When she reached a tulip bed, just to the right of the walk and in front of the house, she stopped. The tulips were in disarray, some supported by garden stakes, others beginning to go brown where they lay in the soft dirt. Iris looked up to the second floor and he was there; the man in the window gazed down at her, then lifted his hand and wiggled his fingers in shy greeting.

Kitty Wilson, on her daily walk, saw Louis from across the street, saw him clearly and in plain view, waving to a woman she didn't recognize. Hot tears of envy sprang to her eyes. All the years, she thought, staring, all the goddamn years I spent looking at those windows hoping to spot him, to catch a glimpse, to see a tassel on his scarf even, and now here he is revealing himself to the first strange woman who strolls up his walk. She raged again under her breath. I should've yanked his scarf off when I had the chance. I should have snatched the ungrateful monster's hat right off his ugly head.

Louis had been watching Iris from the moment she turned onto Amherst. Unlike Francine and Kitty, he recognized her immediately even though she wasn't wearing her nurse's whites. He could tell from the way she walked she was very nervous. He'd learned to gauge people's moods that way, from a distance, noticing details that would have escaped him had he participated fully in the world. He was the exact opposite of a blind man, whose four remaining senses sharpen; he could only see, little else filtered through his windows, could not smell or touch or taste, and usually could hear through the window glass only muted sounds. What he had were his eyes, and memory and imagination. He drew Iris toward him with his eyes, willed, he imagined, her faltering feet to move one before the other. Having seen her approach, he would not let her go. As he had compelled Ariel Nesmith, his first young love, to leave so many years ago, so he now compelled Iris to come. Sometimes he would see the shimmering footprints Ariel, in flight, had left behind. He saw them now, for the last time, as they faded and disappeared as Iris, yielding, took the steps that brought her closer.

He stood at his window for a moment longer after she had returned his wave and given to him what his injured lips had been unable naturally to give her, which was a smile. He stood, and maybe she realized what it meant for him to stand there in the open, what he bestowed upon her by lingering there. She must have—the smile that tried to light her face was as uncertain and unpracticed as his body was, revealed before the curtainless window. What a desperate pair we must be, he thought, to exchange such rare and difficult presents: a smile and a moment at a window.

He looked down at Iris. Here at my window balcony, he wondered, dreamy with unknown possibilities, am I Juliet to your Romeo? Sleeping Beauty to your Prince Charming? Who is it who has come to my rescue, to slay the fiery dragon coiled around my feet? Louis had a vision then of Iris in her nurse's uniform transformed into a shining white knight bent on his rescue, charging up and down the streets of Waverly in search of him.

Below, beside the tulip bed, Iris began to fidget, her smile fading. What was he doing up there?

Rescue me from what? Louis thought. He caught his reflection in the glass as he stared down at Iris's lumpy presence. I'm no Sleeping Beauty. There are no beauties here. Look at her. He grasped the windowsill for support. Look at her. Look at me. My God. Ariel. But Ariel was gone. Then he mouthed his own name. Louis. But the Louis he called for was gone too, sixteen years a memory. Gracie, there's someone at the door. Make her go away.

"Gracie." He turned and waited for her reply. None came.

"Gracie, please. There's someone . . . here."

He remembered. The man who wandered in last night. The burglar called Arnie. He'd come and taken Gracie for a morning walk. The burglar had stolen his mother. Louis tried to catch his breath. Gracie, I need you. They've taken you, and now me, they've come for me. Louis rushed over to his bed and curled up on it. His mending arm throbbed inside the heavy cast.

When Louis disappeared from the window, Iris assumed he was coming down the stairs to open the door. She tugged at her dress, and sniffed quickly at her armpits, and licked her lips anxiously. A minute passed. She stepped up onto the front doorstep, then stepped down again. Another minute passed. Maybe he's combing his hair or something. No, he always wears that baseball hat. Well, maybe he's changing to a fresher hat. When yet another minute went by, she said, "The hell with it," the color deepening in her fat cheeks. "I mean really. The hell with it and goddamn it, too," and spun around on her short legs, and stomped down the walk toward the street.

Francine watched, craning to see from behind her white porch column. Kitty, in her own yard next door, poked her head up from between the branches of an overgrown azalea for a better view. She smiled. The intruder woman had been thwarted. Bev and Bert, driving home from the grocery store, spotted Iris too, and slowed down to see what there was to see. Even Carl, whose house was right across the street, took notice. He'd been watering out back, and now he was in the side yard giving his newly transplanted laurel bush a good soak. He just about drowned the thing while he pondered Iris.

There was a lot to ponder, too. Iris, who looked unstoppable as she charged down the walk, suddenly jerked to a halt and did a pirouette, like she was on a rope and somebody gave it a quick yank, wheeling her around. She stared back at the Malone house, and all the neighbors, from their various hiding places, stared with her, wondering what it was she saw.

What she saw was her last chance, which also happened to be her first and only chance. Iris, she said to herself, you got to press this thing harder, you got to take it further, because after this, there's nothing else, not one thing else. The man in there issued you the only invitation you're ever going to receive; he said come, and now you've come, so you got to see him, at least once. You got to look him in the eye.

Iris marched right back up the walk to the house. Francine's head poked up from her hiding place. Iris chugged up the three steps of the Malones' front porch. Bev and Bert's car pulled over and stopped. Iris banged on the Malones' door. Carl forgot he was holding a hose and watered his foot. Iris banged again, then opened the front door.

One yard over, Kitty scrambled out of the azaleas. She was shaking her fist, her face was contorted. "Hey! Hey, you can't do that. You can't go in there!"

Iris turned and watched Kitty's lurching approach. This woman's been drinking, thought Iris. When Kitty was less than ten feet from her, Iris lifted one of her meaty arms and raised her hand. "Stop!" she commanded. Kitty stopped dead, as if the hand had thumped her on the chest.

Iris glared down at Kitty from the porch steps. "Lady, I'm his nurse, and I'm going in."

"But—but," Kitty stammered. "Nobody goes in. Nobody gets to go in and see him."

Now Iris stepped through the doorway. She began to close the door on Kitty. "It's happening now. Lady, I been invited." The door clicked shut.

Kitty stared up at his window. He wasn't there. Even when he'd landed in the tulip bed, he hadn't been there, not for her. It never meant anything to him, her desire to see him, so that even when he fell to the ground before her, he had been invisible, would remain invisible, unseen except by those he invited to see.

Inside, Iris stood trembling in the dim hallway. "Mrs. Malone?" she called. "Louis? Louis Malone?"

Upstairs, Louis huddled on his bed.

Iris heard the springs creak.

"The door was open," she called. "I hope you don't mind I came in."

No creaks this time, but of course he was there.

"I've come to see you. I've come about your arm."

Nothing.

"Like we both agreed," said Iris, her voice quieter now, almost to herself. "Like we both said."

And then, his voice, weightless, drifting downstairs to her. She strained her ears toward the sound, as she had strained to listen when the Tube Man spoke. Louis's voice had that same quality, of words escaping rather than delivered, whispered from lips that preferred to be still and silent.

"You'll have to go away, I think," came the voice.

Now it was Iris who didn't answer.

"There's no one here," said the voice after a minute.

Iris moved toward the stairwell. "You asked me to come," she said.

"I'm sorry. But I was mistaken."

"You have to see me."

"I can't. Really, I can't."

"You have to see someone." Iris put her foot on the first step.

"No, I don't think so. Thank you for coming, though. Good-bye now."

"I'm on my way up." Iris knew, as nurses seem to know, that it was time to approach. She knew that patients often feared the treatment they so desperately sought, that it was sometimes the nurse's job to administer the treatment against all protests. Now, for the first time, she carried no dressings, or syringes, or medicines to her patient's room, because she herself was the cure.

At the top of the stairs there were four doors, two on each side of the hallway. One was closed. She knocked lightly on it.

"Louis?"

She waited, and then said, "Louis, I'm coming in now."

With a final act of boldness, the last in a series of bold acts that had begun when she made her first surprising overture to him in the Emergency Room, Iris opened the door and stepped into Louis's room. She looked first where nurses always look, at the bed. It was empty. Then she moved her eyes to the other side of the large room, which was the only place he would be, before his window. His back was to her, his hand parting a white curtain just a little, just enough so he could see.

He said, in a voice quiet and even, a voice he might have used often, talking to himself, "I don't look at calendars anymore. I can tell from Mrs. Bingsley's red azalea, which is beginning to overflow into Carl Lerner's yard—Carl doesn't seem to mind, though—I can tell it's the end of the first week of May. May sixth or seventh? June fifteenth Mrs. Bingsley's viburnum will flower, or thereabouts. Francine Koessler prunes her privet hedge June thirtieth and again the last week of

August. Winter is harder. Bert Howard changes his Chevy
wagon over to snow tires on December fifteenth, usually.
Last year's Thanksgiving snow threw him into a tizzy; I've
never seen a man change a set of tires so fast.''

Louis made a sound which Iris thought must have been a
small laugh muffled by his scarf. She stood still, watching his
back, which swayed ever so lightly as his voice found its
rhythm.

He went on. ''That's a good way to keep time when
you've stayed inside for sixteen years, almost seventeen
years, really. This window has been my calendar, and all that
I've observed have been my increments of time. Sixteen
years ago I watched Mrs. Bingsley plant that azalea, and now
look at it. So, in a way, the passing of the days has been a
blossoming for me, like the abundant red of Mrs. Bingsley's
azalea, not a marking of days on the calendar of someone
else's idea of time. My . . . time here, I'm trying to say,''
Louis said softly, ''has been full of happy moments, very
small but very happy moments. Little tastes. Doesn't the first
bite of chocolate cake always taste the best? The shock of
sweetness, the anticipation of more chocolate on the tongue?
Well, at my window it's all first bites, I'm never full, the
chocolate never sours and swells my belly.''

Iris leaned against his bed and listened. She had never
heard such talk.

''Of course,'' said Louis, ''I'm not a crazy man, I'm not
happy every minute of the day. There have been sad times.
Even''—he paused—''desperate times. But never here at my
window. Not with Mrs. B.'s azalea in sight.'' Without turning, he asked, ''Iris, did you see her azalea as you approached
my house?''

Iris frowned, embarrassed. She couldn't recall anything
she'd passed on the way to this house, let alone a particular
azalea. ''I'm afraid I didn't. I was . . . preoccupied. I had
other things on my mind.''

"I don't, you see. Have other things on my mind. Just that azalea. And very little else: Bert's snow tires, like I said, the pruning of a privet hedge, the March appearance of the yellow and white crocuses at the base of the streetlight in front of our house—those sorts of things. The azalea—and it could be the crocuses, or the hedge, or Bert on his knees before his tires that I'm talking about—because it is the only azalea I can see from here, it's rare, to me, and as beautiful as a flower in Eden. Imagine having Eden outside of your bedroom window. Sometimes I can't bear it, I can't bear to look at a single red petal of a single flower on that abundantly flowered bush, and I have to close my eyes. And if I can't bear my one azalea, how could I stand being out there among all the azaleas in Waverly, how would I survive that?"

Iris, who was a nurse, who saw differently, spoke. "But it's not. It's not Eden out there."

Louis made a movement as if to turn to her, but then he didn't and stared out his window again. "You're right. You're right, of course. How else does one explain Kitty Wilson? I've had a hard time imagining her as Eve."

The laugh again, muted and distant. Iris, who'd been leaning against Louis's bed, now sat down on it. I'm sitting on a man's bed, she thought.

"No"—Louis touched a finger to his scarf, where his hidden mouth would be—"maybe it is Eden and Kitty is the serpent. There, that fits, doesn't it? But whatever she is, I'm glad to have her, because like the azalea, which I admit I do prefer, she's been a part of the landscape available to me from my window. She's precious to me. I count on her. Just to show up, to show up and be Kitty, unswerving in her rabid curiosity. It's funny to think that she has stared as intensely in my window as I have stared out of it. There's been no joy in it for her, though. Even if I had stood naked before my window, unmasked, hat and scarf at my feet, it wouldn't have been enough for her. She'd have feasted on my face, and then been hungry for more. That's why I've never given her anything other than a teasing glimpse, so that she'd have something to nibble on for years, to sustain her.''

Louis plucked at the corner of the white curtain. ''The less there has been for me to see, the more I've seen. On the way to your hospital last Wednesday I looked out of the car window at all the azaleas in all the yards, white ones, pink, orange, and I couldn't focus on any of them, the colors smeared and blurred, and the beauty in them was lost to me. I wondered, Is that how they look to the rest of the people in this car? Do I want an abundance of azaleas whose colors I can barely discern? Why clog my senses with more than I can appreciate? The red of Mrs. Bingsley's azalea is before me only two weeks out of the year—but it lingers still through the seasons. Even in winter I can conjure that red. Have you ever seen an azalea blooming in the snow? I can even feel that red, sometimes, warming the panes on this window. If I were surrounded by azaleas on a daylight walk through Waverly, would I see them or feel them? By joining the world, would I lose it?''

Iris smoothed her hand back and forth over the quilt that covered Louis's bed. Stop your talking, she thought. Stop your talking and come sit beside me.

If Louis heard her shifting on the bed he gave no indication. ''God watches, you know,'' he said. ''I'm not sure whether I believe in him or not, but in the moments I do believe, I know that he is a watcher, like me. He chooses not to intervene in the world. Why not? Because he figures he's done enough and the rest is up to us? Or he wouldn't know where to begin? Or because he's in awe of his own miracle? That's how I picture him, his mouth slightly agape, his eyes wide in disbelief. I think he has his own azalea, his own view, his own window through which he peers at one thing at a time, because that one thing is an entire world—the red is a world and the petal is a world and the flower and finally the bush—all worlds, as full and abundant as the actual planet we think of as the world is full and abundant. Keeps him pretty busy, I bet. Keeps me pretty busy, anyway.

"I've often thought that my injury, my face, though the cause of my confinement, is also the source of my freedom. The less we have the freer we are. Had I spent all these years living . . . normally . . . what chains would I have forged for myself by now? What pain have I avoided, or not caused, by keeping to myself?"

Iris stood up. "Stop!" she said. "It's not Eden and it's not all chains. You're not sure what it is, because you haven't been out there for sixteen years."

Now Louis slowly turned from his window toward her. "True. And you have been out there for those sixteen years," he said mildly. "Have they been good? Can you tell me what I've missed?"

Iris looked at him hard. "Shit, I don't know. You missed a bunch of things."

"I can tell you precisely what you missed. You missed Mrs. Bingsley's azalea." He gestured with his good hand. "Come here. Come take a look."

Iris moved on her short legs across the room to him. When she stood beside him the room swayed, just a little. He pulled the curtain back, and Iris immediately squinted, as if from the sudden brightness of the sun. But it wasn't the sun that made her squint, it was something brighter still, more intense. Across the street Mrs. Bingsley's azalea was ablaze with color.

"It's so red," Iris gasped.

"Isn't it?" said Louis softly, at her side. "Sometimes I have to look away."

"But that's not the way things are."

"It's the way they are to me," said Louis. "It's the way they are when you really see them."

"My God." Iris pointed. "And who's that? She just

jumped behind a bush. Did you see her eyeliner? Aqua. It glittered like aqua diamonds."

"Kitty Wilson. She's always been a little heavy with the makeup."

"Diamonds."

"There you are."

Iris jerked the curtain closed. "And that's what you've been looking at for sixteen years?"

"Yep."

"No wonder you jumped."

Louis tilted his head and looked at her from behind his scarf and hat. "You think I jumped?" He touched his chest.

"I would have."

"Why?"

"To see if that's really the way things are."

"And after jumping, if you found out that's not the way things are . . . ?"

Iris was way out of her territory, and had been since he'd begun talking. She tried to pull the talk in her direction. "I've come to see about your arm. That's what I know about all this jumping—you broke your arm." She pulled him across the room and made him sit on his bed. She felt a lot better seeing him in bed—nurses understand people better when they are in bed. "So," she said, feeling Louis's hand where it poked out of the cast, "you been having any problems with your fingers swelling?"

"No," said Louis, looking at her.

"Fingers going dusky?"

"No. Not that I've noticed."

"Pain or tingling?"

"In my forearm, where it broke. Throbs a lot."

"Perfectly normal. Keep it elevated on a pillow when you sleep. And don't stand for long periods, especially without wearing your sling. Where is your sling, anyway?"

"Downstairs," said Louis sheepishly.

"We don't hand them out as souvenirs of your visit to the Emergency Room, you know."

Louis shrugged, then looked away.

"I'm sorry," Iris said quickly. "I didn't mean to snap at you. I just, well, I want you to get better."

"I know," said Louis softly. "It was kind of you to come."

"It was kind of you to ask me."

"I scared you with all of my talk. I'm scary enough as it is."

"You don't scare me."

"I scare everybody." Louis looked directly in her eyes as he spoke the words. "I'm the monster of Waverly."

Iris didn't even blink. In fact, she smiled. "How do you do," she said, reaching for his good hand. "I'm the monster of Barnum Memorial Hospital. I guess I've come to the right place."

They held hands for what seemed a very long time, until at last a shyness returned to them and they released each other.

"Let me take you outside," said Iris.

"Oh, Iris." Louis paced the room.

"We'll go out together. We'll step across the street and take a look at Mrs. Bingsley's azalea."

"It's not that easy." Louis felt his heart race.

"No one will bother us. Who would dare bother a couple of monsters like us?"

"Iris, you're not a monster, don't say that."

"I know exactly what I am. And if I'm not a monster I'm damn close to being one. People don't scream when they see me, but I've heard them laugh—to my mind there's not much difference between the two."

"They'd scream if they saw me."

"So don't let them. Fuck 'em. Whose business is it? I'm not asking you to expose yourself to all the peepers. Wrap yourself up in your quilt there if you want to, whatever it takes. Whatever it takes to get you outside on a spring day, to step across the street and look at a bush.''

''I'd like to.''

''Then come on.'' She held out her hand.

''But not yet.''

''Louis, if I've survived this long out there, you can stand it for five minutes. You made it on Wednesday, didn't you?''

''Those were extraordinary circumstances.''

''This is extraordinary circumstances! Do you have any idea what it took for someone like me to come here, to come here and now ask you outside, like, like on some kind of date? And you're going to turn me down?''

Louis was quiet a moment. Then he said, ''You know, it's very strange. My mother and I, we live alone here and very quietly. Yet today both of us have received separate invitations to go outside, to step into the sunshine. My mother accepted her invitation. She's out now with her new friend, walking the streets of Waverly. It was nice to see that, to see her happy.''

''Don't you think she'd like to see you happy, to see you go outside?''

''I'm not unhappy.''

''Louis, you're in need of some fresh air,'' Iris said to him in her blunt way. ''Several years of fresh air, in my opinion. Now, we can go back and forth on this thing forever, but let's not. Let me just say what I'm going to say, then you say what you want to say, and I'll either walk on outside with you or without you.'' Iris's throat was tight and her mouth was very dry. ''Listening to you, it sounds like you know a whole lot. You've thought a lot about things. Well, I'm not like that. Things don't, I don't know, things just don't occur to me. I understand only after doing something over and over. I'm a nurse, and what I've done over and over is take care of

people; I know how to take care of a person. I know what's
healthy. People should listen to me because I only speak
when I know what I'm talking about. Of course, they don't
always listen. I say to my patients, take your heart medicine,
or do your back exercises, or cut down on your salt intake.
Simple stuff, which I wouldn't mention unless I was right. Now
here I am with you, looking at you, and it comes to me,
like with one of my patients it comes to me. What you need
is to step outside with me, right now. Walk down the stairs
and out the front door with me. Because if you don't—and
this is the thing I know, this is the thing that scares me—
you'll jump right out this window again. And it may be your
neck that breaks next time. You'll jump because the world is
pulling you. You've been looking at it for too long. You've
made it into something too beautiful and too precious and you
got to get to it, but you've stayed here in your room so long
you've forgotten how. It's a pressure inside you, you don't
even feel it, but it's there. You'll be standing here someday,
looking outside, and the next thing you know you won't
be—the pressure will blow you right out this window. So
what I'm saying to you is: let off some of that pressure. Come
on. Come with me. Don't give me a thousand reasons not to.
Just come.''

Iris pressed her teeth to her lower lip and moved away
from him. She took several steps toward the door, then turned
once more to face him. Louis looked as if he was about to
move, his body leaned in her direction. But then he hesitated.
''Why are you doing this, Iris?''

Because, she thought, gazing into his masked eyes,
because you are my Lawrence, my beautiful Peter O'Toole,
my date to the prom, my one and only, my first and last
desperate chance. That's why. I don't care who you are or
what you look like: I'll take you. And you are the only one
who will take me. I am your rarest flower, and I'm blooming
now, this instant, and only you have the power to see it, you

who see everything, you who transform the ordinary into glorious beauty. Look at me with your window eyes and see that I am redder than your blazing azalea, greener than the emerald leaves sparkling on your trees, brighter than the dazzling yellow of your crocuses.

Iris, who never cried, knew that she was about to. Iris, who never let circumstances escape her control, trembled as she waited for him to refuse her offer. She closed her eyes because she could not endure it.

When she opened them again Louis was beside her. He had moved away from his window and across the room without a sound, without disturbing, it seemed, a single molecule of air within the shaded bedroom. As she watched his hand approach hers, she thought that it would be without weight because she was not sure if this really was Louis or a vision of Louis that she had willed across the room to her side. But when he touched her she felt the warmth and substance of his hand, and the trembling in his fingers that matched her own.

Louis looked down at Iris. He did not, as she had hoped, imbue her with physical qualities she didn't possess. Nothing about her sparkled or shone, or made him catch his breath. He saw her as she was. Everything Iris despised about herself, he saw. He saw, then dismissed all that he saw for the simple beauty of her gesture, for her brave and lovely attempt to rescue him. For Louis it was as if Iris had defied the licking flames of the burning back room of the hardware store, had risked everything to pull him to safety. Although she didn't know it, by risking all, she was transformed, yet unchanged. For this woman he would walk out his front door.

"Well," said Louis, trying to steady his voice, "shall we go?"

Iris squeezed his hand in reply.

Louis let her walk ahead of him through his bedroom doorway. He stepped into the hall behind her, then turned, looked at his bedroom for a long moment, then gently closed the door.

"Is it cool out?" he asked as they started downstairs. "Will I need a jacket?"

"A little cool, but I think you'll be fine," said Iris.

"Sounds to me like hat and scarf weather," said Louis. "But then for me it always is."

Iris looked up at him as he laughed softly. She smiled. "You're going to be fine, you know that, don't you?" She'd learned that the patients she'd cared for who laughed at their overwhelming frailty their first time out of bed were the ones who did best.

"I don't know what I know," he said.

"I'll be right beside you."

"It's not like anything will happen. I'm just stepping outside a minute. Right?"

"Right."

"People do that all the time. Right?"

"Right."

"To hang up their laundry or pick up their newspaper or wash their car. That sort of thing."

"I've done those very things," said Iris, "and lived to tell the tale."

They stood before the front door. "If my legs fail me?" said Louis, shifting.

"I'll steady you."

"If I faint?"

"I'll catch you."

"If I change my mind?"

"I won't let you."

"That pretty much covers it, I guess." He put his hand on the doorknob.

"You want me to get that?" said Iris.

But he was already opening the door, opening it and then leaping through it as if he'd decided it would require an unstoppable propelled effort to cross the boundary between his known interior life and the life that waited for him outside.

Just before she shot out after him, Iris thought, This is how he jumped from his window, this is the kind of force he mustered and unleashed.

He got a few feet down the front walk, then froze. She caught up with him and took his arm in hers.

"Hey, hey. Easy now," she said. "Don't hurt yourself—remember, you still have a broken arm."

Louis was elsewhere. He turned and looked up at his window, then down at the tulip bed. He did it again, as if trying to establish the exact trajectory of his Wednesday flight from window to earth. At last he said, "I wonder what it would take to do the whole thing in reverse. Stand in the tulip bed and hop back up into my bedroom."

"You made it, Louis. You're outside."

"Am I? I haven't really looked yet."

"Well, look. I got you. I'm right here." Iris positioned herself for maximum strength and balance, like she did when she helped patients stand after they'd spent weeks in bed.

Louis turned from his house and faced the world of Waverly. He lifted his eyes slowly, staring first at his feet, then at the gray-white sidewalk just beyond the toes of his shoes, then at the fresh spring-green lawn that bordered both sides of the sidewalk. He lifted his eyes and took in the widening horizon of sidewalks and grass and trees, took in the deep black asphalt of his street, and the telephone poles that lined it, and the houses whose exteriors he knew so well from sixteen years of studying them in every slant of light, every dim night shadow, every subtle change of weather that played upon their windows and doors and black-shingled roofs. It was a world he knew, yet did not entirely recognize. Everything he saw now was within reach.

Iris could hear his breathing go tight and shallow. "You

had enough, Louis? You want to go back inside? You don't really have to go over to Mrs. Bingsley's azalea.''

Louis didn't answer. His eyes darted over the landscape as he tried to relearn it, to get his bearings. He was Dorothy disoriented in Munchkinland. And as they had for Dorothy, hidden Munchkins slowly poked into view, Munchkins who in this case went by the names of Kitty and Francine and Bert and Bev. Kitty, in the next yard over, stepped out from behind a bush. Francine peeped around her white porch column, then showed herself completely. Bev and Bert, who'd ducked down in the seats of their station wagon when Louis opened his front door, sat up again and peered at him. Carl had not changed his position in his side yard since Iris had first appeared at the Malone house. He still held the garden hose, and had by now created a small lake around himself. All of the rescuers were assembled and ready for whatever Louis might have in mind to do next.

They hadn't figured on Iris. She felt their eyes upon her, although it was on Louis they were feasting. She wouldn't allow it. She let go of Louis's arm and stormed down the front walk. ''Can I help you people?'' she shouted. ''You got some kind of problem?'' She whipped her head back and forth, glaring at each of them.

Francine let out a yip and, clutching Minky, rushed into her house. Kitty lurched out of view. Bert gunned his station wagon and screeched off down the street, throwing Bev back up against her seat like a rag doll. He didn't even turn up his driveway, but shot past his house as if Iris were in pursuit.

Carl momentarily stood his ground. Actually, it was more water than ground, which he finally realized and twisted off his hose before looking up and giving a wave to Iris frowning at him from across the street.

''Sorry, lady,'' he called to her. ''I had to see.''

"See?" Iris shouted back, about to tip over into a deeper anger. "What do you think you had to see?"

"That he was all right. That everything was okay."

He waved again, this time to Louis who had raised his hand to give Carl the all-clear. "Thank you, Carl," Louis called, "I'm fine."

Carl took a length of hose and began to gather it around his arm. "Well, I'll leave you folks to your business then." He traipsed across his wet lawn and disappeared behind his house.

There was no one left on the street now. If anyone was watching, and there were probably many, then it was from the secret safety of a curtained window. Louis shifted his gaze to the yard next door to Carl's: Mrs. Bingsley's. He moved down the walk until he was at Iris's side, where he stopped and continued to stare across the street. She was about to tell him again that he didn't have to go to the azalea, that he'd done more than enough for his first time out, when she felt him tensing at her side. She reached out with her hand to stop him, because she suddenly realized what he was about to do; but he'd already begun to move, to gather momentum as he'd done before.

"Louis!" she shouted after him.

That's it, he's gone. Watching him run, she was sure of it, that he was like an escaped prisoner made crazy by the world suddenly open to him. He'd run, keep on running as he tried to see everything, to smell and touch, to bring to his senses all that they had been deprived of for sixteen years. Iris stood perfectly still and watched, because she knew she'd never catch a man like that. Her thoughts flashed instantly forward, and she imagined herself standing where she was now, and Louis running for the horizon, his scarf, lifted by the wind, straight back behind him, his figure receding in the distance before he was swallowed by the sun.

All this Iris imagined as Louis ran down the front walk,

then out into the street where he veered left and picked up speed as he crossed to the other side. Iris understood then. Mrs. Bingsley's azalea, he headed straight for it. Louis never slowed down; he looked like he was about to run right into the middle of the thing, immerse himself in the flaming red abundance of flowers. But he cut quickly to the side and stuck his hand out, moving as fast as before, and skimmed his fingers along the edges of the huge bush. Iris lost sight of him for a second as he circled behind it, like the moon orbiting the earth. Then there he was, careening into view, facing her now, his eyes wide as he moved back across Mrs. Bingsley's front yard and into the street again. Iris stiffened as he headed straight for her. She heard him panting as he approached. He never stopped running, and as he passed her, she saw his hand jerk upwards toward her head. She squinted in anticipation of the blow. She hardly felt a thing, a fluttering above her ear, fingers in her hair, the warmth of his hand. She reached her own hand to the place where his had been, as she turned and watched him mount the porch steps two at a time and rush into the house, closing the door behind him. There was something behind her ear, something thin and soft behind her ear and tangled in a strand of her hair. Iris freed it, and held it in her cupped hand. She looked for a long time at the flower that Louis had picked for her from the azalea, the azalea she'd earlier confessed she had not even noticed. From the bush she had not seen, she now held a single red flower, unbearable in its beauty.

As if this was not enough, she heard a heavy scraping sound and raised her eyes to Louis opening his bedroom window. He poked his head out and said, "Thank you, Iris, for a lovely morning. Come back tomorrow?"

Iris couldn't even answer him. She placed the red petals behind her ear again, and nodded yes, before turning on her short legs and walking unsteadily home along the exuberantly flowered streets of Waverly.

III

Arnie and Gracie, too, were walking. Arnie paused on the corner of Dickinson and Elm, and shaded his eyes to see better.

"What is it?" said Gracie.

"Could've sworn I just saw my daughter turn up the street there."

"Would that be so strange?"

"If that woman was my daughter it'd be mighty strange. She looked drunk or something. Iris does not go off on morning drunks. Least not that I know of." Arnie started walking again. "Though some mornings in my opinion she could use a good drunk."

Gracie said, "So how long has she been with you?"

"Two, three years," said Arnie. "She moved out for a long while, then moved back in again when my LuLu passed away."

They walked without talking for a time. Arnie stayed to Gracie's right side, so his hook would be out of view. He'd tried to fit the thing in his pocket, but it kept snagging on his belt loops. She didn't seem to care one way or another, but still, having a hook didn't work to your advantage when you were trying to impress a lady

"It's a terrible business, isn't it?" Gracie said after they'd gone a block.

Arnie hesitated. She mean his hook? "What is?" he asked.

"Oh, losing your . . . having your husband, your wife just disappear. That's how I've thought of Atlas's death, as a disappearance. I looked the word up, you know, and it means 'to go out of sight.' For those first terrible weeks I had a sense that's just what he'd done, gone out of sight, that he was always in the room I was about to enter, but when I'd enter it he'd moved on to the next room. It was a very cruel sensation.''

Arnie nodded. Sometimes he'd had the feeling that LuLu was even closer than that. For months after her funeral he'd suddenly awaken and know that she was in bed sleeping quietly beside him. In his longing for her he was sure he could hear her softly breathing, he could feel the weight of her near him, smell the warmth whose scent had been forty years a comfort to him. He'd lie unmoving until he could not resist his need to reach out to her, and for him the cruel sensation was the cool of the empty sheets beneath his hand.

"You're right," sighed Arnie, "it's a terrible business. I realized, when LuLu died, that that's what it's always been about—losing things. You live for any length of time, it all begins to peter out on you. I feel like one of the cars I used to work on. When I was a young mechanic, I saw myself as a big beautiful brand-new Packard, going down the road forever. And then, bit by bit, as the miles start to add up on you, stuff you don't even pay attention to as meaning anything starts to go. You get a few dents, your engine begins to knock a little, your transmission fluid don't move through you like it used to. Then Christ almighty, one day you're going down that road and your whole damn power train locks on you, and boy you've really had it then. I'm a junker now, and to tell you the truth I ain't so sure I'll be passing the next inspection.''

Gracie smiled at him. "That's the most colorful description of growing old I believe I've ever heard. I'm not sure I agree with your final assessment, however.''

"How's that?'' Final assessment. He liked the way Gracie talked, even though he didn't always catch her meaning.

"That you're a junker. Your parts may rattle a bit, but you're hardly a junker.''

"Thank you for saying so. But you take a good look at me, which I don't advise, you may change your mind.''

"Arnie, my dear, the beauty of being old is that one is unable to take a good look."

They both laughed, and then stopped suddenly, their eyes briefly meeting. Gracie knew he was thinking the same thing. Imagine: I used to laugh like that with Atlas, and you with LuLu. A shyness and a slight sense of betrayal colored Gracie's cheeks. Arnie fiddled with his hook.

They turned the corner onto Cedar Lane. "You getting tired?" Arnie said to break the silence. He hid his hook again. "You need to head back, let me know, 'cause I'll walk your legs off. I'm used to it from walking my dog. Iris, she won't go out with me anymore."

"Oh, I'm fine, fine. I walk a great deal myself." Truth was, she felt a buzzy ache starting up in her right knee. She didn't want to head back, though. She hoped Louis wouldn't— mind? And if he did, would he ever, in a million years, tell her? She didn't feel his aloneness if she was in the house with him, or out on her own doing errands. But when she went to the movies with friends, or to lunch, she never looked back at the house for fear he would cheerily wave her on. She knew that even at the height of his own loneliness, he would not begrudge her moments in the world. Not even these moments, with this intruder of the night turned suitor. No, Louis must have watched from his window as she and Arnie disappeared into the spring morning; watched and wished them well.

As if reading her mind, Arnie said, "Seems like a pretty good boy you have there, that Lawrence."

Gracie looked at Arnie, to see if he was joking with her somehow. When she saw nothing in his face she remembered that he was hard of hearing, and had misheard a word or two last night as they drank their cocoa. Which way should she go? She didn't want to embarrass him with a correction, especially when he'd just finished telling her he felt like an old junker. But then he'd be more embarrassed later when he learned Louis's right name. Better do it now, she thought.

"Yes, *Louis* is a good boy. Too good sometimes," she said, rather loudly.

Arnie cocked his head. "That two boys you got? Louis and Lawrence? Now, I met Lawrence. Where's Louis live?"

She was in it now. "Actually, Arnie, it's Louis who lives at home."

"Louis and Lawrence?" said Arnie. "Both at home still? Boy, I bet that gets crowded. I know when Iris moved back in I couldn't walk into a room of my house without bumping into her. Of course she's kind of hefty, built for bumping, you might say."

Oh dear. Gracie kept trying. "No, actually, you see it's just Louis and me at home. There is no Lawrence."

Arnie got it then. Gracie saw the chagrin spread across his face. He touched her arm with his hand. "I'm sorry. I didn't realize. I shouldn't have pursued it."

And now he thinks Lawrence is dead! She wanted to laugh, or give Arnie a good shake. But she said, loudly and leaning close to what she hoped was his good ear, "Don't be sorry, Arnie. It was long ago and far away." An odd sort of sadness crept through her as she said the words. Well, in a way a child of hers had died: beautiful Louis at sixteen, lost in a fire. She cleared her throat and looked away.

Arnie didn't notice. His eyes were set on a different direction. "Gracie, it was good of you to come out with me this morning. I mean, me barging in on you last night, and all. I wasn't sure, you having slept on it for a night, if you was going to want to see me."

"I was glad to see you, Arnie." She was, truly. Spring meant Atlas working in his garden. She was happy to have the chance to associate it with something else, like walking beneath the green overhang of maple trees with this new man.

"It's strange for me, Gracie, to want to see you." When

she turned to him, puzzled, he stammered on. "I mean, what I mean is, besides LuLu I never much wanted to be with anyone else, to go on walks and such. But that's the first thing I wanted to do this morning when my eyes popped open—get over to this part of town and see you." Arnie couldn't believe the words were leaving his mouth.

"You're a sweet man, Arnie." Gracie smiled. To think I could move a man to say such things. Me, the Widow Malone.

"Well, I don't know about that." Arnie shrugged.

"I do. LuLu did all right for herself when she married you."

It was Arnie's turn to clear his throat and look away.

After they went around Dartmouth Circle, Gracie said they'd better head back. Her knee really was bothering her. They stopped every so often to admire a stand of tulips in someone's yard, or a particularly fine azalea. A block or two from home Gracie paused, started to ask something, then didn't.

"What is it?" Arnie said.

"My son," she said. "Louis. I'm curious."

"What about?"

"You haven't asked me why he wears a hat and scarf. Are you being polite, or do you already know about him?"

"No to both questions," Arnie said. He lifted his hook. "And you haven't asked me about this."

She looked at it without expression. "It never occurred to me to, Arnie."

"There you go. It never occurred to me to ask about your boy. You got a hook for a right hand, you don't nose around in other folks' business. I guess me and you are about equal in that respect. Having lived with something pretty private, we've lost a certain curiosity." He tapped his hook. "Lost my hand fooling with a car."

"Louis was burned in a fire."

"There," said Arnie. "Got that out of the way, and it wasn't even in the way." He smiled.

An immense white azalea caught their eyes as they turned onto Gracie's block.

"That's a hell of a bush," said Arnie.

"White is my favorite. Double-blossoming white."

They were about to start up again when Arnie reached out, so quickly Gracie wasn't sure he'd moved at all. But then she saw the blossom in his hand, and tilted her head toward him as he reached up and placed it in her white hair.

IV

It was the skin on his face, with its memory of pain, that alerted Louis to the nearness of flames. He had been asleep, and the memory obliterated his dreams; the knowledge of heat and light startled him to wakefulness. Fear contracted him, caused him to shrink and curl upon his bed, his eyes clamped shut. A thought flashed: When they find me—a blackened ball stuck to the stinking sheets of my smoldering bed—I will horrify them, my monstrosity complete. He buried his head in the crook of his arm because he was terrified that the fire, which surely surrounded him, would flare into his face and melt his eyes. He couldn't move because he might create a wind that would fan the flames. And if he opened his mouth to cry out, the heat would enter him, burning him from within. In what he took to be his final vision, he saw his room transformed into a crematorium, and himself, at first whole and recognizable upon his bed, slowly consumed by fire, feet, thighs, chest, scarf, hat.

Seconds passed, a minute, and then a cool breeze eased across the length of his body. He remembered that when his face had been burned, the flash of fire felt at first like icy water thrown onto his skin. The cool breeze would be followed by an unforgiving heat, he knew. He clenched his teeth. But the breeze continued, and instead of smoke, or the odor of his own burning flesh, he smelled the damp green of a spring night. He thought: I've passed beyond pain, beyond heat and cold, all the way to death. Is this what Atlas smelled, this green which is a renewal, at the moment he slumped onto the grass beneath the horse chestnut tree? Louis opened his eyes then, and sat up in bed. In death have I been reborn? He touched his fingers to his mouth and cheeks, and felt the familiar terrain of destruction that told him nothing had changed. I'm not dead—eyes open, he saw no flames, and the cool breeze he'd mistaken for the breath of fire came from the open window on the far side of his room.

The fire was not a dream. He knew those dreams, the ascent to terror followed by a slow return to sleep. Nor a premonition. He sensed again the nearness of heat, the proximity of orange light veiled in smoke. He swung his feet over the side of the bed and stood, tensing himself for a run to Gracie's room. Where in the house would he find the flames, or would they find him? As he opened his door, would the hallway be ablaze? He weakened and struggled to breathe. Don't stop, or you'll burn where you stand, like Joan of Arc. Louis of Waverly, we condemn thee. No. On the back of his chair hung his hat and scarf. He reached for them instinctively—they had always shielded him, and would shield him now from the smoke and fire. He turned toward the door, and in turning scanned his windows, the two that faced the street, and the open one with its half-drawn shade, the one which faced the side yard, and through a pair of sycamore trees, Kitty Wilson's house. In full summer her house would disappear behind a wall of thick green. But now Louis could just make it out through the tangle of branches and tiny new leaves. He moved away from his door and over to the window, lifting its shade, the ever-present barrier between him and Kitty. He found his fire. Across the dark, flames on a curtain flickered in the panes of Kitty's second-floor bedroom window. It was not he, but Kitty who would burn.

Louis did not even hesitate. He pulled his scarf tight and his hat low, and held his cast close to his body to keep it from bouncing as he ran into the hallway. "Gracie!" he shouted as he rushed past her open door, "call the fire department, Kitty's house is on fire!"

Gracie, jarred awake, saw her son in pajamas before her, and then didn't see him, his footsteps loud on the stairs before fading to silence as he disappeared out the front door and into the night. She resisted the instant need to follow him, and groped in the dark for the telephone.

When Louis went out the door, his dread left him for a moment, and he thought: Look, Iris, I'm outside again, I can do it. A rush of panic, and the orange glow of fear filled him again, and he wanted to run through the streets of Waverly to her. Save me, Iris. But she did not know his danger. He knew it, and knowing it headed straight for Kitty's house. He didn't try her front door, which would be locked against burglars and creatures of the night like himself. He pushed between two overgrown yews, and lifted his cast, smashing in her picture window. A light went on across the street, and another and another, but inside Kitty's house all remained dark. Louis dragged his cast once across the windowsill to flatten the shards of sparkling glass, then stepped up on a yew branch, and pulled himself inside. He knocked a chair over, then a small table and vase, as he groped along the wall for a light switch. Blinking in the light, he oriented himself, living room, dining room, hallway, stairs. He ran for them and tripped on a cast-iron doorstop in the shape of a dog as he veered out of the dining room. Sprawled at the bottom of the stairs, he looked up and saw the dim cloud of smoke waiting for him at the top. Kitty, I can't.

"Kitty!" he shouted.

I can't make it up those stairs, I'm sorry.

"Fire, Kitty!"

I can't do it. But he was already on the first step, doing what he could not do, propelled by his knowledge of pain, because what he truly could not do was let Kitty burn.

And so Louis climbed the stairs, found another light switch within the gathering smoke, and moved toward the room. Lost in a surging panic, he saw himself approaching that other room, of so many years ago, the back room at the end of the hardware store. He touched the door to Kitty's bedroom, but didn't really know which room he was about to enter. The door opened and there she was, asleep and uncomprehending, a bottle of wine spilled on her bedside table, and next to it an overturned ashtray, the cigarettes scattered across the table and onto the floor and in the wastebasket—because that's where the fire had started, from the wastebasket to the curtains, the flaming curtains sparking onto the rug, igniting another fire in the closet. Louis saw it happen in his mind, traced the path of the lit cigarette as it fell from Kitty's drunken fingers to the overturned ashtray, rolling across the table to the wastebasket, and in tracing that path he saw again the course of the spark more than sixteen years ago, as it lifted off the oily rags he had attempted to extinguish, lifted, floated, and then fell into the paint thinner. . . .

Louis stopped the memory just short of the explosion. He had returned to the back room of the hardware store at the instant before the explosion released the flames that scorched his face. He knelt upon the smoke-enshrouded bed and saw not Kitty, but himself, unharmed at sixteen. Kitty opened her eyes and closed them again.

"I've come to rescue you," he whispered.

He lifted her with one arm, up and over his shoulder, but did not know it. It was Louis he carried across the smoldering rug and beyond the growing blaze, Louis he carried back down the clouded hallway to the top of the stairs, to safety.

Kitty began to emerge from her stupor as they moved

down the stairs. Upside down her face bounced against the purple scarf.

"You," she murmured.

Louis didn't hear her. Firemen ran through the downstairs rooms, pressing past him to get at the blaze, red lights flashed, men shouted back and forth. Someone tried to take hold of Kitty, but Louis couldn't release her. He moved forward through the commotion toward the door, he had to get to the door and outside.

"Let go," Kitty screeched, squirming on his shoulder.

At last he did stop, in the middle of her front lawn, fell to his knees, and dropped her to the grass. He breathed the fresh spring air in great gasps, slowly returning to himself. A circle had formed around them, policemen and firemen, Gracie rushing to his side, and the neighbors who seemed always to be there whenever he appeared, Bev and Bert, Francine, Carl, and others he didn't recognize. The world, it appeared, had descended upon him.

Two firemen attempted to strap an oxygen mask to Kitty's face, but she was having none of it. She struggled against them, spitting words into her mask, crying out. She jerked free and lunged at Louis, her arms outstretched, her hands reaching for his face, and her voice spreading like an infection through the crowd.

Gracie swatted her before she touched Louis, and Kitty fell, ranting, confused and deranged, alcohol and fear pounding through her. "It was him, get him, don't you see?" she screamed, her face monstrous, lit by the glow erupting from her bedroom window. "He started the fire. He tried to burn me in my sleep!"

Louis jumped to his feet and faced the stunned crowd. He was very still and they were very still. He swayed. Then someone moved, and someone else. A fireman turned toward him, and a teenager, and Carl reached out with his hands. Louis made a frightened sound and stumbled forward, breaking into a run. He ran into the street, heading one way, then another—stopped and pivoted, and started again, running straight for his own house, across the lawn, up the steps, slamming the door behind him as he escaped to his room, his concealment, his sanctuary.

V

Iris awoke to a perfect May day. She couldn't remember ever waking to one of those before. She was in such a tolerant mood that the usual morning sound of Arnie gargling and hawking in the bathroom didn't set her teeth on edge. Her thoughts moved past him to Louis's invitation for another visit. She stretched and lingered in bed, enjoying the prospect. When Arnie finished in the bathroom, she rushed in after him, and out again, beating him down to breakfast. She was at the stove when he walked into the kitchen.

"Morning," he said.

"Morning," she returned, her voice neutral.

He poured himself a glass of juice. Then he eyed her. "Fixing a little porridge, are we?"

"How's that?" she said, pretending not to hear him.

"I said, having a little oatmeal? You know, so you can win that badge they give you for the most mornings in a row without ever changing what you eat for breakfast."

Iris whipped around, a mixing bowl in her hands. "Hah!" she said. "You think you know everything. Pancakes!" She tilted the bowl for him to see. "Blueberry pancakes."

Arnie grinned, and she grinned back at him. Duke wandered into the kitchen. "Hey Duke, check that woman out for me, will you? I believe they changed daughters on me in the night."

"Nope, it's me," said Iris.

"I ain't convinced of that," said Arnie.

"Drink your juice," she commanded, turning back to the stove.

"That's more like it."

Arnie ate two stacks of pancakes, and Iris ate three. Every so often, between bites, Arnie looked at her. He didn't know it, but Iris was watching him, too. Both of them were having the same sorts of itchy thoughts, prompted by a reversal of their fortunes. She gonna be all right? Arnie worried. Let's say Gracie and I join up in some fashion. Where's that leave Iris? How are we going to work that one? And Iris was wondering, too. Against her better judgment she had brought her fantasies to the ultimate conclusion (she'd never really had a fantasy before, so how did they expect her to control it?). Suppose I wind up with Louis, was the way hers went. Suppose, even, we get married. What about Arnie? I can't just leave him, and I know he'd never move in with us.

Arnie swallowed his last pancake and announced it had been the best breakfast he'd had in years. Iris agreed. They pushed their chairs back, and nodded, and smiled because although each was worried about the other's prospects, they were still very excited about their own. Iris got up to do the dishes and Arnie jumped to his feet to help. She insisted he sit down to his paper, and he insisted he take a turn at the sink.

"Since when do you do dishes?"

"Since right now, girl. What the hell, you deserve a break."

After a minute or two of spirited wrangling, they agreed that Arnie would do Iris's breakfast dishes, and she would do his. Just before ten o'clock, when their smiles began to poop out on them, Iris disappeared to her room, leaving Arnie to his newspaper. She hummed to herself as she put a little extra talcum under her armpits, changed her dress, and fussed with her hair. There wasn't a whole lot she could do with her hair, which was thin and straight, except wear a colorful ribbon to divert attention. Or would that attract attention? She chewed her lip and stared at herself in the mirror. Then she took a deep breath and went downstairs to the living room.

"Look at you," Arnie said, peering over his paper.

Iris shifted. "Thought I'd go for a stroll," she said.

"Ain't you working evening shift?" said Atlas.

"Took a vacation day."

"A vaca—since when have you ever taken a vacation day? I thought you didn't believe in vacation."

"People change, Arnie," Iris said softly.

Arnie's mouth dropped open. Change? Miss Oatmeal 1992 change? But there she was, standing before him, blueberry pancakes in her belly, a purple ribbon in her hair, taking a vacation day and going for a stroll. Changed.

"Well," he said. "Yeah, maybe. I guess they do." He nodded at her and she nodded back. They did that for a minute. Arnie looked at the front door, then at Iris. "So, strolling any place in particular?"

Iris reddened. She fumbled with her pocketbook.

Arnie got up from his chair and moved past her to the door. He held it open for her, touching her arm lightly as she slowly went by him and out into the light of the spring day. He didn't know where she was going, only that she *was* going, her journey begun. As he stood in the open doorway he thought he could hear the birds chirping in the branches of the maples. He hadn't heard a bird chirp in ten years. Christ, he could barely make out what Iris shouted at him half the time. He was changing too, getting younger, his parts were mending and knitting themselves, and in his excitement he looked down at his hook, almost expecting to see his hand again, the resurrected fingers pink and soft as babies.

Iris's eyes were everywhere, taking in a world she'd barely seen before. It was his world, Louis's, or at least something like it, rich and abundant, sharply focused. She stopped several times to touch a flower, a leaf, and even the brown earth, warm and redolent. She didn't think she was going to be able to survive the azaleas. Where did those colors come from? She knew, of course: from the man in the window.

And so she walked the streets of Waverly, immersed in the endless possibilities of a May morning. She walked, the world filling her, completing her. When at last she turned onto his street, she knew she was ready for him.

What she was not ready for was the sight of Kitty's house, the charred roof and window frame jolting her from her reverie. Her eyes cut to Louis's house next door. Then relief: whatever had occurred in the night had caused no damage beyond itself. Iris touched a hand to her chest and involuntarily said his name. "Louis." What must it have been like for him to have a fire so near? She hurried up the walk.

The front door began to open, and Iris said his name again. "Louis?"

It was Gracie who appeared, her face white, her eyes bleary and sad. She blinked in the sunlight. "I know you," she said.

"Yes," said Iris.

"His nurse."

"I've come to see him. Is he all right?"

Gracie turned her eyes toward Kitty's house, then away again. She clutched the porch railing. Iris moved up the steps to her. "Tell me," she said, holding Gracie's arm. "Tell me what happened."

Gracie leaned against the comforting solidity of her, and told the nurse what had to be said.

Iris listened, her eyes moving from Kitty's blackened window to the shaded window above her, where no one stood. A light breeze carried the fiery odor from Kitty's house, and Iris understood that even though the flames had not touched him, Louis had been burned.

When Gracie finished, Iris said in her strongest nurse's voice, the voice she used to infuse hope in a patient's family, "I'm going in to see him now, Mrs. Malone."

Gracie said nothing, but moved aside to let her pass. Iris stepped once again into the dark house, uncertain that she could rescue this man from the same disaster twice.

Louis lay perfectly still, stretched out on his bed, his hands folded across his stomach. His breathing was so shallow his chest didn't rise, at least not discernibly; but he was moving air because his purple scarf puffed up from his mouth at rhythmic intervals. His eyes were open, but he wasn't in the room. He was far away; he had placed himself on a green hillside at the farm, roaming the grass in search of strawberries. His scarf hung loosely around his neck, his hat shaded his exposed skin from the warm sun. The wind picked up, and it was cool on his face, and the strawberries were tart and sweet, and the tall dry grass brushed lightly against the sides of his legs as he walked along.

Louis, in the bed, breathed more slowly.

He touched another strawberry to his tongue and sat in the grass gazing down into the small valley at the pond. He could just see Gracie at the end of the dock, her feet dangling in the dim water. Beyond her, Atlas floated on a black inner tube, his body turning slowly this way, and then that way, like a compass settling on a bearing. At last, he did settle for a long moment, facing the hillside where Louis sat half-hidden in the grass. Louis saw him lift an arm out of the dark water, and as Atlas waved, drops of water like glittering diamonds fell into the pond. When the last diamond disappeared below the surface of the water, Louis returned his wave.

Louis, in his bed, raised an arm, then let it fall back on the quilt.

Did he know Iris was standing just outside his door? If he did, it was only for an instant, and then he was gone again, beyond her presence, to a place she couldn't get to. The place was Malone's Hardware, on a Saturday long ago, and he was standing on Yank Spiller's shoulders reaching toward a top shelf for a spool of 10-gauge brass wire.

"Tell you a secret," Yank whispered to Louis as he eased him back down to the floor. "That ain't brass at all. It's gold."

Louis's eyes grew wide.

"Sure," said Yank, smiling. "Gold. Malone's Hardware is full of stuff like that, stuff you think is one thing but is really something else."

Louis fingered the spool of deep yellow wire, then looked up at Yank. "Well, how come we sell it? How come we don't keep it?"

"We did keep it, didn't we? For a while, anyways. And now it's time to let someone else have it."

Louis started up the aisle, where Mr. Jimmons waited at the counter for his wire. "Do you think Mr. Jimmons knows it's gold?" Louis whispered to Yank just before they reached the counter.

"I'm not sure. But you and me know, and that's good enough."

The store was crowded with Saturday customers, and Louis, in his shorts and T-shirt, moved easily among them, answering questions, fetching ball-peen hammers and jigsaw blades, making trips to the basement for Atlas. Atlas eased the customers through the store like a traffic cop, pointing, gesturing, maintaining a steady flow, avoiding snarls in the cluttered aisles and around the counter. He was a marvel, and so was his deputy, Yank, although Yank's efforts were more subtle—he was not a man to draw attention to himself. Yank would often appear with something off a shelf before a customer had articulated his need for it.

"I need that gadget," Louis overheard one man start to say to Atlas, "you know, that thingamabob that goes around the, um, the . . ." and then easy as you please Yank was at the customer's side, holding a two-way stopcock. "That's it!" the man exclaimed with a smile. "Give me three." And Yank pulled two more out of his pocket, and nodded in anticipation of the "Thanks" the customer didn't have time to say before Yank disappeared to the back of the store.

Louis, unmoving in his bed, his breathing slowed now to a rate that just sustained his heartbeat, whispered a word. "Thanks," he said.

Louis looked around the hardware store, at the Saturday customers coming in and out, at Atlas grinning and telling a story as he rang up a sale on the old cash register, at Yank lining a shelf with new stock, arranging and rearranging until everything was just right. Louis looked at the worn wooden planks of the store, at the rows of shiny tools, and at a reflection of himself in a box of bicycle rearview mirrors, a reflection of a young boy in the perfect place for boys. He smiled at himself, astonished by the pink health of his cheeks, the sleek shape of his nose, the curve of his soft lips. He wanted to stare at himself forever, to stay in the moment forever, in the hardware store, in the world he and Yank understood, watched over by Atlas. Yes, this is where he would stay.

"Louis."

Louis looked once more into the mirror, then turned slowly to the customer's voice, which repeated his name.

"Louis," came the woman's voice. "Are you there?"

He turned to face the woman, but he was alone in the aisle. He moved his eyes this way and that, in search of her among the dense clutter of the store.

"It's me," said the voice, pulling at him. "Iris."

In bed, Louis opened his eyes, and stared at the blank white of his bedroom ceiling. He took a deep breath and closed them again.

"You're there, I know you are," said Iris. She waited. Then she spoke again. "I heard, Louis. About last night. I heard what happened."

Louis closed his eyes tightly and tried to leave again. He imagined the grassy hills of the farm, and the crowded store.

But Iris came after him. "It was a terrible thing, what

Kitty Wilson did." Iris placed her hand on his door, gently, as if she were touching Louis. "But she was just talking crazy, you know that. You *know* that."

He knew only that Kitty would never find him in the hardware store, hidden amidst its protective abundance. Yank and Atlas would never let her get to him. Iris, stop talking. Let me go.

"No one believed her. The minute she said it no one believed her, I heard Gracie say so. You saved that awful woman, you rescued her. That's what everyone believes, because it's true."

Louis shifted on the bed.

Iris pressed against the door, grateful for the sound of life within the bedroom. "I know what you're doing, Louis. But you can't go back to the way it was. You won't make it in there another sixteen years. I seen you, Louis. I know." Iris leaned her head against the door and stared at the floor.

She said, "It's gonna be that way. You just have to move past it. That's what I been doing for thirty-seven years, Louis. I just keep moving, right past people like Kitty Wilson, right the hell on by. And, Louis, you see, if it was me and you, together, if it was the two of us, don't you see, nobody could get to us, because we wouldn't care. We wouldn't even notice them. I'd have you," she said, her voice dropping to a whisper, "and you'd have me." She pressed so hard against the door, the hinges creaked.

Oh Iris, Louis thought, his mind flashing to the grassy hillside again. But this time he had brought Iris with him, she was at his side, they were arm in arm in the warm sun, roaming the hills, picking strawberries.

At last, Louis spoke. "Iris."

Her head pulled back from the door. "Yes?" she said. "Yes Louis?"

"Stay here with me," he said.

She waited for him to go on, but he didn't. "How do you mean?"

"In here with me. Stay in this house with me."

"I'm not sure what . . . I don't get what you're saying, Louis."

Louis sat up on the edge of the bed and faced the door. "Don't go back out there, Iris. You don't have to go out anymore. You and I would be together in here, and we wouldn't have to worry. We wouldn't bother anyone, and no one would bother us."

"But, Louis," Iris started.

"I do want to be with you, Iris."

I do want to be with you. Iris placed a hand on his doorknob, and she would turn it, and enter his room, the room of the only man in the world who wanted to be with her. Together they would sit before the window, hands joined, at a distance from all that might harm them. In the spring they would be there, watching the azaleas, in the summer they would listen to the crickets, in the fall they would smell the leaves, and in the winter the snows would not touch them. Nothing would touch them, and they would sit, hand in hand, together, day after day, Iris and her Louis.

She did not turn the doorknob. "Oh Louis," she said softly, letting her hand drop as she stepped back from the door.

Louis, from his room, could feel her decide.

"Oh Louis, I'm sorry. I can't do it." Her eyes filled as she spoke. "You see, I live outside. It hasn't ever been easy for me. But I done the best I could with it, and I found things I enjoy, and lots of things I don't, and it's evened out somehow. I'd miss it, Louis. If I stayed in this house, even with you, I'd miss it. I can't just watch. I got to be out here, because it's where I belong, even though looking at myself I don't always believe it, that I belong here, but I guess I really do, no matter what. So what I'm saying is . . ."

"Good-bye," whispered Louis.

Yes, he knew what she was saying. She touched one finger to his door, as if to his cheek, and turned quickly down the stairs.

Louis listened to the sound of Iris leaving him, her footsteps on the stairs, the front door slamming behind her. Silence. His dark room instantly silent, and too small, and Iris gone. He needed light. He touched the light switch and that wasn't enough, because the light he craved came from outside. He ran to his window and pulled up the shade, and there was a blaze of light, he was immersed in it, revealed by it. Iris walked in the light, across his lawn toward the street, her back to him. Louis saw Iris, and below him, in the light of his vision, Gracie and Arnie together on the porch steps, and at the edges of the light, apart from Iris and Gracie and Arnie, there were others. At first he couldn't see them, but gradually, as he stood before his window, he did. There was Atlas, yes, Atlas, and at his side stood a woman Louis didn't know but who must have been LuLu. They were smiling. They lifted their hands in greeting, and so did Bev and Bert, because they were there too, and Yank Spiller. Yank smiled shyly, and he waved, and so did Carl, and Mrs. Meem, with her dog sitting beside her wagging its tail. Yes, there was Harvey Mastuzek, and Jim Rose, and Mr. Hollister, his old gym teacher, and all of Louis's school friends, and Francine Koessler lifting Minky's paw and waving it up to him. Ariel Nesmith touched her hand to her lips and threw him a kiss, and Mrs. Bingsley stepped out from behind her red azalea, smiling and waving. Everyone was there.

Louis pressed himself against the window glass, turned away from his room and the years alone that he had spent there, his eyes on Iris moving across the front lawn, his eyes on everyone he had ever known. The glass trembled and bent as he pressed still harder against it, as he understood that he would join them and the world they lived in, the world they were. Louis, the window splintering around him, entered the light.